D0061437

BAD DEEDS

Also by Lisa Renee Jones

Hard Rules

Damage Control

BAD DEEDS

A DIRTY MONEY NOVEL

LISA RENEE JONES

ST. MARTIN'S GRIFFIN

NEW YORK

BAD DEEDS. Copyright © 2017 by Lisa Renee Jones. All rights reserved. Printed in the United States of America. For information, address St. Martin's Press, 175 Fifth Avenue, New York, N.Y. 10010.

www.stmartins.com

Designed by Omar Chapa

The Library of Congress Cataloging-in-Publication Data is available upon request.

ISBN 978-1-250-08384-5 (trade paperback)
ISBN 978-1-250-08388-3 (ebook)

Our books may be purchased in bulk for promotional, educational, or business use. Please contact your local bookseller or the Macmillan Corporate and Premium Sales Department at 1-800-221-7945, extension 5442, or by email at MacmillanSpecialMarkets@macmillan.com.

First Edition: August 2017

10 9 8 7 6 5 4 3 2 1

Thank you to the entire St. Martin's team for working so very hard on Bad Deeds. *And thank you, Emily, for all you do!*

Dear Readers,

I am thrilled to finally be able to share *Bad Deeds* with you. If you haven't read *Hard Rules* and *Damage Control*, you need to before you delve into *Bad Deeds*, as we are going to be starting our story the moment after *Damage Control* ends. Also, please don't read on, as I'm going to not-so-quickly recap *Damage Control*.

We started *Damage Control* by finally getting the details on Emily's identity and her big secret . . . that she was a witness to her brother, Rick, (who is MIA) killing her stepfather. Both of whom we found were part of an elite and very dangerous hacker group, the Geminis. Shane and Emily both see that their lives are too dangerous and hesitate to bring each other deeper into the twisted webs of deceit, murder, and threats. But when Emily ran, Shane couldn't let her go. He needed to know she was safe, and he needed her. Needed her warmth and her in his arms where he's come to know that she belongs.

As Seth (Shane's right-hand man) and Shane try to discover just how much danger Emily is really in and try to clean up the shoddy mess her brother created of her fake background, more complications arise with the Martina cartel, which Brandon Enterprises has gotten into bed with. As a reminder: Shane's older brother, Derek, had agreed to let the cartel run cocaine through the Brandon Enterprises trucking division and a new performance-enhancing drug (Sub-Zero) through Brandon Pharmaceuticals, the last of which led to Brody Matthews's (Major League ball player who was using the drug) wife threatening to out the drug. Adrian, the son of the cartel leader, confronts Shane. He tries to force Shane's hand into bringing Brandon Pharmaceuticals fully into business with the Martina cartel. Which Shane continues to resist. Enter Nick Snyder, known by Seth from their CIA/FBI days. He's brought in to help Shane and Seth extricate the Martina cartel from any and all involvement in Brandon Enterprises. Together they set up a fake FBI raid on Brandon Pharmaceuticals to spook Martina and agree that Shane needs to meet with Brody Matthews to find out more about the drugs. However, before Shane can meet with Brody, he dies suspiciously in a car accident followed shortly by his wife's suicide. Playing dumb about the FBI raid, Shane visits Adrian, and finds Derek with him. When Shane tells Adrian about the feds and shows him a picture of Derek paying off an FBI agent, Adrian stabs a knife through Derek's hand and tells Shane to either find another route for his drugs or he's staying infiltrated in BP and won't be going anywhere.

Meanwhile, Emily has a very uncomfortable yet revealing lunch with Shane's mother in which she uncovers that Maggie is having an affair with Mike Rogers, a sports team owner and stockholder in Brandon Enterprises, and the worried-about swing vote when it comes to vote either Shane or Derek in to replace Brandon Senior when he can no longer operate the company. Shane and his father conspire to buy the sports center that Mike's team currently operates out of, which they would then use to control Mike's vote on the board.

At this point, Shane finally comes clean with Emily about everything. But she doesn't run like he expects her to. She decides the way out is to build an incorruptible division of Brandon Enterprises, and she comes up with a fashion and makeup line, which Shane thinks is an amazingly brilliant idea, and he wants Emily to head up the division herself.

Shane and Emily later head to dinner at his parents' house, which leads to the news of an experimental drug trial in Germany for his father's cancer, leading to more tension between Derek and Shane as one of them will be running the company in his absence. Derek throws out a threat to Emily, at which time Brandon Senior reveals that Emily is protected by his order, causing an even greater rift between Derek and Shane. Emily has overheard yet another threat to her from Derek and can't see a way out for her and Shane. As they stand outside his parents' house he promises to lay down his own life to protect her . . . and that spot is exactly the moment we pick up with.

I hope you enjoy *Bad Deeds*, and thank you so much for all the love and excitement you've shown the Dirty Money series!

Lisa
XOXO

CAST OF CHARACTERS

Emily Stevens (27)—Heroine in the series. She is Brandon Senior's newly appointed secretary. Learned after landing her new job that the one-night stand she had the night before turns out to be her boss's son Shane Brandon. Emily has secrets and she's running. But Shane will not let her run from him. During *Hard Rules*, the two had a lot of push and pull about their relationship, his family, and her secrets.

Shane Brandon (32)—Hero of the series. Shane Brandon is the only one with a moral compass in his family. The good one. The one willing to risk everything to play this game on the up-and-up and keep his brother from ruining the family empire, Brandon Enterprises, by getting in bed with the Martina family drug cartel. But Shane is treading on thin ice as he brings his legacy back from the brink of corruption. He is also dealing with Emily Stevens. A woman who breaks through his defenses and brings an innocence to his life that he can't have as a distraction.

He wants and needs to protect her, possess her, and be worthy of her. She is already making him a better man and keeping him grounded. But she has secrets, and she could be the one to ultimately send his world crumbling harder than he ever anticipated.

Derek Brandon (37)—The older brother. While he's brilliant and good-looking, his greed for power drives him to make rash decisions. He and Shane were close as kids, but once they became adults and Shane joined Brandon Enterprises, that shifted. Everything became about who would control the empire. Derek has gotten the family corporation into bed with the Martina drug cartel, and Shane will do everything in his power to stop his brother.

Maggie Brandon—Shane and Derek's mother. Seemingly befriending Emily, yet we are uncertain about her ultimate motives concerning the current struggle between her sons for control over Brandon Enterprises. Married to David Brandon (Brandon Senior). Maggie is having an affair with Mike Rogers, a shareholder in Brandon Enterprises.

David Brandon—The head of Brandon Enterprises and the Brandon family. Father to Derek and Shane. Husband to Maggie. He is dying of cancer but wants to leave a legacy and hold on to control of Brandon Enterprises as long as possible. He's a bastard and pushes Shane and Derek in all the wrong ways. He is gruff, cold, and hard at every turn. He enjoys watching his sons battle for power. It entertains him.

Seth Cage (35)—Shane's right-hand man. Ex-CIA. Shane hired Seth, away from their firm in New York to help clean up a mess for his family, and from there Seth remained on Shane's personal payroll, as well as taking up the role of head of security at Brandon Enterprises.

Jessica (29)—Shane's assistant. Ever the loyal employee, she followed him from New York and becomes friends with Emily as Emily starts to work as Brandon Senior's assistant. Jessica's job knows no bounds, she helps Shane with everything from securing a new apartment to keeping an eye on Brandon Senior and Derek when Shane is not in the office to relaying any curious goings-on.

Eric Knight—A friend of Shane's from college who is a brilliant surgeon and has squeaky-clean morals. Eric is the doctor of the patient who was running her mouth about Brandon Pharmaceuticals (BP, part of Brandon Enterprises) being the distributor for an undetectable performance-enhancing drug that her Major League Baseball–player husband is taking. Eric brings this news to Shane, causing Shane to take action.

Adrian Martina—The son of the Mexican cartel leader Roberto Martina. Runs the US side of the operations. He has some sort of relationship with Derek Brandon, the extent of which is not fully known yet. Brother to Teresa Martina, who is sleeping with Derek.

Teresa Martina—Sister to Adrian. Sleeping with Derek. Bartender at Martina's Casa.

Randy—Security guard of the building where the Brandon Enterprises offices are located. Emily and Shane have a conversation with him over her missing cell phone. Keeps Shane updated on his father's activities.

Mike Rogers—Sits on the board of Brandon Enterprises. Holds 20 percent of its stock and owns a professional basketball team. Key player in the hedge fund as well. Has a lot to lose if Brandon Enterprises were to shut down their investment division. His company, Rogers Athletics, is one of the proposed investments for the hedge fund. When Seth and Shane try to pull dirt on the board members so they will swing their way in a vote for power of the company, Seth cannot find anything substantial on Mike. Mike is having an affair with Maggie Brandon.

Rick Morgan—Emily's brother. Is aware of her secrets and why she is hiding. He's very hard to get in touch with, and his silence and evasiveness make Emily nervous.

Lana Smith—A brilliant scientist and businessperson at Brandon Pharmaceuticals. She wants Shane and has caused him trouble in the past. She hid weed in his car and almost cost him his attendance at Harvard. She is still trying to get close to him now, and caused a slight rift between him and Emily in *Hard Rules*.

Nick Snyder—Knows Seth from their CIA/FBI days. Saved Seth's life, and now Seth has brought him to Shane so Nick can help get to the bottom of the true involvement of the Martina cartel in Brandon Enterprises. Confirms that Brandon Enterprises' trucking division is already distributing cocaine. Is going to help Shane and Seth figure out how to maneuver a takedown and extricate the company out of the hold of the Martina cartel.

BAD DEEDS

CHAPTER ONE

EMILY

You could always sacrifice your queen and let her die a royal death. Would it—would she—be worth it to win?

Those words, a threat against my life spoken by Derek only minutes before, seem to whisper in the Colorado wind around us, taunting Shane and me where we stand under a tree in his parents' yard, our foreheads joined, mocking our desire to dismiss them as nothing but words and my desire to believe Shane's promises that everything will be okay. He means it, I know he does, and I'd wanted him to say those words, but now I am coming to my senses, remembering what my family taught me all too well— my brother, most especially. Promises, even well-intended ones, are like water in a cracked glass. One wrong lift or squeeze and it shatters, and in this case, with potentially bloody consequences.

I shut my eyes, and for a moment or two, or maybe even three, I let myself revel in Shane's words again:

We're okay....

Everything is okay....

But as surely as I soak in my desire for those things to be true, I flash back to the moment inside the house, when Derek had looked up from the chess game he'd been playing with Shane, and right at me. To those moments when he'd captured my stare, held it, and then issued that threat, and I'd seen the deep malicious intent and evil in his eyes.

We are not okay.

I shiver in a chilly gust of April evening wind blowing across the Rocky Mountains, and Shane's strong hands come down on my upper arms, the heat of his touch seeping through my navy silk blouse. "You need your wrap," he says, rubbing up and down my arms. "And I don't even have a jacket on to be gallant and warm you up."

"I don't have my wrap because I rushed out here in a reactive mode I should never have let anyone see," I say as more of the typical Denver evening winds lift my hair into my face. I shove it away, reminded that it is now brown but should be blond, the brunette color as fake as my name and identity. Another reality I think of in this moment, because this is my new life, by Shane's side, and I don't want it to be as a liability, but rather as an asset. "And you don't need to be gallant or make promises I shouldn't have asked you to make," I add. "We need to go back inside. The longer we're out here, the more it seems like I'm some scared fool."

He arches a brow. "Scared fool?" He laughs, one of those deep, sexy rumbles that proves he's not as starched as his white shirt, while also telling me that he's not taking my concerns seriously.

"This isn't funny," I say, my hand closing around the navy tie I'd chosen for him out of some romantic notion that we'd match for his family dinner, which doesn't feel romantic anymore.

His hands return to my arms. "No one thinks you're scared. If anything, they think you're angry."

"I am angry. And not at your father for inviting me to stir up trouble, or your brother for making sure he got it. That's just who they are. I know this, and I still gave them both a reaction. And then you reacted. I made myself your weakness." I grab his wrists, urgency growing inside me. "We need to go back inside," I say again. I try to move away from him.

He holds on to me. "Don't go in there thinking you have something to prove. You don't."

"I let them think I was scared."

"The human—and normal—reaction to someone threatening your life is fear, sweetheart, and I'm going to get you the hell out of here."

"No," I say. "No. I have to go in there and correct this. And later I'm going to apologize properly for asking you to make unfair promises."

"I repeat. The normal—"

"Don't say that again, Shane. 'Normal' doesn't apply to my life or yours, and we both know that. I'm human, yes, but I should have waited to freak out until we were alone. I'm pissed at myself, and you should be pissed at me. Why aren't you pissed at me?"

He cups my face. "I don't want you to become cold and callous like my mother. Ever. I want you to have feelings. I want you to be human."

"But being strong in front of your family doesn't make me cold like her. I won't ever become your mother, Shane. Because not only are you not your father, I'd leave if you were."

He inhales and lets the breath out, putting his hands on my waist. "I won't ever be my father."

"I know that," I say. "Or I wouldn't be here, but Derek—"

"Is wearing a wounded ego right along with that bandaged hand, courtesy of Adrian's knife. He's puffing up his chest to try to seem unaffected by me making him look bad to the cartel. And now my father threw down the gauntlet by threatening his inheritance."

"Was that real or just part of the games he plays with you two? I mean, why would he do that when he's been enjoying this game of pitting you and Derek against each other?"

"Because to exact revenge on Mike for sleeping with my mother, he intends to buy the sports center where Mike's pro-ball team plays and then recruit in, or buy, another team. And because of my contractual agreement when I joined the company, he needs my signature to sign any contract. In other words, he needs me happy, which means he needs you safe."

I've already blanched and recovered at this point. "I'm nearly speechless. This is huge. Monumental, even. And expensive." Realization hits me. "That's why he was meeting with investors."

"That's right. It's also legal and highly profitable, which puts me and my father on the same side of the fence for the first time in most of my adult life." His fingers flex at my waist. "I've got this under control. Everything is okay."

"No," I say, rejecting that idea. "It's not that simple, and you know it. Mike won't take this lying down, and he's the largest stockholder in the company outside of the family. He's going to attack you because you're attacking him."

"For all we know, he's already attacking us and planning a hostile takeover."

"Then that only drives home my point. He's going to attack, and who knows where that will make your mother step? Even with those things aside, there's your brother, and hate is positively

radiating off Derek tonight. He isn't done fighting. He'll do whatever it takes to steal the company from you."

"He can't take what's not mine, sweetheart. My father is still
king."

It hits me then that I'm so wrapped up in how Derek affected
me that I've forgotten about Brandon Senior. My hand goes to
Shane's chest. "How are you feeling about your father's news?"

"You don't have to analyze me over this, sweetheart," he says,
obviously reading where I'm going with this, confirming as much
when he adds, "I openly admit that my feelings about my father
are a mixed bag of emotions that resemble a swampland. One I
don't intend to open until I find out if that was real or another
one of his mind-fucks."

Mind-fucks. That's all he ever feels he gets from his family,
and I aided them in that effort tonight. "You think he's lying?" I
ask, certain Shane's in denial, protecting himself from that
swampland. "Why in the world would he do that?"

"I can think of several strategic reasons related to the company and to Mike, that I'll explain after we get home and after
we fuck this night out of our systems a good three times."

The grit in his voice tells me his desire to leave is bigger than
just me. "All the more reason we should get back inside, where
you can find out the truth that Derek and your mother probably
already know."

"None of us will find out the truth inside that house," he
says, "and I've already texted Seth to get me answers." His eyes
warm. "What I really want to do is mind-fuck my father and
leave without playing his game. What I want even more is you
naked and next to me."

He's angry. I hear it in the bite of his voice, feel it in the tension in his body. That's the emotion he feels, and that comes from his certainty that his father is lying. I don't even think it's real. This is about fear, fear that he will feel hope and discover it's false. I step to him, aligning our legs. "Shane——"

"You aren't my weakness," he says softly, but somehow vehemently. "You're just the opposite. You're the complete contradiction to everything that is this family, and you remind me of the change I'm fighting for." His hand cups the back of my head and then he is kissing me, his tongue licking into my mouth, the taste of his anger, his need to escape, bleeding into me, telling me his father's many lies are burning into his mind and emotions. "When we go back inside and my family fucks with your head, which they will, think about fucking me when we get home. That's what I'll be thinking about too."

My cheeks heat with the erotic boldness of those words, the boldness of this man who never fails to make me a little bit shy and a whole lot aroused. Again he laughs low and sexy, caressing my cheek. "I have no idea how you still blush after all the things we've done together, but I love it." And just like that, his mood has lightened, and his arm is around my shoulders, his steps directing us back toward the door. "At least we're guaranteed a good meal," he says. "My mother wouldn't cater anything but the best."

"Were all your meals catered growing up?" I ask, reminded that tonight, with his family, for all its guaranteed uncomfortable moments, there is an open window into Shane's past that I welcome.

"Believe it or not, she was a regular homemaker when I was a kid, even down to the freshly baked cookies after school."

"I'm having a hard time picturing your mother with an apron on. What happened to transform her?"

"I'd say it's a safe assumption that my father happened."

We step onto the patio, and he reaches for the door to the house, but instead of opening it, he maneuvers me to rest my back against the hard surface, one hand on the wood by my head, the other branding my hip. "I will not let anyone hurt you. You know that, right?"

His laughter from minutes before is gone, his words low and fierce in that way he always loves me, and emotions I can't name are welling up in my chest. No one has ever wanted to protect me the way this man wants to protect me. No one has ever cared this much about me, but then, I now know that the same is true of him as well. I wrap my arms around Shane's neck and push to my toes, pressing my lips to his, lingering there a moment before I say, "And I will not let anyone hurt you either." I relax back onto my feet and stare up at him. "You know that, right?" I add, repeating his words.

He stands completely still, unmoving, unreadable, until his hands are on my arms again, and he's pulling my mouth to his again too, in a fast, hard kiss. He ends with, "Ah, woman. What are you doing to me? Let's get this over with and get home." He turns us toward the door and opens it, allowing me entry into the Brandon family home, where life, love, and laughter seem to be more focused on one man's battle to live or die, which he may or may not have already lost.

I enter the house first, my gaze once again traveling the stunning circle that is the broad foyer with a unique domed ceiling, which is somehow fitting, since this family is nothing if not unique. Shane shuts the door and joins me at the same moment I hear Maggie.

"There you are!"

At the sound of his mother's voice, Shane and I turn to the left, nearing the kitchen, and find her hurrying toward us. As is usual for her, her black suit and long dark hair drape over her shoulders, giving the picture of elegance. "The chef's quite insistent that his food has to be eaten now," Maggie says, "or, per his expert opinion, it will be a disaster to the taste buds." Shane's hand settles protectively at my lower back while she motions between us. "I need you two in the dining room, pronto." She stops in front of us and lowers her voice, her attention on Shane. "Is this cancer treatment the real deal?"

"Why would he fake a medical procedure?" Shane asks, clearly having no intention of sharing his doubts with her.

Her lips purse. "Why would he announce something like this and not tell his wife beforehand?"

Shane's fingers flex against where they rest against me. "Why indeed, Mother?" he asks, a barely there hint of sarcasm in his voice, and I know he's thinking about her and Mike, concerned about her motives and loyalty. But I also have an epiphany. Could Shane have coped with his father's flaws by placing an unrealistic standard of perfection on his mother that he's yet to recognize or accept?

Maggie's response to his question is a look that's downright incredulous. "This is your father we're talking about, Shane. Everything he does has an endgame and some sort of strategy to get there."

"Staying alive," he says, "seems like a fairly cut-and-dried strategy and crystal-clear endgame."

"Cut-and-dried?" she demands. "If 'cut-and-dried' applied to your father, he would have told me about his treatment first, as most husbands would have. And if 'cut-and-dried' applied to your father, he'd have made peace with his family when he was diagnosed in the first place." Her voice is controlled, hard, and I do not know if she's containing her burning hot emotions or if she's been scorned by her husband to the point that this is the ice of a queen whose king has betrayed her.

"And," she continues, apparently not done yet, "if 'cut-and-dried' applied to that man, you and your brother wouldn't be playing a game of tug-of-war with the bladed rope he's handed you. Your father enjoys his mind games, and he will enjoy them while the rest of us suffer, until the day he dies. Perhaps even beyond." She folds her arms in front of her but not before I notice her hands trembling, which could mean any number of things, guilt and heartache among potential culprits. "Did you," she asks, focusing solely on Shane, "know about this in advance officially or unofficially?"

"I did not," Shane confirms.

"And you have Seth, who I know is a perfectionist to the bitter extreme, monitoring his activity?"

"I do," Shane states.

"Then that proves my point," she says, anger quavering back into her voice. "We're all being taken on a ride."

"Actually," I dare interject, afraid they're both making assumptions based on a history of manipulative behavior by Brandon Senior that may not apply this time. "My mother's best friend had terminal cancer, and I was close enough to her to know details. When a patient is terminal, they are put on a trial list— if they want to be considered for one, of course. When one opens up that matches their needs, it's often sudden, as it was with her. She found out and was under treatment within days."

"And how did it work out for her?" Maggie asks, her blue eyes fixed on me.

"She lived five years when she'd previously been given three months," I say. "So no, it wasn't a cure, but it certainly gave her valuable years she wouldn't have had otherwise."

"I see," Maggie says softly, her expression unreadable, but there is a timid quality to her barely there reply that doesn't suit what I know of this woman, as if her internal struggle is perhaps distracting her from a performance. It's stunning though. Could her entire existence be one big, exhausting show?

"Mrs. Brandon."

The male voice echoes from the left, near the kitchen, and Maggie inhales but doesn't turn, exhaling on a tightly spoken, "Yes, Chef Rod," and she glances at Shane. "Your father and your brother are already in the dining room." She then cuts me a sharp look. "No one else knows where your head was at and you need to make sure it stays that way." It's a reprimand, and I don't know if it's self-serving to her, but it's good for me and Shane.

"I was angry," I say. "I don't care if they know. I'll tell them."

Her lips purse and hint at a smile. "That's an acceptable response." And with that, she returns to her prickly self. Then she turns and starts walking away.

Shane and I stand there, watching her cross the tiled foyer, neither of us moving or speaking, a band of tension tightening around us, suffocating us with the energy that is his family. "He didn't tell her before the rest of us," Shane bites out the moment his mother disappears into the kitchen, "because of Mike. On some level, be it consciously or unconsciously, I know she knows that."

And with that statement, I have a good idea where his head is, even if he does not, and it's not in the right place. I step in front of him, my hands settling at his hips. "This is not the right time or place to say this to you, but it's necessary if we're going to stay for dinner. Can anyone hear me here or do we need to go outside?"

"Speak softly and we're fine here," he says, curiosity in his eyes. "What is it?"

"I asked you what happened to change your mother, and you

said, 'My father.' I'm not justifying your mother's actions, but, Shane, she didn't get to this place overnight. She has lived with your father for over thirty years. She made a decision to stay, and found a way to survive."

"I know that," he says.

"Of course you do," I say. "On the surface it's logical, but do you really understand it? Because I remember how much I put my mother on a pedestal after my father's suicide and how hard it was for me when I discovered she was as human as you say I am. And flawed, like your mother."

"Why is this important right this minute?"

"Because this house isn't a courtroom filled with clients and peers. It's your family home with your family inside, and if you are wrapped up in the betrayal your mother's flaws make you feel, you will not see your father or brother clearly." I swallow hard and force myself to say the words, to face the truth. "And now that I know the dangerous people your brother has involved your family with, Shane, I know, and so do you, that a misjudgment could be deadly."

He stares at me, his gray eyes as unreadable as his expression: one beat, two, three. Then he gives me a small nod, and that is all I need. He hears me. He understands. No other words are needed. His arm slides around my waist again, and he sets us in motion, walking deeper into the foyer, into his family home, and toward what reaches well beyond a dreaded family get-together that someone else might wish to avoid. For in Shane's case, in our case, we're headed toward more than his blood. We're headed toward people out for blood, one of whom has threatened my life tonight. And I'm not even ready to call him the most dangerous of the group. Or the most dangerous person in my life, or in Shane's.

CHAPTER TWO

SHANE

Emily is an angel in the middle of hell, and as I walk her through the foyer, toward the dining room, I wonder if I'm not the same kind of devil my father is by keeping her by my side, the way he has my mother. And yet I keep walking, leading her deeper into the circle of fire that is my family, selfishly needing her light in this darkness. The taste of sweetness in all that is bitter. And when we reach the arched entryway to the dining area, I don't even think about turning back. I lead her through it and into the rectangular sitting area, where Emily instantly halts, when this is the last place I want to linger.

"I love this space," she announces as we both take in the high-backed brown leather chairs on either side of us, framing mini fireplaces capped by bookshelves. "It's cozy and warm."

Cozy and warm. I inhale on a description I'd simplified to "happy" in my youth, a place that reminds me of a family once connected, now ripped apart. "It's the after-dinner coffee and reading room," I say, eager to leave it at that, at least for tonight, but she breaks away from me, crossing to a bookshelf and running her hand over a row of books. "So many choices. History. Mystery." She smiles. "Nora Roberts."

"I have my parents to thank for being well-read. We were required to read an hour every night after dinner, and they took turns making our choices to ensure we were diverse in our interests."

She turns to face me, her lovely eyes alight with interest in a past that humanizes people who are no longer human, a mistake I'd just made with my mother. I'd let her remain human, pure even, a façade that left me open to the jolt of the letdown I should have long ago faced. "Fond memories?" she asks, stepping to me again.

My hand settles at her waist, and my answer is fast, clear. "Yes," I say, and I'm not thinking of my family, but every moment I've spent with this woman. "Fond memories." I don't give her time to ask for further explanation, snagging her hips and walking her to me, my voice low, for her ears only as I promise, "In two hours you will be naked and next to me." I cup her face and kiss her and then turn her toward the doorway leading to the dining room, or tonight's circus event, allowing her to enter first but quickly joining her.

Almost immediately, I note that my parents are separated by the rectangular dark wooden table that now feels a mile long, each claiming the opposite head, though we'd once crowded on one end. Distant in ways that allowed Mike entry into my mother's life, and I wonder now if my father regrets allowing this to happen or if she is simply property he refuses to claim.

"There are the lovebirds," Derek says, from one of the high-backed red leather chairs facing us, several buttons of his white starched shirt open, his tie and jacket missing, his gray eyes so like mine, on Emily. "Tell me," he adds, his attention moving back to me as Emily and I stop at the table, her at the chair next to my father, me by my mother. "Does this family dinner hint at a wedding?"

My irritation at him introducing a topic I wouldn't dare discuss with Emily under present circumstances is as sharp and fast as Emily stiffening beside me. "If she survives the Addams Family dinner," I reply dryly, "then I'd say she's a keeper."

"A wedding," my mother exclaims, as if the Addams Family comment had not been made, but then I'm coming to realize my mother is a master of simply dismissing the bad and pretending everything is good. "That's an interesting prospect," she adds, motioning to me. "Let her sit next to me so I can get the details and do so quickly. The chef's anxious to serve us."

"The damn chef can wait," my father snaps, never one for these family sit-downs, at least not for a good twenty years.

My mother snaps back at him, but it's Derek and Emily I'm focused on. He's staring at her, and she is boldly staring back at him, and I can see the spark in his eyes, his sharpening need to see her cower. "You should sit next to me, Emily," he says. "If you're going to marry my brother, we need to make peace."

My irritation is turning to anger, but my father, the hero himself tonight, intervenes. "Give it up, boy," he snaps at Derek. "You won't intimidate her into leaving Shane, by sitting next to you, or agreeing with you. I sign her paycheck and she rarely does as I say. Hell. Shane beds the woman and I doubt he can control her."

"David," Maggie reprimands. "That's uncalled for."

"You aren't there to protect her at work," he says. "She doesn't need protection now." He fixes his bloodshot gray eyes on me. "Pick a spot and sit down before you have a confrontation with the egomaniac of a chef serving us tonight."

Emily doesn't look at me. I suspect it's to ensure her decision is labeled as her own, or perhaps because all this wedding talk is flustering her, and how could it not? Whatever the case, she makes her move for the chair in front of her, and I quickly pull it out, guiding her to the table and allowing her to sit.

I've barely had time to claim my seat next to her when Derek goes after her again. "I guess you don't want to get to know me better," he says, sounding pleased with himself.

"Oh, I do," she assures him, not missing a beat. "But I find the best way to do so is by looking a person in the face while you converse with them. Did you know that a person who is lying blinks a lot and makes unnatural eye contact?"

Her quick wit doesn't surprise me, any more than her departure from the library at his threat. She is human and real, not a mold created by greed, but still she manages to bravely face all the things that come with that.

The amusement in Derek's eyes deepens. "Did you know people who are rattled, or even scared, leave the room?"

"Did you know," she counters, "that people who are reprimanded by their fathers, especially as adults, usually prefer privacy?"

I don't even try to hold back my laughter and, much to my surprise, neither does my father, who hasn't done more than grunt in years, at least in front of me. "My boy," he says again to Derek. "You really have a lot to learn about Emily. She works for me for a reason. Like I said, she can't be intimidated."

Derek is not any more amused than my mother is, who downs her wine with a disapproving look on her face. So does she want Emily to put him in his place or not?

"If she knew how often you threaten my inheritance,"

Derek says, looking from our father to her, "she'd rethink her attitude."

"You know, Maggie," my father says, looking at my mother, "I think it's time I share the three versions of my will I've had drawn up, as well as the instructions I've given my attorney."

My mother pales with this news. "Three versions? I thought you only had one."

"That changed two weeks ago," he says, no hesitation to his words, "when I took stock of my imminent death and decided I needed to evaluate who is worthy of gratitude when I'm dead."

Like the man has ever shown gratitude to anyone in his entire adult life, I think, but he's making his point. His money isn't spoken for until he's dead. My mother and my brother won't get it unless they please him in the immediate future. And as if he's driving home my thoughts, he glances around the table and adds, "In case I haven't been clear, I still haven't made a decision on who inherits what."

Derek and I lock gazes, his eyes boring into mine, emboldened with a challenge I answer in what becomes a push and pull of power between us, in which I discover something has changed in him, something I read deep in his eyes. He doesn't give a fuck about the inheritance any more than I do. For me, that's about the money I've made on my own, but I know from his legal troubles that he's spent too much and saved too little. He should need his inheritance, and since I am now certain he does not, I have only one place this leads me. Someone has supplemented his income in an extensive way, and the likelihood that this is Martina, and that Derek is indebted to him in a far deeper way than I imagined, is not a good one.

"Are we ready for the soup?"

At the sound of a female voice, I glance up to find a fifty-something woman in an apron, her dark hair tied at her nape, entering the room from a kitchen door to the left and back of my mother.

"My glass is empty" is my mother's reply.

"As is mine," my father says, and my gaze jerks to him at the request that is a contradiction to his new healthy habits he'd announced to us only an hour ago.

"What happened to no drinking, Father?" I ask.

"I couldn't tolerate whiskey if I wanted to right now, son," he replies dryly, allowing the woman to fill his glass and then lifting it. "Water. One of the only friends I can count on right now."

His word choice, "one of the only friends," is without question a jab at Mike, who I now connect to my mother, and perhaps my brother, and I wonder if my father too has made this connection. But are they both connected to Martina? There is the real question.

"My friend," Derek says, holding up his glass. He downs the amber liquid before adding, "is one hell of a friend." He motions to the server and then to his empty glass. "Another."

My father waves between my glass and Emily's. "Their glasses as well." His attention settles on me. "Glenmorangie Pride 1981 Highland single-malt Scotch whiskey."

"We're celebrating Father's news," Derek inserts, the server filling his glass, only to have him down the contents and, at least to me, give off the impression that it's more like he's drinking away his misery.

"As we should," I say as my glass is filled and Emily covers hers with her hand.

"No, thank you," she tells the woman. "I'm a lightweight. I'll stick with water."

"We have wine," my mother offers, holding up her goblet that is still empty. "It's far less potent than whiskey."

"But it's all way too potent for me," Emily assures her, giving one of her delicate little laughs. "There's no telling what I'd say if I were drinking."

"I think I might enjoy that," my father muses. "But I wonder if my son would?"

"Come on, Father," I say, draping my arm around Emily, sheltering her to me, and then lifting my glass with my free hand. "Do you really think Emily would be here if I were worried about you plying her with whiskey and making her talk?" I sip the whiskey, a spicy, nutty flavor spreading along my palate. "Damn, that's good Scotch." I lean into Emily's ear and whisper, "But you taste better."

She reaches over and grabs my leg, giving it a hard squeeze of warning, the exchange quirking my lips to the side while the scent of her, floral and sweet, reminds me of pleasure outside this room.

"Prepare to have your palates seduced by greatness."

I glance up to find the chef now in the room, along with a male server carrying a tray filled with bowls. "Arrogant bastard, aren't you?" my father demands.

"Simply honest," the chef retorts, personally claiming a bowl, which he sets in front of my father. "Tomato soup," he declares. "Your favorite, I understand." The chef waits as if he expects my father will actually taste it.

"Move on, Chef," is the grumbled response he earns instead, to which the chef grimaces but doesn't debate, doing as he's told, and in a matter of minutes, we all have iced tea in our glasses, and bowls in front of us.

"Bon appétit," the chef says with a grand bow, and then he and his crew leave the room.

And the instant we're alone, my mother lifts her spoon and waves it around the table. "No more conversation until you've all sampled the food." There is a motherly snap to her voice that has us all lifting our utensils. "It's unbelievably good," she adds. "Now all of you, confirm."

Nostalgia bleeds into the moment, reminding me of family dinners where my mother, not my father, was in charge. Also like then, in unison, we do as we're told, dipping our spoons into our bowls, and collectively, mouths open, we all take a bite. Instantly, the sweet flavor of sugar touches my tongue before it immediately turns to a delicious spice. A sound of satisfaction in one way, shape, or form seems to move around the table, an odd moment of unity and satisfaction, significant in that we all agree on something. The soup is good. It's small, but it's true. We all like it. We all agree.

I have one moment in which I dare to believe this dinner, and our mutual agreement on anything, is my father's brilliance and reason for calling us all here. He's finally had a reckoning, and this is a way to show us that we can perhaps agree on more. One small step for mankind, or at least the Brandon family. But the wave of unity is followed by thick silence and then a bristle of universal discomfort as realization slams into us. We are split into opposing agendas, and agreeing, connecting, on anything feels like a betrayal of those causes. This is a group of family and acquaintances, but one other thing supersedes all. We are enemies.

And my father knows this, which means that agenda my mother spoke of him having was solidified in that fact. It also reminds me of Emily's warning. I do need to retain a clear mind and judgment.

Almost as if everyone in the room comes full circle to the same "enemy" conclusion at the same time, there is a sharp shift in energy, and action waves around the table. My father lifts his glass and downs his water. Derek follows with his whiskey. My mother then lifts her newly filled goblet, and drinks. Emily and I, in tune in that incredible way we always seem to be, are in unison as we simply set our spoons down, her hand going to my leg, settling there, and I read her message. There is a divide in the room, but not between us. And just that easily, this group is no longer one, but many. As easily as family can become enemies, life for my father could become death. And in sickness there is weakness, and in death, defeat, which he's not ready to accept, even in the grave.

And that weakness is like bait to the sharks that Derek and Mike, and perhaps even my mother, represent and will exploit. Death might still be the endgame he faces, but defeat in that death is not his intention, or mine. In other words, my father is staking his claim on the company, backing Derek and Mike off, and buying time to destroy the bastards. All the things I'd implied to Emily outside and then forgotten the minute I'd gotten inside again. Instead, I was thinking of tomato soup and damn near convincing myself there was a group-fucking-hug in our future.

Firmly seated back in reality, I look at my father and, no longer seeking the truth, at least not tonight, I prompt him to deliver the message we need Derek to hear, and my mother to repeat to Mike. He's still king. "When do you start treatment, Father?" I ask. "And can you give us any details?"

His gaze meets mine, his expression hard, unreadable, seconds ticking by that I expect are all about the games he plays. But time stretches, and I become aware of the white lines and tightness around his mouth. He reaches for his empty glass, and Emily grabs hers and sets it in front of him. "I haven't touched it," she says.

My father's reply is a cough, then another, that turns into deep, harsh grinds from his chest; I feel like my own lungs are being pulled up and from my throat. Weakness that becomes death, I think, my gut telling me that my father is already gone, that there is no salvation for him, and somehow I find my eyes locked with Derek's. And with that connection, there is a bond that is both old and new, an understanding we don't want to exist. We both hate and love our father, and yet, despite that love, it's Emily who is now squatting next to him, handing him a napkin he's now soiled with blood. Not me. Not Derek. Not my mother, who I glance over to find pale and as frozen as her sons.

"He needs hot tea with honey," Emily calls out to the waitress who's returned to refill his glass with water. "Quickly, please," she adds.

"I don't need a goddamn hot tea," my father snaps, clearing his throat, the coughing abating. "And get back to your damn office." He grimaces at his out-of-character misspeak, and corrects himself. "Chair. Get back to your chair."

Emily hesitates to do as ordered, something few would do with my father, but when he gives her a stare that equates to a proverbial punch, she acts, quickly pushing off her knees and settling back onto her chair. And apparently knowing my father well enough to understand that one look in my direction would read as if she were undermining his authority, she smartly faces him, while my hand settles on her hip, silently thanking her for once again being the kindness in a madhouse of ugliness.

"Let's cut to the chase, shall we?" my father says, flattening his hands on the table, and somehow my gaze is on his fingers that are now unrecognizably thin and frail, the knuckles knotty and jutted. "Forty-eight hours from now," he continues, "Maggie and I will be in Germany, where I will undergo treatment for two weeks before returning here to complete another two weeks under local care."

"Go with you?" my mother says, sounding stunned. "You want me to go with you?"

"You're my wife," he replies, his words simply spoken, without inflection, while his expression is hard, two collaborated qualities that in my father equal displeasure. "Of course you're going with me."

"David," my mother tries to reason. "You know that I have—"

"*You're* going with me," my father states, his tone as absolute as his added "End of subject." He glances around the room to continue with, "Tomorrow morning the board will be individually notified that I have every reason to expect a full remission and will be maintaining control over the company indefinitely."

"Do we dare believe that means remission is absolute, Father?" I ask, giving him the chance to drive home his claim of control and expecting fully that he will.

"Eighty percent of everyone who enters the program," he says, giving me a more believable answer than I'd expected, but I do not allow myself to assess the validity of his claim. He is, after all, the man who taught me to paint a picture with exactly the right colors to receive the reactions I needed from a jury or an opponent.

"I don't have to ask what happens to the other twenty

percent," Derek interjects, "but the board will, and they'll want a plan in place if something goes wrong."

"You mean *you* want a plan in place," my father says. "You want to know how likely it is that vote for CEO you want really takes place."

"I don't want you to die," Derek says, his voice tight, but there is a hint of grimness to it. "But this isn't just about family. We have a board of directors to deal with, with or without you. They will demand a plan and a precautionary vote."

"Should anyone so choose to make such demands," our father states, "I'll simply refer them to Amendment A1 of the charter."

"What the hell is A1 of the charter?" Derek asks of a document I know well, considering I wrote the charter.

"You signed it, son," Father says, of the legal clause that gives him a motivation to fake a cancer treatment, if that's what he's done. "You don't know what it says?" He flicks me a look. "Enlighten your brother."

Derek's gaze rockets to mine. "You wrote it."

"When we didn't know if you were going to prison or not," I state.

"And trusted my brother enough not to read the damn document."

"I went over it with you."

"Just tell me what the damn document says," he snaps.

"If at any time the active CEO is incapacitated, I will be claiming control, until which time the CEO is legally, and medically, capable of resuming his or her duties, for a period of up to six months."

Derek's eyes sharpen, darken, flecks of red-hot anger in their depths, but to his credit, he stares at me, the lines of his face hard, his expression stormy. "And at six months?"

"The board will rule on my retaining control, or there will be nominations and a planned vote."

His jaw clenches and his attention turns back to our father. "I've spent my entire life bleeding for this company. He doesn't even want to be here."

"He left his legal career for this company," Father states, "which makes him the only person other than me who doesn't want our business to end up under anyone else's control. The amendment stands." And then he stands. "End of conversation. End of this dinner for me." He says nothing more. He just leaves the room.

Another moment, and a charge races around the room, my gaze colliding with Derek's while my mother makes a small frustrated sound. "Evidently I need to cancel dinner," she says, in a rare moment of sounding flustered, before she stands and leaves. Sensing Derek and I are going no place good, I reach down and squeeze Emily's leg, telling her to follow.

Clearly reading my message, Emily pops to her feet, already moving toward the kitchen, and announces, "I'll help your mother."

"Yes, help her," Derek calls out, flicking her departing figure a look. "She'll like that, I'm sure," he adds, returning his amused look to me. "She's fitting right in, now, isn't she? And she's beautiful. A beautiful, graceful butterfly with delicate wings. And you know what they say about delicate things?" He doesn't wait for an answer, doubling down on his earlier threat to Emily by adding, "They get clipped easily. I hear they never survive once that happens."

CHAPTER THREE

SHANE

With that threat against Emily, Derek's second issued tonight, anger comes at me, sharp, biting, and immediate, but years of negotiations and courtroom battles serve me well now, allowing me to deny him the heated reaction he seeks. I steeple my fingers in front of me, my eyes narrowing on him. "Careful where you go from here, Derek," I warn, and while my voice is low, it's precise, lethal.

"I could say the same to you, Shane. Don't throw me to the wolves with Martina again. You won't like the results." He pauses and then adds, "Brother."

"You threw us all to the wolves when you got us involved with Martina," I say. "And there is no 'again.' This is over. You heard Father. No outsiders. I'm getting us all out of this."

"You're the outsider," he grinds out, his tone guttural, but he seems to catch himself, inhaling, then exhaling, his voice and demeanor calm as he adds our father's long-spoken words. "Profit is king to Father. He'll come around."

"Father is king to Father," I say. "Martina is out."

"Martina doesn't agree."

"He will."

"If you believe that, you're a fool. This is an opportunity for two parts of one industry to merge in financial reward in a way that has never been done. Martina sees that. He wants that."

"Illegal drugs and legal drugs are not one industry," I say. "And Martina only wanted in because you made him want in, but worse. You made him think we could all get away with it, without consequences, with regulations no one can hide from. There's a reason this hasn't been done before now."

"You're right. There is. The wrong people were involved."

"Martina isn't the fool you are, Derek. He wants money on this side of the steel bars."

"He's a man who isn't afraid to take risks," he says. "You did nothing to dissuade that man from the mission he's on."

"I gave him a reason to get out."

"All you did was make yourself a little bitch willing to serve him. His little bitch."

"I'm not the one with a bandage on my hand," I remind him. "And I didn't offer my services. I offered him incentives to get out of our business."

"The Martina family doesn't replace profits. They expand them. Give them something more, and they simply take more. There is no getting Martina out. There's just getting us all killed."

"Don't put this on me, Derek. You did this. Just like you got us into legal trouble. I got you, and us, out of that then, and I'll do it now, but I swear to you, Derek. You will help me, or there will be a price to pay."

"You mean you'll tell him about me fucking his sister? He knows."

"He doesn't know that you're using his sister, which you clearly spelled out in graphic detail in the recording I have of you telling me," I reply. "Do not underestimate me, brother. I'm done trying to save you."

"But you aren't done trying to save Emily." He pauses and then adds, "And trying might not be good enough. Cross me with Martina again, and I'll make sure he believes you're setting him up with the Feds and that Emily is his revenge."

"If I play him that recording, you'll be dead before you have the chance."

Our eyes lock in a collision, seconds ticking by, thick air surrounding us before Derek stands up, and unwilling to allow him to dictate my actions, I stay where I'm at. I don't stand. I don't lean back in my chair. He presses his fingers to the table, his spine stiff, his anger palpable, and his expression unreadable. "Seems our chess match is far from over," he says, and then with nothing more, he pushes off of the table, clearly intending to leave, and turns to walk away, rounding the table and heading in the direction where I'd entered the room with Emily.

Listening to his footsteps, I remain where I am, my mind rooted in nothing but his exit until I know he's gone. Then, and only then, do I let my thoughts free and they land one place: Emily. There is danger everywhere for her, both from her family and mine, and I'd believed her safer here with me, under Seth's watch, but the very fact that she is being threatened says that I have done too little to protect her. That shifts my thought process to how I fix this, and fix it now, and I replay my conversation with Derek.

He's cocky, and that comes from somewhere that isn't fear. He has someone powerful in his corner. If it's Mike and my mother he's in cahoots with, my father and I have a plan for dealing with them in play, but Martina is another story. One knife in a hand does not make an enemy in Martina's circle. It just makes a punishment or a show. I need to lock down a firm agreement with Martina. I reach into my pocket and remove my phone, doing a search and then dialing the restaurant Martina owns. I'm forced to leave a message with someone I think might be his sister, my brother's bedmate.

Returning my phone to my pocket, I drum my fingers on the table and think about that recording I have of my brother and how cocky and unaffected he is by it. My lips thin with realization. He doesn't believe I'll use it, but him believing I will protects Emily and the company, a situation I need to remedy now. Launched into action, I push to my feet, on a mission to find Derek, heading to the library to find it empty, and then down the hallway to the garage, I enter just in time to find him backing out. Cursing, I make a fast path to the foyer and exit to the driveway, where the garage door has lifted. Stalking forward, I meet Derek's Porsche as it exits, walking right up to the driver's door and knocking on the window.

He halts the vehicle and rolls the window down. "Miss me already?" he asks dryly.

I press my hands on the window's edge, leaning in and crowding him. "You think I won't use that tape recording."

"You don't want me dead."

"That might be true," I say, "but I want Emily alive more than I want you alive." I shove off of the car. "Checkmate, Derek."

"Checkmate?" He laughs. "I'll give you Emily, mostly

because I enjoy watching you get owned by that woman, but not the company. That game isn't over. It's mine, and you'll figure that out soon." He revs his engine and pulls away.

Hands settling on my hips, I watch his car depart, confident for now that I've set the boundaries that protect Emily. What I didn't do was check what could be his dangerous alignment with someone else. But I will, I think, and repeating his statement, I murmur, "Soon, brother."

"Shane."

At the sound of Emily's voice, I turn to find her on the porch, her wrap and hair lifting around her body as she moves toward me in a sudden gust of wind. And damn if she doesn't look like that butterfly Derek had called her, her delicate wings spread wide. But she's not weak. She is many things, but never, ever weak. She is strong. Beautiful. Confident. She is passionate in all that she does and believes in. Translation: too damn good for this house and my family. My desire to get her out of here is reignited.

I take several steps, helping her close the space between us, and then she is in front of me, the sweet floral scent of her teasing my nostrils and promising an escape that includes her soft sighs and softer skin. My hands go to her waist, hers flattening on my chest. "I heard what happened with Derek just now. I'm not blood, Shane. I can't ask you to put me before your family, and I don't expect you to. If I need to leave, I won't like it, but I can. I will."

"You won't," I say, cupping her head. "You won't leave and you're already first." It's a declaration I seal with a kiss, my tongue licking into her mouth, a deep, dark hunger clawing at me, a need that only she can answer, and I want that answer sooner than later. I release her, lacing her fingers with mine and

leading her to the Bentley parked in the driveway, opening the
door for her.

She moves to climb inside, but I sense torment in her, and I
pull her to me, my hand sliding around the back of her neck, our
lips close. "I need you here. Don't forget that." I drag her mouth
to mine and kiss her. "Now, let's go home. Okay?"

"Yes," she whispers. "Please."

We ease apart, but just as she's about to climb inside the
vehicle, the door to the house opens, and we both turn to find
my mother stepping out onto the porch. She halts there, arms
crossed in front of her, unmoving, in just the right spot to hide
in the shadows, but I can feel the jagged edges of her emotions.
I can sense she needs something from me right here and now.
But I need something from her as well, and I don't know what
that is. Perhaps a confession of her betrayal of this family? Or
not. I don't know what I need, and maybe she doesn't know what
she needs from me. She starts walking, but not toward us. She
crosses the driveway and walks toward the lawn, and I follow
her steps, watching as she fades in and out of the shadows, her
destination the swing I often favored as a child. Where she
pushed me and sang to me. At a time when we were normal, or
at least we did a hell of a lot better job at faking it than we do
now.

Emily's hand comes down on my arms. "You should go
to her."

A proper son would, I think, and I've always been that son.
But maybe there's more of my family's blood running through my
veins than I want to admit, because I don't move, nor do I have
any desire to move. I seem to be done being the "good" brother,
and the last thing I need to do right now is rehumanize a family
who has no humanity.

"Shane—"

"Let's go," I say, turning to Emily. She searches my face, her eyes narrowing in surprise at what she finds in mine.

I don't know what that is, and I'm not sure I want to know, but whatever the case, it silences any insistence she might have that I join my mother. She slides into the car and I shut the door, rounding the rear of the Bentley, reminded of my father gifting it to me for saving the company once before. I didn't want the gift. I didn't want to be here. I'd wanted to save, and reunite, my family. Now my biggest fear is that reunion will be in death, which is exactly why I don't look toward that swing again, and to the fairy tales of the past that stir emotions I can't afford.

Opening the door, I slide onto the soft leather and inhale the sweet scent that is so naturally Emily, but when I am about to start the engine, I am slammed with her silent, forceful disapproval. Sighing, I look in her direction to find her watching me, and I don't even have to ask what's on her mind. "Anything my mother will say to me right now will be a lie I don't want to hear."

"She was shaken when I tried to talk to her. Deeply shaken."

"Of course she's shaken. She's replaced her husband, and my father, in the bedroom, and most likely intends to extend that to our boardroom."

"As confusing as this is for you," she says, "you have to know it's not that simple. Sometimes when people are hurt and grieving, they do things to survive."

I start the engine. "I'm trying to make sure we do more than survive." I face forward and reach for the gear.

Emily's hand settles on mine. "Just know this. She loves him. I see it in her face."

Love.

The meaning of which I wouldn't know, if not for Emily. I damn sure didn't learn it from this family. I put the car in drive and get us out of here before the quicksand that is my family traps us in hell with them. Pulling us around the house and down the driveway, we're just exiting the property when I note the black sedan one block down, a light flickering in the dark window, which I believe to be a cigarette. Logically, that could be a stranger who doesn't know us or care about us, or it's one of Seth's men who I know are following us, but in this case it's not. It's someone else, and my gut says that someone else is a Martina minion, and he's monitoring Adrian's investment in this family.

I turn us onto the road and glance at the rearview mirror to find the car's lights flickering to life. It pulls away from the curb, and we're officially being followed. Removing my phone from my pocket, I dial Seth. "Talk to me," I order.

"About your text related to your father's treatment or the car following you?"

"Both."

"I'll have news on your father's medical status in the next ten minutes," he says. "We're about to breech the hospital's servers. The car following you is driven by one of Martina's men, who doesn't seem to care that we know he's there, which reads like a message to me from Martina. He's here. He's watching. He's waiting."

"That's exactly what this is," I say. "Call me when you know about my father." I end the connection and look at Emily. "Seth will know the truth about my father's treatment by the time we get home."

"That's good," she says. "That's really good."

But the fact that a drug cartel minion is following us home is not. It's a detail that would scare her, despite the fact that she'd put on a brave mask and say it doesn't, when she was already running and afraid when I met her. I want to protect her. I want to make her feel safe. I just need to end this hell with the cartel and tell her it's over, once and for all. And I need to do it quickly, by whatever means necessary.

CHAPTER FOUR

EMILY

I don't push Shane to talk during the short ride downtown to our apartment. I understand him well enough to know that he's waiting on Seth's call, battling inner demons he must first name before he can even think of defeating them. It's something I know well from the many demons that consumed me after my father's death. And Shane's demons are clearly holding the same emotional blade on him that mine had on me, ready to cut him deeper and deeper if he lets them, with the worst demon of all, the one coming to claim his father: death. *No,* I amend silently. It's not the worst. Guilt is the worst. All the guilt you put on yourself for everything you should have, could have, might have done differently with the person but can't now.

I sigh, and sink deeper into the leather seat of the Bentley, letting the demon-filled silence speak to me, letting Shane speak to me. Because the truth is that, despite his silence, I do not feel shut out at all. Not when he allows his emotions to whisper darkly in the air, viciously taunting him and me with the way they affect him. Speaking to me in a way he would let them speak to no one else, and I am eager for that moment when we will be naked and next to each other as he's promised. When I know I will fully understand what he is feeling and, then soon after, what he is thinking.

An eternity later, it seems, though it is only minutes, we turn into the parking garage of the Four Seasons, and Shane wastes no time finding us a parking spot in the private residence section. He kills the engine and we're about to exit when his cell phone rings, and I swear every muscle in my body tenses, my nerves on edge with whatever news it will hold. Shane answers it, and almost immediately I surmise from a few words that again he's speaking with Seth, who is not only the man who sees to our protection, but the man I know will have answers about Shane's father's treatment.

The communication is short, with Shane querying, "And?" and then: "Are you sure?" Neither of which tells me much. Finally, he says, "Make sure," before he ends the call and slides his phone back into his pocket. But rather than turning to me, or getting out of the car, his hands settle on the steering wheel, and those demons of his aren't whispering now. They're shouting. Actually, I'm pretty sure they're holding knives and jabbing them in his chest and mine right along with it. "What happened?"

"The treatment program is real," he says, without looking at me, his voice a tight band. "But the success rate isn't eighty percent. It's twenty. Seth had the records hacked to indicate eighty, to ensure that if Derek or Mike investigates, they feel like my father is going to make it."

Oh yeah. Knives in the chest, all right. "Shane—"

"I need out of this car and garage," he says, popping his door open. "I'll come around and get you." He doesn't wait for a reply, exiting the Bentley.

I don't wait on him. I don't bother with my wrap, opening my door, and I'm on my feet, shutting it again by the time he's standing in front of me, his expression stark, shadows clouding his gray eyes. We stand there, seconds ticking by, neither of us speaking or moving, his tormented emotions standing between us like one of those demons, and I hold my breath, waiting for his cue to what he needs or wants right now, afraid he will push me away.

"Come," he finally says, his voice a rough, gravelly tone, his arm wrapping around my waist as he sets us in motion toward the lobby, our hips aligned, his instinct, thankfully, to keep me close, not push me away. So much so, in fact, that he holds on to me as we enter the garage elevator, and I have this sense he's holding on to me to protect me. As if he feels like I'll be gone soon too, and this affects me. Because he cares about me. Because he's hurting and I want to take away his pain. There are so many things I want to ask him and say to him right now, but I know this isn't the time or place. I'm not even sure this night is the right night for these things.

We reach the entry door and exit to the lobby, where one of the staffers greets us. Shane manages a polite, even friendly, reply, displaying a skill for appearing unflappable and unaffected by life that speaks to his success as an attorney. It also drives home the fact that he chooses to allow me to see the real him. He gives me that trust willingly, as I do him, and it's not something either of us has with anyone else in this world. It matters in ways I don't believe I even knew could matter before meeting him.

We continue our walk to the elevator, and while Shane still

appears cool and casual, like he's living any other night, he jabs
the call button a little harder than normal, an edge of anticipation clinging to him as we wait for the doors to open. One second, two, ten, and when finally they part, Shane wastes no time
guiding me inside the car. Still holding on to me, he punches in
our floor and our security code. The doors close, and the moment
we are alone, Shane's hand comes down on the back of my head,
and he's leaning into me, his breath warm on my cheek, on my
mouth. And my hand is on his chest, his heart thundering
beneath my palm, and mine answers, pounding against my rib
cage, his sudden lust for me overwhelming, contagious. I need
him. I want him.

"Emily," he whispers softly, a gruff, affected quality to his
voice, and then he's kissing me, the taste of all his emotions bleeding into my mouth: Anger. Guilt. Pain. More anger. It's a kiss of
dark chocolate, bitter but somehow addictive, sinful. It consumes
me. He consumes me, and I lose track of time and place. I can't
think of anything but how he tastes and how his hand feels when
it slides up my waist and covers my breast. I moan with the intimate touch, the tease of his fingers over my thin blouse that peb-
ble my nipple, my hand covering his, my mind reaching for
sanity. "Shane," I pant out, trying to pull myself back in check.
"Shane, I—"

He reaches behind him and hits the button to stall the elevator, and my already racing heart starts to thunder. "What are
you doing?"

"This," he says, maneuvering me into the corner, his mouth
already back on mine, his hands sliding over my backside, where
one hand cups and squeezes and the other makes its way back to
my breast. And while my mind tries to reach for reason, my body,
my emotions, respond to the dark hunger inside Shane. The

animal quality that I've never felt in him consumes him now and claims me. His need feeds my own. I taste it. I crave it. I burn for it and him. He answers those sensations by creating more, his powerful legs framing mine, his tongue licking into my mouth. His hands travel my body, and somehow my blouse is open and my bra is shoved down, nipples hard as pebbles against his fingers that are tugging and pulling.

I am wet. I am hot, but when he reaches for my waistband, when I'd let him further undress me, the sound of a buzzer permeates my mind, and reality hits me. We're in an elevator. The alarm is going off. "Shane," I say, grabbing his wrist, only to have his fingers stroke my sex through my slacks, sensations rolling through me, my body all but demanding I forget objections. "Shane," I say again, somehow staying focused. "There are cameras."

"I'll have the security feed destroyed," he promises, and he's already kissing me again, and with one deep stroke of his tongue against mine, which I feel everywhere, I want his tongue, and I struggle to find resistance. I even let him unbutton and unzip my pants. Still, though, that alarm is sounding, seeming to get louder, insisting that I hear it, reminding me where we are. "Shane."

He answers by nipping my bottom lip, a deliciously rough, sexy bite that he follows with a lick. With just that easy of a distraction, I am not thinking, but feeling again, my tongue seeking his, every soft spot on my body wanting every hard part of his. But when his warm palm flattens on my naked hip, skimming my pants downward on one side, the idea of being naked in the elevator sparks one thought: we are being watched, an idea that shakes me fully back to my senses with the hard, cold reality, and I grab Shane's shoulders. "Stop."

"After you come."

"Before," I hiss, and when he leans in to kiss me again, I pull back. "Damn it, Shane. Stop. Not here."

The fierceness of my voice fills the car, and he jerks back, looking down at me, his gray eyes glossed over with lust that quickly sharpens into understanding. His chest expands on a deep breath, his hands leaving my body to settle on the wall on either side of me. "You don't like the elevator."

"It's not about the elevator," I say, grabbing his collar and stepping into him, my voice low, for his ears only. "It's about who might see us before you clear the tape. Like your brother or father who could be watching us right now."

He lowers his head, tilting it low, all but burying it in my neck, and I can sense him battling to tame the beast this night has unleashed in him, softly murmuring, "What the hell is wrong with me?" He inches back to look at me, his eyes clear now, control restored. "I'm sorry, sweetheart. This isn't me."

"Don't be sorry," I murmur softly back. "You're human too, Shane, and I don't want you to stop being human any more than you want me to. But no one else needs to know that right now but me." I flatten my hand over his chest. "Let's go do this in private."

His eyes warm, expression softening. "What did I do to even deserve you?" He doesn't wait for or expect an answer, glancing down and then adjusting my bra to cover my exposed nipples. "I hate to tell you this, but the buttons to your blouse are missing," he says without apology as he adjusts my pants back into place.

"It's a short walk to the apartment," I say, tugging my zipper up and tying the ends of my blouse at the waist.

He cups my face and kisses me. "I'll buy—"

"Me a new one," I supply. "I'd rather you just take this one off me."

His eyes darken, a hint of that lust returning as he takes a step and stretches across the car to punch the button to set us in motion again. The car starts to move, and his hands come down on my arms, pulling me to him. "I'm not—"

"Oh yes, you are," I promise him. "The minute we get inside the apartment, because I'm about to combust." I soften my voice. "I'm supposed to be naked and next to you, remember?"

"Yes," he agrees. "You are." The car halts with a ding, the speed at which we've arrived proving we were close to home when detoured by our little encounter. "Let's go get you properly undressed," he says softly, draping his arm over my shoulders and pulling me into the cocoon of his body.

We exit the elevator onto our floor, and I hug myself to hide the gap in my blouse. In a few steps, we've rounded the corner to the hallway that leads to our apartment, and Shane leans in, kissing my temple. My lips curve with the tenderness of his action, while my gaze travels down the long hallway to our door, my brow furrowing with the sight of a man standing in front of it. "Who is that?" I ask, noting the way Shane's fingers flex on my shoulder and the slight tensing of his body.

"Adrian Martina," he says, "and no one I want you to meet."

"The drug cartel," I whisper, recognizing the name Martina, though I'm not sure how or when I found out that detail. When the Escalade showed up in our garage, I believe.

"Yes," he confirms. "And as much as I want to send you back to the elevator, you need to stay with me. The reasons for that decision are too many and too complicated for me to explain right now."

"Understood," I say, quite clear on the reasons, starting with the risk that someone could be potentially waiting for me at the elevator or elsewhere. And if that isn't a good enough reason, there is no question that me leaving would simply look like running, which will make Shane look afraid and weak.

And so we walk the hallway that is always long and yet not long enough this time, considering each step is leading us closer to a man who is a criminal, who is dangerous in ways I don't think either of us wants to fully understand. Martina is tall, dark, and extremely good-looking, an air of power, intelligence, and money radiating off of him. His dress pants are black, expensive, while his white shirt is starched, his jacket and tie absent. He is not a man in bandanas and a white T-shirt. This is a man who operates on the same playing field as Shane. One I fear might just be capable of intellectual destruction as readily as he is capable of physical destruction. He is terrifying, and he is now only two feet away.

Shane halts us a good foot from Adrian, releasing me and stepping forward, while the drug lord does the same, meeting him toe-to-toe. "I heard you wanted to speak with me," Martina says, his accent rich but his English perfect.

"A phone call would have suited me."

"Phone calls can be recorded," he says. "And I like to invest in building my new friendships."

Friendships? They're building a friendship?

"Let me be crystal clear," Shane replies. "We're not friends. We will never be friends. But allies with a common cause that includes getting you the hell out of my business, perhaps."

"Well then, potential ally," Adrian says, "why don't you show good faith and invite me inside?"

Shane doesn't immediately react, and I don't believe that's indecision but rather a strategy I hope leads to a decline of this man's invite into our home. But when he turns to me and motions me forward, draping his arm around me, I'm pretty sure

Martina's rejection isn't in the cards. "You must be Emily," Martina greets me, offering me his hand, which I can't take without my blouse gaping.

He notices too, his gaze touching my blouse, his lips quirking as he gives me a nod instead. "Nice to meet you."

"Nice to meet you," I say, pleased with the sincere tone I've mustered.

"Sorry to interrupt your evening," he continues, a hint of amusement in his eyes that I know is about my torn, open blouse. "I'll be as fast as your man allows."

Shane walks me past Martina, toward the door with the words "your man" in my mind. I'm not sure why that bothers me coming from this man, when with anyone else, I think it might please me. Shane opens the door and motions me forward, catching my waist and stepping up behind me to whisper, "Go upstairs."

I enter the apartment, flipping on the lights to illuminate the long hallway that leads to the place I've started calling home and safe. A place where a drug lord is not welcome. Moving forward, my feet touching the pale bamboo floors, I feel Martina behind me, and my instincts demand I turn to face the door, and him. And, sure enough, I find him just inside the doorway, close, too close, and I am now staring into his brown, intelligent eyes that don't ever leave my face, and yet this man has a way of making you feel touched by his presence. This is a man who could seduce his way into many a foolish woman's bed, or equally so into many a foolish banker's or businessperson's secret bottom drawer holding the key to their vault. And he wants to be Shane's business partner. I just want him gone.

Shane appears beside Martina, his eyes sharpening on me. "Emily—"

"I'm going upstairs," I say, forcing myself to turn, heading down the hallway. I've just approached the stairwell and placed a foot on the bottom step when I hear Martina say, "You're protective of her, as I am of my sister. But know this, Shane Brandon. If you are loyal to any agreement we make, now or later, as I assure you I will be in reverse, I will protect her, even kill for her."

My blood runs cold at the veiled threat that to me clearly has an unspoken addition: if you're not loyal to me, I'll kill her. And who knows how he defines loyalty or what nasty task he might demand as proof? Footsteps sound on the hardwood floor behind me, spurring me into action, and I quickly head to the upper level, but I don't enter the master bedroom immediately in front of me. Instead, I flatten against the wall and lower myself to a squat, taking shelter behind the railing of the stairwell, where I intend to do my best to listen in on the conversation being had between the man I love and a man whose claim to fame is a family-run drug cartel. But really, when you're in bed with a drug cartel, is there anywhere you can truly find shelter?

CHAPTER FIVE

SHANE

I am not pleased that Martina got past the security team I'm paying a small fortune, but that's a problem I'll be taking up with Seth later. Right now I have a drug lord to contend with. Motioning forward, I lead Martina down the hallway, toward the living room. His agenda for this visit, which has nothing to do with my phone call, is evident to me in one statement: *I will protect her, even kill for her.* That wasn't a threat. Not when he'd prefaced it by exposing the vulnerability that he has in his sister. He's too smart to offer me a weakness without intent, which I read as him trying to build trust with me. He doesn't want me to be his little bitch. He wants me to be part of his inner circle, where he believes he can convince me to play his game, which tells me one thing. Derek was right. He doesn't want out of Brandon Enterprises. He wants my invitation inside, which means the choppy water I was treading in is now treacherous.

"You like whiskey?" I ask as we enter the living area, high ceilings above us, leather furnishings in the center of the oval-shaped room, framed by windows, the Denver skyline dotting the darkness with white lights.

"Tequila's in my blood," he says, scanning the windows before he looks at me. "But I do enjoy an occasional whiskey if it hits the right note." He changes the topic. "Nice place. A safe zone overlooking the city. I might have to consider a similar option."

"Safe from everyone but you apparently," I say dryly, indicating the pale bar wrapped in bamboo against the wall and between the kitchen and the patio door, where we both travel to and stop. "Let's see if I can hit the right note on that whiskey," I add, setting two glasses in front of me. I reach for a glass decanter, removing the plug. "This is a Balvenie forty-year-old single-malt Scotch whiskey." I fill the glasses. "You'll find it has some spice to it, worthy of a man with expensive tastes and a penchant for good tequila." I hand him a glass.

He takes it and swirls the amber liquid, studying me, not it. "You're wondering how I got past your security team, which is an excellent team, by the way."

"Apparently not, or you wouldn't have gotten by them. And I'd like to know how."

His lips curve. "You know I'm not going to tell you that." He lifts the glass to his mouth, lashes lowering, his palate savoring the rich apple, oak, and cinnamon flavors. "Hmmm. Exceptional." He downs the rest of the glass and sets it on the table. "I owe you a tequila worthy of that whiskey."

"I'll take you up on that," I say, knowing this is the way of trade and respect that I've learned in many a business dealing, which this is, and more.

"Let's have a frank talk about family and business."

I empty my glass and set it down as well. "On the balcony," I say, indicating the glass door.

"Of course," he says. "We wouldn't want to upset your woman, who is no doubt listening in right now, ready to state an opinion the instant I'm gone. That too is like my sister." He moves to the door and opens it, the motion detector setting off the dim glow of lights.

I join him and we walk to the railing, both of us leaning elbows on the steel surface, the glass beneath it reminding me of the day I'd stripped Emily naked and leaned her against it. I wanted her vulnerable, exposed to me in every way, which in a different sense is exactly what Martina wants of me now.

"You've made millions in New York," he says. "You're considered one of the top attorneys in the country."

I glance over at him to find him looking at me. "I see you do your research."

"Always," he says. "And I find it interesting that you walked away from that success to fight your brother for the company."

"To save my family name," I amend.

He faces me, his one elbow staying on the railing, and I do the same with him. "I had a brother."

"I'm aware of that."

"Of course you are, because you, like myself, are always prepared and strategic in all you do."

"Like you showing up at my door was strategic."

"Indeed," he agrees, but he leaves it at that, circling back in the direction he was headed moments before. "My brother and I were pitted against each other for the family crown as well. And my brother thought the way to do that was to be a bigger, bolder, more careless version of my father. Like Derek seems to be doing with your father."

"With you at the helm," I point out.

"And yet I'm here talking to you now."

"Why?" I ask. And then, thinking of my earlier conversations, I add, "Spare me the chitchat and get to your endgame."

"Direct," he says. "I like that, and I will get to the endgame. I'm here because you and I have something in common. We see a better way for our family businesses. A new way. I believe we can help each other reach our common goal."

"The only way you can help me reach my goal is for you to get the fuck out of my business and my family. I'll give you the trucking company. Then you can move your drugs."

"I don't need another trucking company," he says. "It's too convenient a choice, and therefore too obvious a place, for the Feds to look for trouble I don't intend for them to find."

"I can create a shell company for the ownership."

"And if they ever look into that company, they'll look into you. That doesn't work for either of us." He pushes off the railing and folds his arms in front of his chest. "Being as direct as you have been. Brandon Enterprises is about a bigger distribution picture. A smarter one."

"The Feds are looking into our operation. That makes us a bad choice, not a smarter one. You have to know that."

He holds up a finger. "That's where you're wrong. The magical part of having them look at you and find nothing is that the red tape and bureaucracy of the United States government will force them to move on. Especially with a brilliant attorney like yourself ready to sue them."

My jaw clenches. "In other words, my brother was right. You have no intention of getting out."

"Your brother?" He laughs without humor. "I assure you, your brother has no insight into my mind or my intentions. He's a liability I'll tolerate to do business with you." He lowers his voice, a sharpness to his eyes that reminds me there is a lethal quality to it, one I remember from the restaurant, right before he shoved a knife in my brother's hand. "I've always been after you, Shane," he adds. "I just needed a way to motivate you to get involved."

"You used him to get to me," I state, resisting the urge to drop my hands and give him the reaction he wants, let alone do what I really want to do and punch the bastard.

"He used my sister to get to me, and the only reason I let him live was to get to you. Seems a slightly unfair trade, considering how much I hate that little fuck, but I'm hoping you'll prove otherwise."

"I don't deny my brother's an opportunist," I say, going into damage-control mode in order to keep Derek alive. "He saw his new woman's brother as a business opportunity that frankly I would have seen as trouble."

"And then I assume my sister wouldn't have been worthy of you?"

"I don't know what you're trying to discover about me by baiting me, but it will get you nowhere," I say, unfazed and unamused by the obvious attempt. "I know nothing about your sister that isn't on a piece of paper. For all I know, it's you who's not worthy of her."

His eyes darken, harden, silence ticking by in heavy beats, before he sighs. "She's a different breed than I am."

"You mean she's not a manipulative prick?"

"Manipulative prick," he says, and laughs. "This from one of the top attorneys in the country? I find that entertaining. But for the record. Yes. I'm a prick. And yes. I've been working on that, but to be honest, it's not gone well. I want what I want, and I go for it. And what I want is the same thing you want."

"We want nothing that's the same," I say, though I have a

begrudging appreciation for the skilled manipulation that got
him here tonight.

"But we do," he says. "We both want to turn the dirty money
generated by our families into legitimate investments."

Now I laugh. "You want me to believe you're looking for legitimate investments when you're the one who brought Sub-Zero
into the one legitimate operation my family had? That doesn't
support an effort to legitimize your business. Just delegitimizes
mine."

"On the contrary. Your company gives Sub-Zero distribution,
and I believe we should explore legalizing it."

"Legalizing it? You've got to be fucking kidding me."

"I'm really lacking a sense of humor," he states dryly. "It's
another flaw I'm working on."

"You can't market a drug that gets people high."

"You must have confused Sub-Zero with a prescription pain
pill. This drug doesn't get anyone high at all. It improves mental
clarity. And the many ways that it could be used in relation to
real medical problems is astounding."

"A man, a professional athlete I knew and respected, died
in a car accident high on that drug. He hadn't slept in days."

"Yes, well, we don't advise people to pop Sub-Zero like candy.
It's a drug. It can be abused, and as we know from recent high-
profile celebrity deaths, that's a problem that reaches beyond the
streets to prescription drugs."

"The Feds know about the drug," I say, knowing that any
decision I influence him to make on his own is one less I have to
make later, with potentially bloody results. "The minute I was
foolish enough to introduce it to market," I add, "they'd connect
the dots. The minute your name is attached, we're screwed."

"We both know you're smart enough to repackage it, rename it, and disconnect it from the street-drug version. And I assure you that I operate within a consortium of legitimate, deep-pocketed investors with an impressive and quite legal portfolio of investments."

"And they want to go into the drug business with the son of a drug lord, who is a drug lord in his own right?"

"They, unlike you, know me as a fellow investor who makes smart financial decisions," he says. "And we, as a group, are not coming to you with a hope and a dream. We are coming to you with it as close to market ready as it gets."

"Define close to market ready," I say, skeptical about his claim but intrigued in spite of myself.

"We have had extensive research done in an accredited lab, which supports Sub-Zero as being an effective treatment for ADD, ADHD, and anxiety disorders, not to mention sports recovery and numerous other disorders."

"Those determinations would take extensive drug trials to validate," I say, still skeptical, but more intrigued than moments before.

"But we can get it onto market with only one validated use. We can expand from there, and I have confidence we will. The studies we've done are impressive. Even as reluctant as you are right now to buy in to this, I promise you. You'll be impressed."

There is a lift to his voice, passion in its depths and in his eyes. He's actually excited about this, and I consider the idea that his quest to go legitimate, no matter how unorthodox and dangerous his approach, might be real. But that doesn't make me any more willing to take this deal. It might, however, make him more accepting of my declining his offer.

"I need to be blunt here," I say. "If this drug, and this opportunity, had come to me without you contaminating my business with illegal activity, it would be a tempting proposition."

"You can tell yourself that now," he replies, "but we both know that not only would you have shut me down, you wouldn't have apologized for the decision any more than I do for the actions I took to ensure we ended up in business together. I have a vision of a Martina empire, not a cartel, and I'll do whatever's necessary to make that happen."

"And I have a vision for Brandon Enterprises. Illegal activity of any kind, for which you're a magnet, is not part of it. So no. I would not have done business with you nor would I have apologized for that decision."

"This is a good move for all of us."

"And if I say no?"

"There's no reason for you to take our relationship, or that of your family and my family, to negative places when 'no' doesn't make sense."

"Negative places," I repeat, laughing without humor. "I don't need an imagination to hear the threat in that statement."

"I didn't seek you out and go to the lengths I did to align our interests to have us end up in the same bad places our families would end up if they were the ones negotiating this deal."

"That's not a denial of the threat."

"Not only is this drug a formula for us to make millions upon millions together," he continues, as if I haven't spoken, "but my consortium connects you to some of the most powerful men in the world. That's not a resource to be taken lightly."

"I need a list of every member of the consortium," I say, wanting to know who I won't be doing business with and how dangerous they are to my agenda of getting us the hell out of this.

"Tye Reynolds, the director of the consortium, will make contact and provide you that information. He'll also be the one presenting a formal request for your corporate involvement. I'll be playing the role of silent investor, along with the rest of the consortium."

"Where does your father stand on this?"

"I have my father under control."

"Forgive me for not being comforted," I say, noting the tic in his jaw, aware that I've hit a nerve I intend to continue to punish, "but your brother is dead and your father killed him. I'm assuming your brother thought he had him under control as well."

"That's where my brother fell short. He thought. He didn't know. He didn't create insurance. That won't happen with me, and it won't happen with you, which is why I'm here. Change, and a new direction, isn't easy. It comes with resistance, even anger. It takes backbone and real commitment to make it happen, no matter who fights you on it."

His words, and the passion with which he speaks them, resonate with me as relatable and sincere, while his actions and methods for achieving his goals do not. "If I agree to do this," I say, testing his honor and my level of influence over this man, if any, "I want Sub-Zero out of my facility completely."

"Soon," he agrees.

"Now," I counter.

"That's not possible."

"If you mean to legitimize Sub-Zero with my help, and through my operation, any connection to the illegal distribution of the drug is tempting fate and is self-destructive. And you don't strike me as self-destructive."

"You're right. I'm not, but I also don't have a death wish for either of us. I promised revenue to the cartel and delivered at above expectations. I cannot simply cut that off without consequences."

"You're the cartel."

"My father, and his inner circle, represents the beast that is the cartel. I'm the future for the Martina name."

"If running drugs through my operation is your plan for the future, it's not a good one. We have regulations and inspections. We will get caught."

"I have people in my pocket at every level in this city, and we only need to keep them in check for a short window of time, at which point this will be a nonissue. I'm selling off the illegal version of Sub-Zero to the highest bidder, and on the condition they provide their own distribution outlet."

"As in there's an auction going on that could leak to the Feds?"

"Your obsession with the Feds really is over-the-top and unnecessary. As I said, I have people in my pocket. I have a sale in the works. This is handled, but you need to be crystal clear on where we stand. Any disruption of revenue between now and the closing of the deal could destroy it and anger the wrong people, people we do not want angry. And you need to know and understand that I cannot, and will not, let that happen to either of us. Distribution cannot be disrupted."

"What do you think the Feds are?"

"Again with the Feds?" He scrubs his jaw. "Damn, man. Get over it. Read my lips if you can't understand the words coming out of my mouth: I have people in my pocket."

"And yet they raided my facility."

"It won't happen again. I've made sure of it, but I'll shelter you and deal with your brother. You won't know what's happening if questioned."

"My brother is not a token in your game."

"You are in his. You should thank me for giving him the impression he's fucking you over while you're the one fucking him over."

"I'm saving his ass, not fucking him over. He's my brother. My blood, which means something to me even if it doesn't to you."

"Your blood? Don't be sentimental. It doesn't suit you. He'd let you die to get ahead, just like mine would have me."

"And yet he's the one who died."

"That's right," he says, his voice taking on an icy quality. "He did."

"You say that like you feel no remorse."

"I say that like I'm a survivor and a winner, and so are you or I wouldn't be here." He glances at his watch, and I have the impression he does it to break eye contact. "And on that note, I have a naked woman in bed waiting on me who will get pissy if I don't get back to her soon." He glances back up at me, any emotion he might have been hiding now sheltered behind an unreadable mask. "And she's a vicious bitch when she wants to be." His lips quirk. "And since I looked into the eyes of your little Emily and saw ice you'll have to warm, I suspect you'll have a long night ahead of you as well." With that accurate statement, he reaches into his pocket and hands me another card, which I accept. "My private numbers," he explains, "which I'll assume you will use with discretion."

"You mean don't copy them, hand them out, and tell people you'll get them a good fix if they need one?"

He laughs. "I can think of a few people I'd like to do that to, but no. Please. Do not do that to me."

"You're apparently thinking I have that sense of humor you claim to lack," I say, sticking the card into my pocket. "Which in itself is amusing, considering that's the last thing anyone who knows me would call me. Focused. Yes. Driven. Yes. Vicious, by more than a few of my courtroom opponents. Abso-fucking-lutely."

"Sometimes," he agrees, "being vicious is the only way to win." We stare at each other, another of those battles of will between us, until he says, "But there's no reason to go there for us."

He's wrong. There is every reason, and that's exactly where this is going, a detail I'm too smart to voice to a drug lord's son without a survival plan, but then I don't get the chance anyway. He starts for the door and I watch his departure, having no intention of stopping him. I want him out of my apartment even more than I want him out of my company, but almost as if he's replying to those wants with defiance, he isn't quite ready to leave. He reaches the door and pauses, turning to face me, a dark, sharp shift to his energy.

"No one likes to believe their own blood will betray them, but denying that they will is a good way to end up dead. Your brother's your enemy, not me. Watch your back and keep your woman close."

He lingers just long enough to allow those words to punch through me, before he pulls back the door to depart, leaving me with one certainty. Veiled threats are unnecessary for a man like Adrian Martina, who has already been quite frank about his character, and that of his family. No. That was a genuine warning, and I'm not sure what bothers me the most. The fact that my brother is willing to kill me, or the fact that I have far too much in common with Adrian Martina for comfort. I know that man. I understand him. I even respect his intelligence and manipulation skills, skills that every attorney worth their salt must master. But then, you have to respect the abilities of your opponent or they defeat you, and I can only hope he underestimates me in a way I won't him. Because no matter how much I sympathize with his unique plight, his actions and my certainty that he would hurt those close to me to win his own war have made him my enemy.

He disappears inside, and I follow in his footsteps to ensure his rapid departure, entering the apartment to find him already halfway across the living area, his pace steady as he turns the corner and heads for the door. He pauses at the door, hand on the knob, heavy seconds ticking by, but he never turns. He inhales sharply on whatever words he seems to think better of speaking, and exits the apartment.

The instant he's out of sight, I dig my phone from my pocket, dialing Seth as I walk to the door, where I flip the lock into place. "He's gone," I announce when he answers. "You want to tell me how he got to me with no warning?"

"I'm working on that," he assures me. "What did he want?"

"That's a conversation I'm not having with you over the phone." And knowing I need to talk to Emily before I leave, I say, "We hired Nick's team to do a job, and as far as I'm concerned, they failed tonight. I need to see him in person. At his facility, where we can speak frankly."

"He's expecting as much. When and where?"

"Have a car waiting for me in the garage. I'll be there as soon as I can, but I make no promises as to how fast that will be." I end the connection and slip my phone back into my pocket, and a tight ball of emotions in my chest has me leaning against the hard surface of the door. Instantly, my mind is processing, trying to analyze and store things in a way that is logical, not emotional, but instead I bob and weave through it all: my father's cancer. My mother's infidelity. My brother's defiance and, most important, Emily, who has to be shaken by Martina's visit.

Shoving everything but her aside, I straighten and then walk down the hallway, turning toward the stairs, only to hear, "Shane," from behind me.

My jaw clenches at Emily's voice, and the realization that she isn't upstairs has me mentally cringing with the memory of Martina exiting the door that wasn't shut completely. Emily heard everything that was said, and I have a feeling I'm about to be in damage-control mode all over again. Turning toward her, I find her standing in the living area, on the other side of the couch, her hand pressed to the glass window, her complexion pale. Her brown hair is in sexy disarray, which is ten kinds of fucked up considering it's a creation of her nervous fingers, not my eager ones. Worse, though, it's not the desire I'd come home seeking in her eyes but rather the exact thing I never, ever want her to feel: fear. And I don't think Martina is the one who's scaring her. It's me. It's my family. It's this world I live in that is so much like the one she ran from. She's afraid I'm like her brother, my brother, and my father. Like everyone in her life and mine who ever let either of us down. She's afraid the path I'm traveling is taking me to the hollowed, dark places where they already live.

She's afraid of what I might become. Or perhaps already am, and she just doesn't know it yet.

CHAPTER SIX

SHANE

Frozen in place with the slice of the blade that is the fear and doubt I see in Emily's eyes, I stare at her, the armor I've learned to erect long ago, a way of surviving life in the Brandon clan, cracking like glass rather than remaining impenetrable steel. Each flaw forms a representation of the conflicting emotions I felt by the door moments before. I will them all back into containment, under my control, but there is one that refuses to be quieted: anger. And at the core of that anger is the realization that this woman who I love, who I want to protect—and yes, Derek, dear brother, I dare to admit to myself in this moment—who I want to make my wife, is shaken by me. Not my brother. Not my family in general. Not Martina. By me.

So yes. I'm angry. I'm angry as hell, in fact. Angry with my people for letting Martina up here to ever allow that look in Emily's eyes to exist right now. Angry with myself for allowing a conversation I couldn't avoid once Martina was here, to be held in a place Emily could overhear, when I know all too well what her family has put her through. But damn it, I'm angry with her too. She knows me. She knows what I'm trying to do and who I am, and it guts me that she now doubts me.

It's with that thought that I step forward, my stride long, and in a few short moments, I've closed the small space between my-self and the woman I love, who now thinks I'm no better than anyone else in her life, and from nothing more than one conver-sation. Instantly my senses are overloaded with the mix of my temper and her contrasting sweet floral scent, the memory of that smell on my skin after, and during, me licking and kissing her, heating my body. And just that easily, that dark, hungry need I felt in the elevator roars to the surface, a beast I want to deny that I know from the past, though I don't.

This part of me that punishes myself with the far too human feeling of self-doubt that I couldn't afford to feel then and damn sure can't now . . . the part of me that I would tame with hard, meaningless sex the night before every courtroom battle I feared I might lose, which was every damn one of them . . . He's the beast that demands satisfaction above all else and has none of the ten-derness or caution in him that the man Emily knows does. He's the man who wants to grab Emily now and kiss her with what I know would be punishment to us both. I should have protected her better tonight. She shouldn't have trusted me more. A ridicu-lous contradiction that I hate has even entered my mind.

"Why didn't you stay upstairs?" I ask, my voice low, tight, one part that anger I'm still feeling, another part barely bridled lust I will not unleash with Emily. Not when I'm in a mental and physical place that isn't one I frequent or welcome, and might just convince her I'm as dark and dangerous as she seems to think I am.

Her eyes flash in response to my demand, her chin lifting

in this delicate defiant way that just makes me want to say fuck it, and fuck her despite that animal clawing away at me. "Stay upstairs?" she demands. "I'm not a child sent to my room. I'm either in this with you or I'm not."

I tell myself not to touch her for all of one second, before I shackle her arm and pull her to me. Instantly, I am aware of her many soft curves pressing against me, tempting me in all kinds of deviant ways, but her words are what have my attention now, even above her body. "This is the second time tonight you've mentioned leaving," I say, hyperaware of her hand settling on my chest, scorching me through the starched cotton of my shirt. "If you keep bringing it up, I'm going to think that's what you want."

"I never said I wanted to leave. I said I can't be here if I'm not in this with you. You know I don't want to leave."

She's wrong. I don't know that at all, and judging from the shadows glazing her pale blue eyes, whether she realizes it right now, I'm not sure she does either. And since nothing else we can say on this topic, this night, under these circumstances, will change anything, I move on. "How much did you hear?"

"Everything, and yet I don't know what I heard. What was that between you and Martina?"

"Strategy," I say. "I'm letting him think I'm playing his game while I make it mine."

"Strategy?" she demands. "That's what he said. I can't begin to tell you how much I don't like you repeating his words."

There is a hint of accusation to those words that I do not like, and I turn her, pressing her against the thick wooden beam dividing two panes of the floor-to-ceiling window wrapping the room. My body lifts from hers, my hands settling on the wall above her, while her hands press to the glass on either side of her. And for several beats we just stare at each other, her gaze probing, looking for something, I assume for a reason to trust me. And I wonder what she finds. I wonder if it would be the same thing I would see if it were me looking.

"Shane," she says softly. "You and Adrian Martina—"

"It's a game, Emily. Just a game."

"A dangerous game."

"One that would be far more dangerous if I didn't play it right."

"Please tell me this right way doesn't include doing business with him."

"The right way is any way I get his drugs out of my facility."

"In other words, you are going to do business with him."

"We're already doing business with him. I'm controlling how and when until I can remove him from our lives."

"You're playing his game. He wants you in his inner circle. That was clear. This is what he wants."

"I let him think I'm playing his game. There's a difference."

She narrows her eyes at me. "I looked into that man's eyes, Shane. He's smart. He's intelligent. He's vicious. He scares the hell out of me, but he doesn't scare you, does he?"

"Fear to a man like Martina is like blood to a lion. He craves it. He will come after it. He will use it against you, and I won't give him that weapon. So no. I don't fear him, but I do understand him. I know who he is and what he wants. And that is power."

"Understand him? What does that even mean? He's not you. You know that, right? No matter what he might seem to have in common with you. He's not you. He's not really trying to do the right thing."

"At his core," I say, "he is like me. He's a son, a brother, and a businessman. A person who wants and desires something bigger or better. But our similarities are not bad, Emily. Knowing our enemies as well as they know themselves, or better, is how we defeat them."

"If you know him, then he knows you."

"He thinks he does."

"And I'm sure he's saying the same thing about you."

"You underestimate how well I stand toe-to-toe with my opponents."

"What happens when your opponents begin to feel like the ally your family is not?"

That anger I'm battling spikes hard and fast. "I am not your brother. I am not seduced by Martina's world the way Rick was your by stepfather's." My hand falls from the wall. "And right now I need to go find out how the hell Martina got up here in the first place." I back up, intending to turn away.

She grabs my tie and holds on to it and me. "Don't do that. Don't put words in my mouth and then try to leave to shut me out."

"I'm not shutting you out," I say, my hands staying by my sides, while that part of me that wants to fuck really wants to say to hell with my anger and touch her. And taste. And fuck her again.

"You are shutting me out," she says, snapping me back to the war of words. "We both know you are."

"I'm protecting you," I amend. "That's what I'm doing, and I need you to trust me to do that and to handle this."

Her grip on my tie tightens. "You have to give trust to get it."

I tilt my head slightly, studying her. "Meaning what?"

"You didn't want me to hear that conversation with Martina because you didn't think I could handle it."

"I just told you. I'm protecting you. Distancing you from this does that."

"And then who protects you, Shane?"

"I don't need protection."

"I disagree."

"I protect you. You don't protect me. Do you understand? You don't get involved."

"We protect each other," she argues. "That's who we are."

"Not in this, Emily. In this, I protect you. The end."

"You can't—"

"I can," I say, my hand covering hers over my tie, the touch, and that damn sweet floral scent of her, igniting more fire in my blood and making my voice lower, rougher. "I am. End of topic, and I need—"

"No," she says. "I need—"

"I need," I say, closing the small space my near departure created between us, my legs framing hers. "And the ways I can end that sentence right now are many. I need Martina out of my company." I swallow hard. "I fucking need my father to actually live and not die despite what a bastard he is. I need my mother out of Mike's bed. I need you here with me, but I need you safe. And I really need you to never look at me the way you looked at me right after Martina left tonight."

"What look, Shane?"

"Fear," I say. "Of me."

"No," she says, instantly rejecting that idea. "No. I'm not afraid of you."

"Wrong answer."

"I'm afraid of Martina. I told you that."

"And me."

She stares at me, those pale blue eyes of hers sharpening.

"Maybe it's you who's afraid of you. Maybe on some level you know you got along with Martina just a little too well. Maybe you—"

I tangle my fingers in her hair and tilt her face to mine, my anger now a live charge cracking around us. "You're wrong."

"What I am is here, and to be clear, I'm not going anywhere. I'm also not going to hide in a closet and stay silent. I will question you so neither of us loses you. I will ask questions. I will—".

"Stop talking," I demand, tightening my grip on her hair, adrenaline coursing through me. "You talk too much." I breathe the last word into her mouth, my lips covering hers, licking into her mouth, tasting her with a hunger that only she can create in me. She is sweet honey on my tongue when everything else sits like a bitter pill I cannot swallow. I can't get enough of her, and it's that idea, that realization, that only makes me hungrier, hotter. Gone is any worry that I'm too dark for her. There are just her damning words, over my fear of myself, that I do not like. This isn't about me. This is about her. She doesn't trust me. She thinks I'm like everyone else in her life, and that realization is like poison that doesn't kill, but punishes, the way I want to punish her right now. It torments me. She torments me, and that brings me back to the simple, easy-to-understand feeling of lust. Fierce, intense. *Now.*

Angry all over again, I reach down, grip the front of her blouse, and yank away the remaining buttons, immediately unknotting the material at her waist. Emily gasps, grabbing my shirt on either side of me, while I shove down the lace of her bra and stroke her nipples, which earns me her panted breaths. I swallow those sweet, sexy sounds, licking into her mouth again, expecting the taste of fear and doubt to overwhelm the arousal, but all I find is sweetness and need, though I know there is more there. More I both want and don't want to discover.

My fingers tighten where one hand remains threaded in her hair, and I give it an erotic tug, caressing her breast and then teasing her nipple again, and this time not gently. Actually, I'm not sure the first time was either. Nothing about me is gentle tonight, and gentle won't expose her fear. Gentle won't force her to admit it, and until she does, we can't face it and deal with it. And it's this idea that spurs my freedom to push her, to unleash every dark, brutal emotion biting away at me tonight. I want her to feel it, to taste it. I want her to admit she knows it exists.

But she doesn't try to resist or hesitate in any way. She arches into me, pressing her hips against the thick ridge of my cock. Giving me her submission, not her anger or her distrust. And on some level I know this should please me, but it does not. It does not. I need more, and I need it now. I release her hair and shove her back against the divider, our gazes colliding. Those sweet full lips of hers are parted, inviting me to kiss them again, my mind conjuring all the places they could be before this night is over. But the swell of my cock doesn't touch the swell of demand inside me. I want more from her than just her riding my cock. I want more. I want her to show me the emotion that drove that look I saw on her face.

I cup her breasts, thumbing her tight, swollen nipples, my cock so fucking hard it hurts. Her hands go to my arms, her lashes fluttering, lifting. "Shane," she whispers, her chest rising and falling, and I swear my name on her lips is everything right in my world, when everything else is wrong. I don't want her to fear me, but if she does, right now, in this moment, I need to know. I need to erase it and make it go the hell away.

Inhaling on a wave of lust, my hands settle at her waist. "Are you afraid of me, Emily?"

"No," she says firmly. "I am not afraid of you."

"I want to believe you. I want you to trust me."

"I *do* trust you, Shane."

But there are still shadows in her eyes. I hate those fucking shadows. They tell the story her words do not. They torment me every time I see them, and that knot in my chest tightens and expands, driving me to leave no crack in my armor, or hers, gaping and ready to break. And that thought spurs actions, ideas. I lift her off the divider, sidestepping and settling her weight against the floor-to-ceiling window, my legs shackling hers, protecting her. My hands press hers to the glass on either side of her body, and there is no mistaking her faster breathing or the panic in her eyes. "Now are you afraid?" I challenge.

"Considering I read an article about a couple in Japan who were having sex against a window and then fell to their deaths . . . Yes. I'm afraid the glass will break. So it's a good thing I trust you to catch me if it does."

Her words punch into that knot in my chest. "And if I leave you against the glass and walk away?"

"Then I'm alone and I can fall, but we both know you won't let that happen."

It's the right answer. It's what I want to hear. She trusts me. So why am I so dissatisfied with it? Why do I still want something more? Jaw clenched, I settle my hands at her waist again, and I pull her off the glass, her body all but next to mine, but I don't cave to the urge to pull her close. Instead, my lashes lower, and for a moment that turns into several more, I just inhale that sweet scent of her, waiting for the satisfaction that should follow but does not come. "Undress," I order, releasing her and taking a step backward.

"Undress," she repeats, making no move to do any such thing.

My gaze slides over her exposed nipples, lingering a moment and lifting. "Yes. Undress."

"And you? Are you going to undress?"

"When I'm ready," I say, maneuvering the large brown leather footstool in front of the coffee table and her. "For now," I add, sitting down on top of it, "I'm going to watch you."

Her eyes meet mine, hers narrowing, a tiny hint of vulnerability in their depths that is there and gone before I can even begin to analyze it. She knows I see it too, and she reacts in that feisty, fierce way I expect from her. Her chin lifts, challenge and defiance in her expression. She slides her blouse off her shoulders and tosses it aside. Turning the tables on me, she doesn't give me skin. She pulls her boots off next, as if she knows it's torturing me to wait for more. And it is, but damn if the burn in my body isn't the sweetest ache of any I've had tonight.

Her bra is next though. She unhooks it, but instead of removing it, she laces her fingers in front of her and it, her hands under her chin, and just watches me. But it's not hesitation to undress I see in her eyes. It's something else. Something I can't quite name, but I want to. She doesn't give me the chance to try. Without further delay, her fingers part, and she drags her bra down her shoulders. My gaze rakes over her beautiful, high breasts, her nipples already puckered, hard like my cock, before my gaze slides down her arm to the finger where her bra now dangles. Sensing there's a message in the action, my eyes find hers, my brow arching in question. Her lips firm, her eyes darken and she lets her bra drop to the ground. A calculated decision. A choice. The question is, is that choice about her taking control or giving it? It's a question I'll answer for her and soon.

She reaches down and unzips her pants, wasting no time in shimmying them down every delicious inch of her body, to expose pale, gorgeous skin, and kicking them aside. Her fingers then twine in the strings at her hips, and she drags the slip of lace that is supposed to be panties down her hips. They too dangle in her fingers, her eyes meeting mine, before she releases them.

I'm pulling my tie from my neck and standing before they ever hit the ground. "I'm going to tie you up, Emily," I say, closing the small space between us to tower over her.

Her response is quick and unexpected. "On one condition," she says.

"I'm listening," I say, and suddenly, while waiting on her answer, I realize she might be without clothes, but I am naked in every other possible way. And I know then that I am fucked up tonight, both looking for her confession of fear and dreading it.

"When this is over, you will not question how or why it happened. This is my choice. You didn't intimidate me into saying yes. You didn't scare me. I chose to give you this control because I trust you. Because I am not afraid of you, and when you are like you are tonight, I still won't be." She offers me her hands.

Every nerve in my body is jumping. Every dark part of me is now on fire. Every emotion a twisted knot that torments me with a demand that it be named. I won't allow myself that kind of weakness, and the theme of this night returns. Anger. Emily is the one pushing me to feel these things. She is the one pushing me to prove one thing: that I didn't see what I saw in her eyes tonight.

I toss the tie and drag her to me, tangling fingers in her hair again and cupping her backside. "Denial is destructive. You know that, right?"

"I do," she says, her fingers on my chest. "I know, but do you?"

"Damn it, Emily," I growl, my mouth coming down on hers, tongue sliding past her lips, a band of tension wrapping around us, my need to bend her will, to force her to admit the truth dominating, the way I want to dominate her. But she doesn't let me dominate her.

Her kiss is as fierce as mine. Her tongue as demanding, while her soft little hand manages to slide under my shirt that is somehow untucked, and scorch my skin. I deepen the kiss and squeeze her backside again, not sure who is pushing who. Not finding the fear I'd sought or expected, and that drives me to want it, to want her, all the more. I raise my hand and give her a smack on the bottom just hard enough to get her attention.

She yelps and then pants into my mouth. "Was that supposed to scare me? Because it didn't." She pulls back and looks at me, no hesitation in her words or eyes. "In fact, it turns me on. Everything with you turns me on, Shane. Do it again."

Possessiveness rises hard and fast, unfamiliar and intense. "Who spanked you before me?"

"Nothing matters before you," she says, her fingers curling at my jawline. "Do it again. You want to. I feel it. I know it."

"Holy fuck, woman. I was worried about scaring you."

"You mean you were convinced I was already scared. I wasn't and you can't scare me, but you can piss me off like you did when Martina left. That wasn't fear you saw in my eyes, Shane. That was anger. I was pissed. I still am."

I don't do us the injustice of playing naive. "Because I didn't want you to hear that meeting."

"Yes," she says. "And you know my past and all the secrets

and lies. You know the lie I have to live to survive. Don't give me more of the same."

"I also know the reasons your family gave you to feel insecure. I don't want you to feel that."

"Secrets make me feel that."

"It's not about secrets. I was—"

"Don't say 'protecting me' again. Don't even say it. Even now, you want to be the person you were in that elevator and you won't. Give me everything or nothing. I can't do in between. So you want to fuck me, you want to spank me? Stop holding back." She grabs my shirt. "*Stop* holding things back *from me*. I want the good, bad, and ugly. I want—"

I kiss her again, and damn it, if she wants the bad and the ugly, I'll give it to her. I lift her and carry her to the couch, sitting down, and before she even knows my intention, I have her over my lap, my hand on her backside. "I'm going to spank you now."

"Do it," she hisses. "Do it now."

But I don't do it now because that would defeat my purpose: seeking control and her giving it. And it wouldn't be about anticipation, pleasure, or escape. It would be about fast, hard pain. "Soon," I say softly, shutting my eyes, running my hand over her bottom, warming her cheeks, readying her beautiful backside, that dark part of me unleashed but controlled in a way it wasn't before. She isn't demanding that I spank her for me. She wants it for her. She wants the escape it can be, and I know now that she's needed that in the past, details of which I plan to find out. She was afraid tonight, but I was wrong about why. It wasn't because of me. It wasn't even because of Martina. It was about losing control, losing me and us. She wants the same escape I need, and I'm going to give it to her.

CHAPTER SEVEN

SHANE

My palm flattens on Emily's gorgeous backside, and she is trembling all over. "I'm not going to hurt you. I would never hurt you."

"I know that," she whispers, and then her tone becomes firm. "I trust you. Do it."

Trust.

There it is.

This isn't just about escape. This is her sending me a message. She trusts me, and even beyond that, she can handle anything and everything in this life we now share. It matters. And holy fuck, now I think I'm shaking and I don't shake. Ever.

"Shane!" she hisses, arching her back slightly. "You have to do it. The anticipation is killing me."

"That's part of it, sweetheart," I say, caressing her cheek. "The anticipation."

"It's too much. It's too—"

"I'm going to count to three."

"One," she says. "Two—"

My lips curve and I add, "Three," before my hand lifts and comes down on her. The first contact is forceful, but nothing that will hurt her. A sting that doubles that arch in her back and draws her gasp. The second stroke is immediately after, and a little lighter. The third is the hardest of all, and I finish it by cupping her cheek and leaning down to kiss her shoulder.

"No more," I whisper, turning her to face me, cradling her body. Our lips are close, our breath mingling. "Tell me you're okay?"

Her fingers curl at my cheek. "I am always okay with you, Shane."

My hand covers hers. "I want to know who did this to you before."

"No one who mattered. I told you. Nothing before you matters."

"I still want to know."

"Not now."

"No," I agree. "Not now." I shift us, lifting her and pulling her across my lap, her legs straddling my hips, and then her hands are on my shoulders, and one word comes to my mind. Naked. She has allowed herself to be totally, completely exposed with me, in ways her past says she should never allow it to happen.

We linger together, our lips still a lean from touching, the air thickening, the need between us swelling like a wave that suddenly breaks, the two of us moving at once, our lips and bodies melding together. And in a collision of everything that's happened tonight, we are kissing, touching, and all I can think about is being inside her. She tugs at my shirt, but I have no patience to remove it. I shift our bodies, and both of us attack the unzipping of my pants, and when I lift her, intending to set her aside to undress, somehow we are kissing again, and she's back on top of me.

Urgency pulses between us and we shove down my pants. Holding her waist with my arm, I hold her and she wraps the thick, hard ridge of my erection with her hand and guides it to her sex. I groan as the wet, tight warmth of her body slides down my shaft. When finally she has taken all of me, I am buried to the hilt, and we stay that way, joined together. And in this moment, I again think that she is everything right in my world, in a night when everything else is so damn wrong.

My hand settles at the back of her head. "I will protect you," I vow, and I don't give her time to tell me why that's wrong. It's not wrong, and it will never be wrong. I kiss her, a long, deep, drugging kiss that seduces me when it's meant to seduce her. No longer do I feel that dark, hard part of me. She softens me. She changes me. And as we begin a slow sway, I feel like I come back to her and to myself. Her fingers slice through my hair, tangling there, a brush of warmth, a tug of temptation. My fingers splay between her shoulder blades, molding her to me, even as my other hand covers her breast.

She moans. She sighs. She whispers my name and everything else fades. There is just the here and now. There is just Emily. She is the sunshine that was never supposed to exist in this storm I'm living. A calming breeze in the heat of demand, and still she manages to be fire in my blood. In this moment, I know it's with her that I will always find me. With her, I will always escape them. And when she stiffens, when I know her pleasure is a few thrusts away, I want to hold back. I want to keep her in that moment, but I don't. I want her pleasure too much. I want that moment that follows when she shakes and trembles for no one but me, and her body drives mine to an explosive release.

I collapse onto the cushion, and Emily melts into me, her cheek pressed to my shoulder, and I want to stay in this moment.

But I can't. Already my phone is ringing, calling me back to reality, and with it the memory of Adrian Martina standing in my apartment, where he should never have been at all.

"I need to take this," I say. "In case—"

"There's a problem," she supplies, leaning back to look at me. "I know."

And I wish like hell she didn't know. I roll her to her back, reluctantly pulling out of her as I do. "Stay here," I say, brushing hair from her beautiful, troubled eyes. "I'll get you a towel." She nods and I push off the couch, righting my pants I haven't even taken off and tucking back in my shirt, which is a testament to how wrong this night has gone.

My phone starts to ring again, and I walk toward the bathroom, fishing my phone from my pocket. A quick glance at the caller ID with my brother's number surprises me. I answer the call. "Is something wrong?" I ask, flipping on the bathroom light and grabbing a towel for Emily.

"What do you know about his treatment?" he demands, his tone gravelly, affected, and I have no doubt despite his every intention of beating me to the top, he's as shaken as I am.

Inhaling, I lean against the sink. "I know the program is real."

"Confirmed after dinner tonight?"

"Yes. Confirmed."

"What are his real odds?"

Fleeting memories of our shared past, when we were not enemies but family, brothers, fill my mind, tempting me to answer him with every detail I know. But those times ended forever tonight when he threatened Emily's life. "Does it really matter?" I ask instead. "He's dead if it doesn't work."

He's silent for several heavy beats. "He's a bastard."

Translation: Why is he letting Father's potential death get to him? "I tell myself that every time I give a damn too. It doesn't work. The idea of him dying still guts me."

"That's the magic of his manipulation," he says. "Not only does he know how to drive a blade and twist it, he enjoys it."

"We don't have to be part of his game, Derek."

"There would be no game, Shane, had you not shown up here and tried to take what is mine. I worked for this. I bled for this. And if you think anything you have done has made me give it up, you're mistaken. Go fuck your woman. I'll go fuck mine. And then we'll see which one of us fucks each other. Goodnight, brother." The line goes dead.

I grind my teeth, slide my phone back into my pocket, and with the towel still in hand, I press my palms on the counter, my chin pressing to my chest. Damn it. By his woman, he means Teresa Martina, Adrian's sister. He's pushing his luck. He's going to get himself killed. I have to create an exit for Martina and do it now. Shoving off the counter, I exit the bathroom and make my way back to Emily, where she still lies on the couch, but she's pulled a throw blanket over her.

I go down on one knee beside her and offer her the towel. "Sorry that took so long."

"It's okay," she says, accepting the towel and putting it to use before sitting up and working to shift the blanket around her shoulders. "Everything okay? I mean, as okay as it can be?"

I sit on the coffee table in front of her, my knees beside hers. "That was Derek."

"Derek called you? That's very unexpected."

"Yes, well, he wanted to know what I know about our father."

"Did you tell him what you found out?"

I shake my head. "No, because I don't know how he'll use

that information, and right now we need Mike Rogers and Adrian
Martina to believe my father is alive and will be staying that way.
That buys us time to remove them from the company."

"We? Meaning you and your father?"

"Yes. Me and my father, and I never thought I'd say those
words again."

Her hand settles on my leg. "I'd tell you he might make it,
but somehow I don't think that's what you want to hear."

"Hope is what I need everyone else to have while I plan for
the worst. I'm going to meet with Seth and his team to ensure
what happened tonight doesn't happen again." I reach up and caress her cheek. "I want you to feel safe."

"I want you safe. Don't do business with Martina, Shane.
Please."

"This isn't about me saying no to one man, Emily. This is
about a drug cartel. There are many layers beyond Adrian
Martina."

"But he's the one obsessed with you," she argues, and I can
almost see her mind racing. "He doesn't want to do business with
Derek. He knows he's a risk. That was clear. If you aren't involved,
maybe he walks away. So you walk away first, now. Give the company to your brother and let's go to New York and you—"

"No," I say, sitting back, withdrawing. "Derek will end up
dead, and you know I won't let that happen."

"Why would Adrian kill him? He'll lose interest."

"It's a risk I won't take."

"Derek would take it with you, Shane. Even Martina said
that."

My gaze sharpens, that edge from earlier returning with a
fierce jolt. "You don't want me to use Martina's words, but you
will."

She pales. "No. I'm sorry. Shane, you're right. That was wrong of me. I'm just . . . I'm afraid for you."

"I'm not Derek, Emily." I stand up and round the table and ottoman to walk to the window, pressing my hand on the divider I'd pressed her against this very night, and stare out at the Denver skyline, a rainbow of colors dotting the night sky. Emily appears by my side, and I voice what is in my head. "This is my city. My home. It belongs to me." I think of Derek's claim that I've stolen something from him. "It should have belonged to Derek, but it damn sure doesn't belong to Adrian Martina. He's going to find that out."

Emily steps in between me and the window, sliding onto the divider beneath my hand, her hand knotting the blanket at her chest. "Go to the FBI," she says. "Negotiate a way to save your family."

"The FBI's a two-headed beast," I say, leading her to the place I already am and where I need her to be. "The good agents will turn us into snitches, which equates to death or going into hiding. The bad ones will run straight to Martina."

"There has to be a solution. There has to be a way out."

"There is," I say, pushing off the divider. "And I'm handling it. I have a plan."

"Which is what?"

"Whatever it takes to end this."

Those pale blue eyes of hers turn stormy. "Define 'whatever it takes'?"

"Whatever it takes. And you need to decide if you can really handle that."

"I can handle what I know and understand."

"And therein lies the problem. You might not understand it at all. You just have to trust that I have no other option."

"I just want to know. Promise me you'll tell me."

"No," I say, no give to my reply.

She blanches. "No?"

"No. I won't make a promise to you that I might not keep, and in some cases what you don't know can't hurt you or be used against you."

"You mean if it's illegal."

"Take that how you wish, but right now I need to go meet with Seth and his men. I'm not sure how long I'll be gone. Lock up behind me." I turn and start walking, and I expect her to try to stop me. I don't realize how much I want her to until a step is gone, and then another, and each one is heavier with her absence. I reach the door and find myself pausing, willing her to appear. She doesn't, though, and I know that it's for the best. If she did, and if she said or did just the right thing, I might make one of those promises I swore I wouldn't break. And then I'd break it.

Hesitating another moment, I wrestle with the idea that I've created the fear in Emily that I just pressed her to prove doesn't exist. Inhaling sharply, I open the door and step into the hallway, sealing the door behind me. And then I wait and count out sixty seconds before I hear the locks on the other side of the door clang into place. She's locked up and she waited until she didn't have to see me again. But I can't think about that right now.

With each step, I shift from that man I am before a battle to the man who I am when I win that battle. The one who doesn't feel emotions. The one who controls everything. By the time I'm in the elevator, that edge that was animalistic and fierce is now a hard line that I control. I am focused on winning. By the time I step into the parking garage and find Seth leaning on the trunk of his silver Mercedes that he's parked beside my Bentley, his tie missing, his expression grim, I've already decided that Derek is going to learn to put the family first. My mother will get the hell out of Mike's bed or out of this family. Mike will learn he messed with the wrong Brandon. And Martina. Martina is about to learn that he too chose the wrong brother.

Seth pushes off the car, and I close the distance between me and him, stopping toe-to-toe with him. "What's Nick have to say for himself?"

"One of his men is missing."

Dead. That translates to dead. "Which one?"

"A family man named Ted Moore, with two kids. He was covering this parking garage when Adrian managed to get upstairs."

"Do we have security footage?"

"It was wiped clean."

"In my building that we're supposed to control."

"Isn't that Martina's point? To send you the message that you control nothing and have to play his game?"

"Beating someone at their own game is exactly how I like to win. Where's Nick now?"

Seth fishes his keys from his pocket. "The only place I know is one hundred percent secure, because I made it that way. He's at my house, waiting on us."

"And if I go, who's watching Emily?"

"A team led by Nick's best man, Cody Rodriguez, who I happen to know personally. No one will get past Cody."

"Someone did get by him."

"No. Cody just flew into town from another assignment. Nick pulled him here immediately. He's as good as they come."

"I'll save the rest of my questions for Nick." I motion to Seth's car. "I'll ride with you," I say, already walking to the passenger-side door while he climbs behind the wheel.

Neither of us speaks during the short drive to the Cherry Creek neighborhood where Seth lives, and where I'd considered moving, both of us watchful and thoughtful. And as I scan the roads, I think that it's time I start carrying my gun and get Emily one as well. I also decide that she was right. I am scared, but not of what I will become or perhaps what I already am. Everything I have done or will do is about saving my family and my woman.

No. What I fear is the moment when I'm forced to do something that I can fully justify but she can't. That moment I do something Emily can't live with, because I know her, and that means she won't be able to live with me.

CHAPTER EIGHT

EMILY

I lock up behind Shane, feeling naked beyond my skin beneath the thin blanket. Suddenly experiencing the sense of being exposed and out of control for too many reasons to count, I dart down the hallway and up the stairs. Once there, I dig out a pale pink bra and panty set, put them on, and then cover up with gray sweats and a long-sleeved black T-shirt. And because a drug cartel seems to be hanging around, I opt to slip on socks and tennis shoes before my mind starts racing, my thoughts twisting and twirling in such a whirlwind that I sink down onto the edge of the bed. Thoughts come at me hard and fast, but there are two that demand center stage. Shane just all but promised to shut me out, and I all but begged the man to spank me. He did spank me, and that connects to so many pieces of my past that should have made that traumatic and lost the me I've known, yet it did not. But then, it wasn't about me. It was about Shane and trust, which brings me back to his vow to shut me out.

"But it's not about trust," I whisper, thinking about his promises to protect me and quickly dashing my anger. Shane's had a hellish night. Anger doesn't help him. My mind goes back to a statement he made. *I am not Derek.* He's right. He's not like this brother, but if this "war" as he calls it forces him to stoop to that level, what will he be on the other side? I have to help him find a way out of this that won't do that to him, and do it in a way that doesn't get us all killed.

Which is what? I go back to a certain law professor who used and abused me, and pretty much said the same thing Shane did tonight. Know your enemy better than they know themselves or you. I need to gather every fact I can for Shane and present him with every idea I can to defeat his enemy.

I push off the bed and dart for the door and down the stairs, my destination the office. Once there, I flip on the light and by-pass the giant mahogany desk directly in front of me, cutting left to the couch and chairs framed by bookshelves. Claiming the spot on the floor between the couch and the coffee table where my MacBook sits, I power it up and bypass all my research on the new fashion line I'm determined to make happen for Brandon Enterprises. Right now I have one thing on my mind: finding Adrian Martina's weakness.

I start reading, and it's kind of eerie how alike he and Shane are in many ways. Both with elite educations. Both with family empires they're battling to control. Both with brothers, only Adrian's is dead, and . . . gulp. At the hand of his father. So add a brutal father to the list of commonalities they share. But the one difference that stands out to me is a sister. Adrian has a sister, and she is the one Derek is involved with. I have no idea why, but she feels important. Teresa Martina has my attention. If only we didn't have her brother's.

SHANE

Twenty minutes after I leave Emily in our apartment, Seth guides us past the foliage-covered gate of his traditional-looking home with a steepled top, the exterior impression more family home than bachelor pad to an ex-CIA operative. But then, that's exactly why an ex-CIA operative would want it. Traveling the driveway, we cut into the back of the house, and there's a white Porsche, my brother's favorite color and make, parked outside the garage.

"Nick's," Seth says, hitting the electronic pad above his visor to open the garage door. "Needless to say, leaving the FBI and opening his own security business has been a good decision, though I doubt with his man's disappearance, he'll agree."

"Considering Martina made it to my apartment on top of that," I say dryly. "I'm not sure I can agree either, but at least he has something in common with my brother. Maybe Nick can understand Derek where I can't."

He pulls the car into the garage and lowers the door behind us. "Your brother is a narcissist and driven by greed. I understand him just fine."

I glance over at him. "He called me tonight."

"He wanted to know about your father's treatment," he assumes, popping open his door, "like you did."

"He did," I confirm, exiting the car to meet his stare over the roof, a realization hitting me. "But my mother didn't," I add as we walk to the entry.

Seth keys in a code on a panel by the door. "Maybe she elected Derek to call you."

Rejecting any answer that indicates my mother has the heart my father does not, I offer another solution. "Or she told Mike about my father's treatment and he's trying to get her answers."

"In which case," he assures me, "he'll find the information we made sure he finds."

"As long as his people weren't as fast as ours."

"Despite tonight's events," Seth says as we enter the newly remodeled house to be greeted by pale hardwood steps to match the flooring in the entire lower level, "you have the upper hand with our team."

"After tonight," I say, the two of us starting the climb up the wide steps before us, framed by stainless-steel handrails, "that's a statement I'm going to need Nick to back up with more than words, or we're replacing him."

"He will," he promises, and in a few seconds we reach the top floor and walk directly into a library, with bookshelves lining the walls and several gray leather chairs with ottomans sitting at various locations. In the center of it all is a long wooden table with a half dozen MacBooks on top, and Nick is behind it, talking on his phone, his military-style buzz cut as extreme as the set of his jaw.

He looks up as we step into the room. "I need to call you back," he tells his caller, ending the connection as he stands, allowing me a view of the Harley-Davidson bloodstained-skull graphic on his black T-shirt, the FBI conservative logo announcing his past nowhere to be found. "I have no excuse to offer you," he says, pressing his hands on the table as Seth and I stop on the opposite side of it. "But Cody Rodriguez is leading your team now, and he's not only damn good, this is his world. He was born and raised in Mexico, and he was undercover in a competing cartel at one point." He slides a folder across the table. "That's his file."

I ignore the file and focus on him. "Do we know how this happened?"

"No," he says. "And that's as honest as it gets, but I will find out, and people will pay for it."

"What about your man?" I ask. "Is he still missing?"

"Yes. Ted is still missing, and I'm here now to reassure you that I'm dealing with this, but I need to be somewhere else, helping my team find him."

My mind goes back to my meeting with Martina and every one of the many conversations I've had tonight on strategy. "You won't find him unless Martina wants you to find him," I say, reaching into my pocket and removing my cell phone, and the business card Martina gave me. "I'll handle this," I add, glancing at the number on the card, playing the game Martina wants me to play but doing it my way.

"Handle it how?" Nick asks.

I punch Martina's number into my cell and toss the card onto the table. "I'm going to the source of our problems." The line rings twice.

Martina answers on ring three. "Shane Brandon," he says, a smile in his voice, his identifying greeting no doubt meant to let me know that he already has my number, though I never gave it to him. "Miss me already?"

"Ted Moore gets returned alive and well or that deal we discussed is no deal at all."

"I'm always happy to aid a friend. Who exactly is Ted Moore, and who do I need to kill to get him back?"

A threat. And not even a subtle one. "Alive, Adrian."

"I don't know Ted, but I own this city and I believe in the return of favors. You're going to get my drug into a trial and I'm going to get your man back to you."

Favors. Quid pro quo. I get Sub-Zero into the drug study. He returns Ted. And how I respond to that clear setup, right here and now, will set a precedent for our future interactions. In other words, I have to gamble on Ted's life and just how much Martina wants this drug study, or risk many others.

"I'm going to look at the information your consortium sends me," I say, establishing that I still control this relationship. "And I can promise you only one thing during this phone call. If Ted were to die, I would be too distraught and shaken by the death to even consider looking at the information for months. In fact, I might have to take time off for therapy."

There is a beat of silence, then two, then five, before he laughs. "I'd love to be a fly on the wall in one of your therapy sessions. I'm putting word out on the street that this 'Ted' has my protection. I'll be in touch." The line goes dead, and I slip my phone back into my pocket.

"Tell me whatever you just did got me Ted back alive," Nick says.

"If he's not already dead, then it did."

"When will we know?"

"He isn't going to give us Ted back without a wait. That would make it seem like I said jump and he asked how high."

Nick scrubs his lightly shadowed jaw and presses his fists to the table. "I need a gut instinct here. Is Ted alive?"

"Yes. I believe he is."

He gives me a several-second hard look and then nods. "Then thank you, man. Because I really don't want to tell his wife otherwise."

Seth gives the table a quick knuckle knock. "What did Martina want tonight?"

My cell phone rings, and I remove it from my pocket to find

Emily's number, my jaw setting, and after a ten-second hesitation, I press decline. I can't talk to her right now, not without risking my decisions being swayed by her moral compass, not Adrian's, and Adrian's is the one that could get us all killed. Again I slide my cell back into my pocket to find Seth and Nick staring at me.

"It wasn't him" I say, and force us back to Martina. "Everything about this night, including Ted's disappearance, is about Adrian Martina letting us all know he's in charge. I suggest we sit down, I fill you in on my conversation with him, and then we come up with a way to ensure he's not right about that."

There are some grumbles and exchanges about shutting Martina down, but the conclusion is that Seth and Nick are sitting at the table, with me directly across from them, while I fill them in on my conversation with Adrian. When I'm done, Seth narrows his stare at me. "You don't really think he's trying to go legitimate, do you?"

"I believe there's some part of him that believes that's what he wants," I reply.

"I've studied this man," Seth says. "And I agree. He believes that's what he wants, and ironically, he justifies one bad deed after another as a means to that end."

"And he thinks with his Ivy League education and expensive suits, he's better than the rest of his family," Nick adds. "But he's no better than them, or my man wouldn't be MIA right now. He's just a gangster in a suit."

My e-mail beeps on my phone, and I remove it from my pocket and glance at the screen. "A gangster who just e-mailed me," I say, tapping the screen to open the e-mail and read it out loud.

Shane:

*I'm stepping ahead of my team and sending you the list of
our consortium members. Now you have time to vet them
and be appropriately impressed. We can help each other.
Still looking into your problem. Nothing yet.*

Adrian

"I have a good mind to go to that bastard's restaurant and
point a gun at his head until he gives me Ted," Nick says.

"He's giving us something to do while we wait on Ted," Seth
comments.

"That's right," I say. "It's part of him controlling us. Everything is about him." I grab one of the computers sitting on the
table. "But be careful where you shine the spotlight," I add.
"Someone might see something you don't want them to see. If this
consortium really is all-powerful and untainted by the Martina
clan, we have to make sure they know who he is."

"It won't matter," Nick says. "He owns them, or he wouldn't
be in business with them."

"He's right," Seth says. "Like we made sure we owned our
stockholders, he's made sure he owns them. I'd bet my life on it."

"Let's hope that's true," I say. "Because powerful people don't
like to be owned, and they will look for an escape."

"And we'll be the escape," Seth adds. "I like it." He pulls a
computer to him. "Let's give the man what he wants. Let's look
at the list of consortium members."

"Are you going to reply to that e-mail?" Nick asks.

"I'm not responding to anything else until we get Ted back,"
I say.

"He'll know you read the e-mail," Seth points out. "He has tech resources."

"Good," I say. "Then he knows my lack of reply is a choice."

Fifteen minutes later, Nick has e-mailed the list of consortium members to his best hacker, while he, Seth, and I dig through it ourselves as well. An hour later, it's nearly midnight, and Nick is in touch with his field operation but has no word on Ted. For my part, despite the interesting, and yes, impressive list of consortium members I can focus on, I find myself typing out a personality profile on Adrian. His strengths. His weaknesses.

My cell phone rings, and I glance down to find Emily calling again. Inhaling, I decline the call a second time, not sure why I can't hear her voice right now. That's not true. I do know. A man could be dead, directly related to Martina being in our apartment tonight. She will hear that in my voice when no one else would. I send her a text: *Is everything okay?*

Her reply: *Are you okay?*

Me: *I'm with Seth and Nick, doing research. I won't be home soon.*

There is a long pause in which I find myself staring at the screen and waiting for her reply that doesn't come. Finally, I type: *Are you okay?*

Her reply: *Yes.*

Nothing more. And damn it, I need more, when I'm the one who didn't answer the phone. I set my cell down on the table next to me and turn it over, and when I intend to look at my computer screen again, I find myself replaying something Martina said tonight. *You're protective of her, as I am of my sister. But know this, Shane Brandon. If you are loyal to any agreement we make, now or later, as I assure you I will be in reverse, I will protect her, even kill for her.*

I key in a name: Teresa Martina. The woman in my brother's bed.

TERESA

I jolt awake and sit up, tugging the blanket over my thin pale pink gown, my gaze swinging wildly around my bedroom, sensing I'm not alone. "Teresa."

At the sound of Derek's voice, I yelp and then turn toward him, my gaze cutting through the shadows to find him sitting in the leather chair in the corner directly to my right. I recover quickly from the surprise of him being here, but I'm also shocked and pleased that he has actually used the key I gave him weeks ago. Rotating, I let my feet dangle over the side of the bed, and blink into the darkness, slowly having his outline become clear, seeing a glass of whiskey in his hand, his usual tie absent. I glance at the clock and note the two A.M. hour, aware now that he has not been home, but he has not been here either.

Inhaling, I don't speak. I just sit there and he sits there, with those now familiar waves of torment rolling off him, telling me that he is once again fighting those inner demons of his that both draw me to him and warn me away. He's headed for trouble with my brother, the kind I'm trying to escape. And while I know this, I can't seem to turn him away. I can't. Somehow, despite all of the many flaws he presents, I fell in love with him.

He downs his drink and then throws the glass against the wall. I jump but don't make a sound. I know he had dinner at his parents' house earlier, and I know that every demon he battles is clawing and biting him tonight. And I know why he is here and what he needs. He leans forward and rests his elbows on his knees. "My father got into a drug trial in Germany."

I am on my feet in an instant, crossing to stand in front of him. His hands go to my hips, and he presses his head to my belly. My hands settle on his head, fingers threading through the dark locks. "No one understands what it's like to be conflicted over your father more than I do," I say. "I've told you what a monster mine is, but yet . . . I still love him."

He looks up at me and then sits back, pulling me onto his lap, my legs straddling his hips. "And if your father died? How would you feel?"

"Confused. Hurt. Scared. Relieved for the world and guilty for feeling that as his daughter." I lean forward and cup his face. "I told you. No one understands what you're feeling more than I do." I press my lips to his and he cups my head, claiming that control he so needs and always demands, his tongue pressing into my mouth in a deep, tormented kiss. He hates his father. He loves his father. He hates himself right now, and I know that feeling and it's a lingering feeling, because you can't escape yourself or your family. Lord knows, I've tried.

"Teresa," he murmurs softly, and I answer by sitting back and pulling my gown over my head. It's barely left my skin before he's dragging me to him, kissing me again, his hands caressing my skin, his fingers reaching up and pulling away the tie binding my long dark hair. He strokes it free, touching me everywhere, like he can't get enough of me, his caresses tender and yet wild. I lose myself in his demands and needs. In the way he touches me, holds me, demands more of me, and I do so knowing that the only place he lets go, the only person he lets see the vulnerability he shows in these intimate times, is me. And for this reason, I can be vulnerable. I can be wild, and I don't even care that he is not undressed. I just want him inside me, and somehow we get his pants down enough for me to make that need a reality.

I slide down on him and he molds me closer, and then we are kissing, swaying, and escaping both of our worlds that have somehow become one. And when it's over, when we've collapsed and I'm lying on top of him, my head on his shoulder, neither of us is in a hurry to move. Eventually though, Derek stands and carries me across the room and into the bathroom. He flips on the light and sets me on the tiled navy countertop, pulling out of me and pressing a towel between my legs.

I quickly clean up and I hate that he's dressed, perhaps ready to leave, but that isn't what happens at all. I toss the towel in the sink behind me, and when I face forward again, his hands come down on the sink on either side of me. One is bandaged and I don't ask about it. One thing a Martina woman learns is, just don't ask. You wait until they tell you, if they ever tell you. But he doesn't tell me anything. He just stares at me, his eyes murky with shadows, his lashes lowering. My hand goes to his jaw. "You came here for a reason. Talk to me."

His gaze lifts and finds mine. "I came here for you. Just you." He inhales and shoves off the counter. "And that will matter more when I get the filth of this day washed away." He turns away from me, undressing and walking to the shower, turning it on and stepping inside. Staying here with me, which speaks volumes about his state of mind. He needs me and he's willing to admit it.

I climb off the sink and walk to the shower too, where Derek is now standing under the spray of water, his back to me. I open the door and he doesn't turn, but I am not dissuaded. I walk to stand in front of him, and in a blink, his hands are on my waist and I'm in the corner, his big body shielding me from the water.

"I used you to get to your brother."

Stunned, I blanch, but recover quickly. "I knew that the minute you met him," I say, concern filling me. "Why are you telling me this now?"

"You knew already?"

"Yes."

"Then why did you let me?"

"Because my brother might be a bastard, but he's my brother, and this is my family. If you wanted to be close to my brother, you would have found a way. This way I knew what you were doing and why. I was protecting him."

"Did you tell your brother?"

"No."

"Why?"

"Because I'd already decided you were an asshole I cared about by the time I knew."

"I'm not using you now."

"I know that too."

"You matter to me, Teresa. I hate that you matter to me, but you do."

"I'm not sure how to take that."

"I'm not sure what do with that."

I study him a moment, looking for an answer I don't find but need. "There's still more, isn't there?"

"My father gave my brother control of the company while he's in treatment," he announces, which I know is devastating news for him. "That man," he continues, "has used his death to taunt Shane and me into a war over a company that should be mine. Every wrong move I made was really my father's, but I took the fall for him. I took the fall. I deserve the company. I earned that badge, and I can't let him or Shane take it. So do I want him to die? No. But that hate I feel for him runs deep."

"Can you change his mind?"

"I know him," he says. "It's done."

"Why would he do that to you?"

"Shane convinced him your brother will take it from us, when my father all but shoved me at you and your brother."

"At me," I say, my throat thickening, that admission more than a little bit cutting.

He cups my face. "I regret using you, but had I not, we wouldn't be here tonight."

"What does that even mean?"

"I need you. Is that what you want to hear?"

"For me or for my connections?"

"For you, baby. I need you, or I would not be here tonight, talking to you like this. I don't—"

"I know. I know you care about me, or I promise you I'd be out of this corner and you'd be hunched over."

His hands settle on my shoulders. "Then I need to tell you something else."

"And here it comes. The real reason you're telling me this tonight."

"One of the reasons," he amends. "Shane recorded me telling him you were just a fuck. I was talking out my ass. I was—"

"And you said you fucked me to get to my brother."

"Yes. And I said it like you were a conquest."

"You're such an ass. I don't even know why I'm here with you." I try to get past him.

His legs lock around mine. "You said you knew."

"I wanted to be wrong, but suddenly it feels really shitty, like my judgment in men."

"Don't say that."

"Did I mention that you're an asshole?"

"An asshole who wants you."

"You mean, who needs me to get to my brother."

"You know that's no longer true."

I don't know, and I don't think I'm going to be rational about it when he's standing in front of me naked, so I don't try. "If Adrian wants your company, it's already his."

"He couldn't take it, and even if he tried, it would be insanity to connect a drug cartel to a pharmaceutical company."

"If he wants it, he has a plan, and maybe it's not even the pharmaceutical branch he really wants. You don't understand my brother or my family. I love Adrian, but he's like my father; he's brutal and greedy, something my younger brother didn't learn and now he's dead."

"Your father killed your brother."

"After Adrian set him up."

His brow dips. "If you believe that, why are you here with him?"

"He's my brother, and beyond that my answer is as complicated as yours is about your father and it's not what's important right now. You better hope your brother doesn't play that tape for my brother."

"Shane isn't that brutal."

"I hope you're not underestimating him, and you had better not underestimate Adrian. The only way to get Adrian out of your business is to make him think he makes the choice on his own. You have no idea what Adrian is capable of, but I do. He'd kill for me, but everyone else he kills, and there have been many, he kills for himself."

CHAPTER NINE

EMILY

Teresa Martina.

I tell myself to think of her, and her story that I have yet to figure out, not the fact that Shane isn't home yet and isn't taking my calls. That works at midnight. It works at two in the morning. By three though, it's no longer my ticket to sanity, and yet somehow at five I wake up on the couch, still in the office, and incredibly, I've dozed off. I check my phone to find nothing from Shane. I stand up and pace, my hand ripping through my dark hair that I wish right now was its natural blond. In the absence of the familiar with Shane, I crave something I know, something that feels like me.

I don't understand why he's not communicating with me. He was just supposed to be checking on the security breach, but I'm still alone. And I could deal with that if he'd just talk to me. I sink down on the floor between the couch and the coffee table, where I've spent hours tonight, and I key my computer back to life, but another story about the brutality of the Martina family isn't helping my waning sanity. And that's how I keep focusing on Teresa. There's nothing violent in her past. There's nothing much at all to her past that's documented. She's twenty-two, in school, and seems to be low profile. But aren't the silent ones often the most dangerous? She's too squeaky clean to make sense. I mean, she's here, working at her brother's restaurant.

When six in the morning rolls around and I'm still alone, I decide to take a jog. I don't know if leaving the apartment is even okay though, so I decide to text Seth: *Unless I hear otherwise, I assume I can take my morning jog and go to work. Brandon Senior is expecting me. I'm leaving for my jog in exactly thirty minutes.* Message sent, I head upstairs, change into a sports bra, grab my headset, and then head downstairs where I down a protein shake, which I barely manage to stomach. At the thirty-minute mark, my phone beeps with a message from Seth: *Normal activity is acceptable.*

I grimace at the phone. "Normal activity is acceptable," I repeat, and I try to take comfort in the hidden meaning of that formality. Clearly everything is fine with Shane if "normal activity is acceptable." He's just not talking to me or coming home. Oh yeah. I really need that run. Heading to the foyer, I intend to depart quickly but find myself gun-shy to open the door, as if Adrian Martina, not Shane, will be standing there. I inhale and will myself to get by my nerves, yanking open the door and exiting into the hallway. Stopping just outside our apartment, I make sure I've locked up, and as I start walking, I really hate how uneasy I am. Running is my sanity. It's my escape, and yet I'm second-guessing my choice right now, despite Seth's approval. I halt and turn around but grimace at my nerves. This is our life. Martina and my brother's hacker hellhounds aren't going away. I can't hide in our apartment or I might as well go find a safe house and live in a hole. Besides, it's better that I run off steam before I see Shane again than end up responding to him emotionally and blasting him, which solves nothing.

Heading down the hallway, I enter the elevator and flash back to Shane doing his best to strip me naked in the car last night. He'd needed me then. He clearly needs space now. I'd respect and understand that if I wasn't so sure this silence is related to his vow to do whatever necessary to beat Martina, while all but assuring I won't know the details. He doesn't want me to know what he's doing because he doesn't want me to talk him out of it. I don't even want to know what that means he's doing right now. I exit the elevator with this in my mind, but quickly find I'm distracted by my surroundings. Scouting for trouble, I find only a few businesspeople here and there, and nothing and no one dangerous.

Exiting to the front of the Four Seasons, I'm thankful the familiar faces are not chatty ones, and I make a fast escape down the sidewalk. Turning on my music, a Jason Aldean song Shane and I both enjoy, I insert my headphones and start running. Soon I'm feeling the burn in a good way, but it's not blocking out my thoughts as I'd hoped. One minute I'm replaying my night with Shane, and the next I'm back in a memory I despise. I'm tied up, while my tattoo artist ex-boyfriend, if you could call him that, Bobby J, is fucking another woman in front of me. Because of course, dating a professor who used me wasn't enough. I had to rebound with his complete polar opposite, a man with a propensity for kink, while letting myself become his sex doll. I stop running, bend over, and press my hands to my knees. Damn it, why am I going there now? Why? I hate that time in my life. I hate that person I was, who I don't even know as me.

Why now?

I start walking, a coffee shop in my sights, and with each step

my surroundings come back to me, a prickling sensation beginning on my neck. Actually, I think I've had it for a while now.
Like I'm being watched or followed. My gaze catches on a horse
and carriage parked at the curb, and I approach it, stopping to
admire the horse, stroking his nose, while discreetly scanning left
to find a tall dark man with a hoodie walking in this direction,
along with two men in suits, who pass him and keep walking.
Glancing right, there is a lady with a dog. Normal people. Normal
activities. And yet that feeling of unease remains.

Turning away from the horse, I eye the coffee shop again and
hurry in that direction, seeking the shelter it offers, not to mention the caffeine for my sleep-deprived body. Entering the shop,
I am immediately calmer and really regretting this run as I make
a fast path to the short line. As I'm standing there, waiting to
place my order, my mind goes to my brother and the hacker operation hunting him and me, then moves to Adrian Martina. Will
there ever be a day when I run again and don't look over my shoulder? I order my coffee and turn. My heart lodges in my throat as
the man from outside enters the shop and pulls down his hoodie.
To my distress, his eyes meet mine, and there is no question in
my mind. He's here for me.

I turn, fully intending to race for the bathroom, but a lady
and her three kids step into my path. My heart is thundering in
my ears. Time seems to stand still as I step around them and dash
for the too-distant back of the shop, finally turning down the hallway, but to my distress, once I'm at the ladies' room door, it re-
quires a pass code I don't have. I rotate again just as the man I'm
running from enters the hallway and, my God, he's big, broad,
and in my path.

"Who are you and what do you want?" I demand.

"Emily," he says, making it clear that I'm right. He's here

for me. "I'm Cody." He holds up his hands, his dark hair curling in slightly at his brow, his eyes meeting mine. "I'm the new head of your security detail."

"Security detail?" I ask incredulously. "I have a detail now?"

"You do," he says. "Starting today."

"And as the head of this detail no one told me about, you sneak up on me? How about introducing yourself and letting me know you're with me?"

"That's what I'm doing now."

"You should have done it sooner, and how about someone calling me and telling me you're about to corner me?"

"Someone was supposed to call you before I approached you," he explains. "I had no idea he hadn't. I'll call him so you know I'm with him."

"No," I say when he reaches for his phone, and I see a tattoo of a cross exposed on the back of his hand, more ink disappearing under his black hoodie sleeve. "Just show me a text message from him or a business card."

"How about both?"

I nod, and he reaches into his pocket to hand me a card with a security firm listed. He follows that by handing me his phone with a text message from Seth about me that reads: *Emily's jogging in thirty minutes. I'll make contact and let her know who you are. Shane wants to meet you once she's safely at work.*

"Obviously he didn't make the contact he promised," Cody says. "And I promise to give him hell." I hand him back his phone and he adds, "As I'm sure you will as well."

"Oh yes. I will." I stick the card into my pocket. "Thank you. And now I just want to get my coffee."

"Understood. Let me key all my numbers into your phone and then I'll leave."

I pull my phone from my pocket and he takes it from me, punches in several numbers, and then hands it back to me. "I gave you my cell and home number, as well as Nick's cell number as well. See something, say something. Call or text me if you need anything. I won't ever be far, and know this. I just got into town. I'm Mexican. I've got extensive experience with cartels, which is why I'm here, and I'm better at my job than Martina's people are at theirs. Had I been there, Martina would not have made it to your door. I'll be close." He doesn't wait for a reply. He turns and leaves.

I am perhaps marginally comforted. I tell myself this man is Shane's way of telling me that even when he's not with me, he's protecting me. Exiting the hallway, I watch as Cody travels toward the door, and by the time I've walked to the counter and retrieved my coffee, he's disappeared outside. Out of sight, but obviously not gone. Ready to retreat to the apartment again, I head for the door myself as well, when my eyes catch on a dark-haired man sitting at a table in the corner. Something about him strikes me as familiar. He's handsome in a stunning kind of way: his cheekbones are chiseled, his facial features well-defined. He doesn't look up, and I can't keep staring, but as soon as I look away, I swear I feel him looking at me.

It's a crazy notion, or maybe not considering my life right now, but whatever the case, I shove open the door and turn onto the sidewalk, heading back toward the Four Seasons. I've made it all of a foot when my cell phone rings, and hoping for Shane, I check my caller ID to find it's Seth.

"Communicate, Seth. Don't send a stranger to me when I'm this on edge."

"He's a good man."

"That might be true, but I didn't know he was following me, and I have too many reasons to be on edge to have a surprise like that. So I repeat. Communicate, Seth."

"I had a situation, but you're right. I should have told you sooner."

I want to ask about Shane. I don't. "Shane should have told me."

"He's juggling—"

"Don't make excuses for him. It doesn't suit you or me. He's okay. I'm okay. Cody is okay. Jogging today was a bad idea. Let's leave it at that." I end the call and shove my phone back into my pocket, my mind returning to that man in the coffee shop. Why is he so familiar? Maybe obsessing over him is easier than thinking about Shane shutting me out.

And I'm still obsessing about him when I step onto the elevator, and the very fact that I think the man is Mexican is clawing at me. It's just too much of a tie to Martina, on top of the familiarity, for me to ignore. I decide to text Cody a note: *There was a man in the coffee shop who looked familiar as I was leaving. Dark hair. Mexican, I think. Familiar, and I don't know why.*

Cody immediately confirms with: *Investigating.*

It's not much of a reply, but at least he replies.

I exit the car and hurry to the apartment to discover what I assumed to be true. I'm still alone. With my body tense, I hurry upstairs and shower, that man in the coffee shop invading my thoughts often. Once I'm dressed in a black suit dress and heels, my brown hair sleekly flat ironed, my makeup done in darker pinks and roses today to hide the effects of no sleep, I head downstairs. I'm about to grab a cup of coffee to go, when I decide to detour to the office. I sit down and start tabbing through everything

I studied last night, when I stop abruptly, my heart racing wildly at the sight of the man I'd seen in the coffee shop in a photo with, of all people, Teresa Martina.

I text a copy of his photo to Cody, certain he'll come to the same conclusion I have, knots forming in my belly. Funny how an international hacking operation hunting me, most likely looking to kill me doesn't seem nearly as daunting when members of a drug cartel have you in their sights. I dial Cody as well, not sure I should leave the apartment. He answers immediately. "Do you know that man?"

"Only from the research I did last night. He's Ramon Aguila. Martina's head of security, and there's no way he was in that coffee shop when I was by coincidence. He was there for me."

"It's a small neighborhood the Martina family inhabits as well. It could have been—"

"He was there for me," I press. "I don't do well with coddling. Be straight up with me."

He's silent a beat. "Okay," he says. "Yes. I'd say he was there for you, but so was I."

"You didn't know he was there."

"I did know."

"And you didn't tell me?"

"I'm telling you now."

"That's the second time you've said that to me today. Don't say it again. Why would he follow me?"

"Because he knew we'd know who he is and he wanted Shane to know he's watching you."

"He's using me to try to control Shane."

"Yes. He's using you to try to control Shane."

I say nothing else. I end the call and draw in a hard-earned breath. If I'm going to be used as a weapon against Shane, I have to figure out how to become a weapon against Martina. My gaze lands on the photo of my coffee shop stalker and Teresa Martina, the woman Adrian Martina said he'd kill for and perhaps the only person on the planet who knows his weaknesses. Oh, what I wouldn't do to have a conversation with her, but then, she'd never tell me how to defeat her brother in this war. I suck in air with a realization. She's in Derek's bed. She might tell him, but then, he's Shane's enemy as well. But maybe he doesn't have to be mine.

SHANE

Seven in the morning comes with Ted still missing, and Martina doing his best to send me a message before he returns him. I didn't win. He can get to Emily anytime he wants. Well, if that was his opening statement, I have a reply for him. I enter the Blue Roof bagel shop two blocks down from Martina's Casa and immediately find the pretty dark-haired woman in the back corner booth, a book open in front of her. A man on a mission, I stalk in her direction, and seeming to sense my approach, Teresa Martina glances up. Her eyes go wide, panic in their depths. She shuts her book and sets it on the seat next to her as I claim the seat across from her, inhaling in that way people inhale when they're about to perjure themselves when giving testimony.

"You know who I am," I observe.

"You look like your brother."

"And that's how you know who I am?"

"No," she surprises me by admitting, shoving hair from her face, exposing high cheekbones and features too delicate to fit this life she leads. "I already knew who you were," she adds.

"From my brother or yours?"

"Both. If this is about Derek—"

"This is about Adrian."

"My brother? What about him?"

"Ramon followed Emily to the coffee shop this morning and made sure we knew he was there."

She swallows hard, her face paling. "I know nothing about that." But the way she cuts her eyes and doesn't even ask who Emily is tells me that's a lie.

My cell phone beeps, and in case it's a warning, I remove the phone from my pocket and glance at the message from Seth, laughing without humor at the content. "Derek is at breakfast with Mike Rogers," I say, returning my cell to my pocket. "Mike's—"

"Your largest stockholder," she supplies. "I know. And Derek is just trying to protect his company from everyone who wants to take it."

"That would be your brother, not me."

"Had you not tried to take the company from him, he'd never have ended up involved with my brother."

I arch a brow, surprised at how in tune she is with our business dealings, no matter how distorted her facts. "I'm not trying to take it. I'm going to save it. What does your brother have to do with Mike Rogers?"

"I'm not involved in any of this."

"Oh no? You've already blown your chance at playing the ignorant card."

"I'm not involved in any of this," she says again, and while her voice is sweet, her track record innocent, she is right here in the middle of her brother's world, and that's damning to me.

"Is your brother involved with Mike Rogers?"

"I'm not involved in any of this."

"You're sleeping with my brother."

"Who I care about."

She says those words fiercely, her eyes flashing. She does care about him. And damn it, that is not good. That is a formula for death if Derek hurts her.

"If you really care about him," I say, looking for a way out for Derek, "you'd get him out of your family business."

She leans forward. "So you control everything? That company was Derek's."

"Then why did he just hand it to your brother?"

She sits back. "What do you want from me?"

"Ramon visited Emily this morning. I'm simply visiting you."

"He can get to her and you can get to me," she supplies.

"That's right."

"Are you threatening me?"

"Yes," I say, and when she blanches, I am surprised at how easily that reply came out and how little sympathy I have for her. She's a Martina. She's the enemy.

I exit the booth and start walking, never even considering a look back. I reach the door and push it open, stepping outside. A man I know from my research to be Ramon steps in front of me, giving me the attention I wanted, and I don't back down. I close the small space he's left between us, stepping toe-to-toe with him, our heights nearly equal, our gazes colliding. "I highly recommend the everything bagel," I say, so he knows I know who he is. "You should take one to Adrian."

I step around him and make it all of one step when I hear, "Careful which bear you poke."

"Careful which lion you scratch, because he might be hungry." I start walking again and I don't stop.

Seth pulls to the curb and I round the vehicle, sliding into the passenger side, and we don't speak until we're in a parking spot in the garage of the Four Seasons. "This is a dangerous game you're playing, my friend."

"One you and your men need to decide if you're willing to play with me."

"How far are you willing to go?"

"As far as it takes to protect what's mine."

"Do you understand what that could mean with a man like Martina?"

I glance at him. "I do and I will not back down. The question is, are you in or out?"

He studies me, his eyes hardening. "I'm in."

"And Nick?"

"I'll talk to him."

I give him a nod and open the door, ready to go to do battle, no matter who's with me or not. I meant what I said that Martina had scratched the wrong lion. This one bites.

EMILY

I leave the Bentley for Shane. And since I'm feeling gun-shy about walking again, plus loaded down with my research on the new Brandon beauty and fashion line I'm proposing, I Uber my way to work, with a goal of being at my desk by eight. Once there, and walking into the building, dread fills my belly at the idea of dealing with stockholders over Brandon Senior's cancer treatment. No. That's not true. This dread is about my worry that Shane will already be here, perhaps having showered and dressed somewhere else. Maybe every excuse I gave him for being gone last night was my denying that we're in real trouble. Suddenly not eager to go upstairs, I stop in the coffee shop to grab myself another caffeine boost and Brandon Senior the hot tea he likes, figuring I can warm it in the microwave if he isn't here yet. I've just placed my order when a blond woman grabs my arm.

"Emily."

I blanch at the realization this is Jessica and her hair has gone from short to long overnight. "Who are you?"

She laughs. "I look different, right?"

"Ah yeah. Where's my friend and Shane's spiky-haired assistant?"

She grabs a long lock of golden hair. "Extensions. I needed a new me, and I'll tell you about that later. Is Shane here?"

"I don't know."

Her brow furrows. "You don't know? Don't you live together?"

Those knots in my belly get bigger. "He had meetings."

"Oh okay. Well, pray he's not in for me. I forgot to turn in a contract for a deal he's closing for a sponsorship. He's going to kill me."

"You forgot something?"

"I'm human. Don't tell. Grab me a caramel macchiato, will you?"

"Yes. Okay." She starts to leave, and I grab her arm.

"Stick my briefcase on my desk, will you?" I ask, sliding my bag off my shoulder and handing it to her. "And my purse. I'll charge the drinks." I hand her that too but change my mind. "No. I'll keep it, but text me a call sheet of which Brandon is in, including Derek."

"Derek?"

"Yes. Derek."

"I'll get that piece of gossip later. Gotta go before your Brandon and mine wrings my neck." She starts backing up. "No foam, but I want whip. No. No. Dieting. No whip. Low-fat or fat-free or whatever you call it." She turns and then rotates back. "Damn it, I want the whipped cream." And then she faces forward again and is gone, leaving my mind to go crazy with the places Shane could have been all night and now. I actually find more peace thinking about my missing brother, my murdered stepfather, and the hackers who could appear at any moment and make our lives more complicated. Okay, I don't find more peace in those things, but they still trump the stories of Martina Senior ordering the beheading of fifty people for crossing him in Mexico, which I'd read about last night.

By the time I have a tray with four drinks in it, I decide I need to just hum that Jason Aldean song I was listening to while running, to shut down my mind for a few short minutes and pull myself together. I step into the elevator and am thankfully alone, so I actually recite the lyrics to the empty car. It's an absolutely ridiculous idea that does nothing to help me. I need to do something, make a difference somehow, not check out. That's what I did with Bobby J.

I press my hand to my face. Why does that piece of hell keep popping up in my head? Grimacing, I shake it off and head to the door.

Entering the lobby, I greet the receptionist, who's on the phone, and then walk to the break room to stick the two teas for Brandon Senior in the fridge to ensure the milk doesn't spoil. And since I have yet to get that warning text, I go to my desk, shove my purse in a drawer, and dial Jessica, only to have her round the corner. "No one is here. I have to go to legal on the second floor. Walk with me?"

"Yes. Okay." I grab our drinks and cross to join her, offering her the caramel macchiato.

She takes a sip. "You got it with whipped cream. I'm dieting."

I laugh. "Oh no, you don't. You don't get to blame me for that. You said: 'Damn it. I want the whipped cream.'"

"But I didn't say get it for me."

"You are being bad," I say, sipping my white mocha and trying not to think about the first time I met Shane and I drank from his cup. "It must be that long gorgeous hair," I add, "and you do not need to diet anyway."

We step into the corridor outside the elevators. "You really like the hair?"

"I do," I say. "I mean, I loved the spiky Brigitte Nielsen thing you had going on too, but this looks more natural."

She snickers. "My fake hair looks more natural. Love it." She pushes the elevator button and takes a drink of her coffee. "I'm glad you got me the whipped cream. Thank you."

"Happy to fatten up my skinny friend any day. What made you change the hair?"

"Oh, you know, it was always long, but I had this bad breakup, really bad, and I'll need drinks to tell you about it. Anyway, I had an identity crisis and chopped it off."

I inhale, back once again to tattoo-domination hell. "I understand."

She tilts her head. "You do?"

"Yeah. I do. I did something like that."

"What?"

"I'm not sure drinks will be enough to share that one."

"Oh God. Now I freaking *have* to know. You're telling me. That is all there is to it."

The elevator dings, and we both step forward only to freeze

as Shane steps off the elevator, freshly shaven and dressed in a blue suit, his attention landing hard on me. And Lord, help me, he's so damn tall, dark, and good-looking, he never fails to make me weak in the knees. He's also now standing in front of me, smelling like spicy, woodsy male perfection, and looking at me like he wants to gobble me up. But he's freshly showered and dressed. And yes, he's wearing the Burberry tie that has a special meaning between us, one I know is a message to me, but at the very least, he waited until I left to go home and change.

"Let's go to my office and talk," he says.

"I'd rather talk tonight if you think we'll be under the same roof."

"Emily—"

"Tonight." I try to step around him, but he maneuvers in front of me, and I catch a glimpse of Jessica disappearing into the elevator.

"Let's go talk," Shane repeats.

"I'm really upset. We do not need to do this here; your father will be here making demands at any moment." The elevator dings again, and suddenly Derek is exiting a car.

"Well, if it isn't the lovebirds," he says, his voice instantly furrowing Shane's brow.

"I'll leave you to your brother," I say, turning on my heel and heading back to the offices.

"Emily," he bites out, but I keep walking. I push forward and don't stop until I'm back at my desk, but I'm rattled, trembling even. Irritated at my lack of control, I walk into Brandon Senior's office and shut the door. When I'm still shaken, I lean against it. Where was he? Why didn't he take my calls?

The door opens behind me with such force, I have no option but to lift myself off it. I face forward to find Shane stepping inside. Desperate for control, I race across the room and step behind Brandon Senior's desk.

"Your father will be here any minute," I object as he shuts us inside and faces me.

"I'm here now. And he'll have to wait." He reaches over and locks the door.

CHAPTER TEN

EMILY

Shane's across the room and around the desk before I can blink, but I'm ready. I grab his father's chair and rotate it, putting it between us with the back against the desk. "Stay there," I order.

"Then you come here."

"You said you want to talk. We don't talk when you touch me. I tried that last night and—"

"I spanked you?"

My cheeks flush. "Yes. You did."

He moves, and before I know what's happened, I'm on the other side of the chair with him, leaning against the desk, his big, wonderful, delicious body pressed to mine, while my hands manage to find the hard wall of his chest under his jacket. "Shane, damn it. I told you—"

"I spent the entire time I was in the shower replaying that spanking."

"The shower you took after I left?"

"I meant to be there before you left. Who spanked you?"

"I'm upset with you, Shane, and you want to know who spanked me?"

"You're damn right I do. It's driving me crazy."

"This conversation is crazy," I say. "This is not the time or place for this."

He lifts me and sets me on the desk, shoving the hem of my dress up my legs and then pressing my knees open, his hands settling on the lace band of my thigh-high stockings. "Who spanked you?" he repeats, stepping toward me.

"Shane—"

"Was it the professor?"

"The tattoo artist. We need to talk."

"We are. I want to hear about the tattoo artist spanking you."

"I hated everything about the many things I did with that man."

His eyes narrow. "Define many things."

"Why are you doing this now?"

"I'm feeling possessive. I'm feeling really damn possessive."

"Be possessive in bed, our bed, the one that you should have been in last night."

"I really like hearing you say 'our bed.'" His thumbs make circles on the skin just outside my panties, the waves of pleasure he produces threatening the last of my clear thinking, and I grab his wrist.

"Shane. This isn't talking."

"No one but me will ever spank you again."

My eyes narrow at him. "What is in your head right now?"

His eyes heat, darken. "You. Always." He inches back and looks at me. "You're mine. Mine to protect." His voice is low, fierce, and he grips my panties and yanks them away. "Mine to fuck."

I gasp and grab his shoulders. "Shane."

His answer is to wrap his arm around my waist, pull me close, his cheek against mine, his fingers pressing into the V of my body. "Wet, just the way I like you," he says, pressing two fingers inside me. "Wet for me. And too fucking perfect for my sanity sometimes."

"That doesn't sound like a compliment," I pant out, grabbing the lapel to his suit as a sweet ache begins to build in my sex as his thumb strokes my clit.

"And no one else," he murmurs, nipping my earlobe, "will ever touch you like this." His fingers caress deeper inside me. "No one," he adds, "will ever make you say their name like I want you to say mine right now. Say it."

"Shane," I whisper, and not because he wants me to, but rather because it's there on my lips, the way I wish his tongue was on my lips now. "Shane, I—"

Seeming to know what I need, he cups my head and kisses me, long, slow, sensual strokes of his tongue that somehow make every touch of his fingers more intense. "Come for me," he murmurs, and this time when he kisses me, I start climbing that wall to release, and I'm there at the top in an instant. I stiffen while his fingers and tongue tease, please, and then I jerk, I'm over it, tumbling in an instant into shudders and shakes. Shane's lips lift from mine as he breathes with me. His fingers slow as he eases me through the waves until I collapse against his chest.

He tangles his fingers in my hair and drags my mouth back to his. "And no one but me will ever make you come like that again," he declares, the waves of his emotions beating down any embarrassment I might feel over having had an orgasm on his father's desk.

"No one has ever made me feel what you make me feel, Shane."

"I love you," he declares. "You know that, right? With everything I am or will ever be."

Shock radiates through me at the declaration he's never spoken until now. "You do?"

"Yes. I do."

And I love him too, but I'm tormented by the timing of the
confession. "I love you too, Shane, but last night confuses me. Why
didn't you take my calls?"

He leans back and looks at me, shards of emotions I cannot
name in his eyes. "I told you—"

"Tell me again."

He sucks in air, stepping back and sliding my knees together,
gently pulling down my dress before grabbing the chair and pulling it forward. He sits in it, his hands settling on the desk on
either side of me, his head lowering. My hands go to him, fingers
sliding into the long dark strands of his hair, a hint of dampness
telling me that his shower wasn't very long ago. I don't press him.
I wait. I give him room to breathe, just happy he's doing it here
with me.

Finally, his head lifts and he looks at me. "You are everything that is right in my world right now, Emily. Everything
good."

"But you shut me out."

"Because I don't want the bad in my life, in me, to destroy
you and us."

"In you? There is no bad in you, Shane."

"I don't win like I win and have no bad in me, sweetheart. I
have a ruthless side. You don't see it because you love me. And I
don't want that to change."

"I was going to law school. I like to win too. I know it takes being ruthless. I'm not naive. I can handle whatever you need me to handle."

"I don't need you to handle any of this. That's the point. And no matter where this takes me, if I have you to come back to, I will come back."

"That statement was spoken like you've put a divide between us now."

"A divide between you and the situation, not me and you."

"They're the same."

"No. I'm still with you, sweetheart, like I have never been with anyone."

"Shane—"

"The situation is bad, Emily. Really fucking bad."

"I know, but—"

"One of the men guarding us disappeared last night. A family man with two kids."

"Oh God." My hand goes to my neck. "Tell me he's not dead."

"I don't know the answer to that, but I told Martina that if Ted is dead, then there will be no drug study. And don't tell me I can't do business with him. You have to see this is not cut-and-dried."

"I spent a lot of time researching the Martina cartel and the family last night," I say, "looking for any weakness I could give you to use against them. I know it's not cut-and-dried."

"And what did you discover?"

"That if you find their weakness, they cut your head off, which is why I'm terrified over your involvement with Adrian."

"And that information is exactly why I don't want you involved."

"He has people following me around, Shane. I'm involved, but believe me, I'm not dangling a cookie out there and asking for attention. I just want to get it off of you. What did he say about Ted?"

"He denied being involved but said he'd look for him as a favor to a friend."

"The game you mentioned."

"Yes. The game."

I study him, those shards in his eyes cutting, the emotions they represent unfamiliar to me, and frightening, and with them, a realization comes to me. "You asked me who spanked me. You really needed to know."

"Yes. I did."

"Why?"

"I just did, Emily."

"And I just keep thinking about him."

His spine straightens. "What the hell does that even mean?"

"Not in a good way. He is not a good memory."

"Did I do that to you? Did I trigger bad memories? I would never—"

"I know."

"Did I hurt you?"

"No. No, it was intimate and sexy and—" I press my hand to my face. "I'm blushing thinking about it."

He pulls my hand from my face. "It was intimate and sexy and I liked it."

"I did too, but I don't know what came over me. I all but told you to do it."

"You did tell me to do it."

"Okay, I did."

"What are you telling me, Emily?"

"That spanking and me thinking about him wasn't about

him or me. It was about you. When I was with him, I was hiding from me. I didn't like what I'd become and I wanted an escape. All I was doing was hiding. Don't hide from yourself by hiding from me."

"I don't hide. Ever. I'm protecting you."

"And now it's my turn to say—it's not that simple. And you know it."

The phone on the desk buzzes, and I jolt while Shane simply frowns, pushing to his feet and moving to the other side of the desk. He punches the lit-up button, and Jessica immediately says, "Senior is here."

My heart leaps to my throat and I jump to the ground. "Oh God. This is bad."

"Try to hold him off," Shane orders.

"He's already rounding the corner," Jessica replies.

"Try anyway," Shane snaps, letting go of the button and facing me.

"This is bad," I say.

"This is us talking, and he of all people knows we have plenty to talk about."

"Does he know about Ted?"

"He knows nothing but what happened at the dinner, and keep it that way. Now, let's go face the angry king."

I nod and we round the desk, but just as we reach the door, he snags my waist and turns me to him. "If ever I'm not home," he says, "I'm wishing I was there."

My thundering heart falls. He's just prepared me for more lonely nights, and I can't even find the words to reply. Not that I have a chance. He kisses me. A long drugging kiss that leaves me breathless but still sad. There is something missing in that kiss, like a piece of him he's holding back. He begins to release me and I catch his arm, my fingers going to his lips. "Still not your shade," I say, wiping away my lipstick.

His mouth twitches and then curves. "But you are. I'll go first and take the heat." He then sets me aside and opens the door, leaving me with the dire need to yank him back and lock it again. But I can't, and I'm not sure what I could change if I did—in this moment, at least.

He exits to the alcove and mini lobby that is my desk area, and I immediately follow, my heart sinking as I find Brandon Senior with his feet propped up on my desk. "If you two are done," he says, settling his feet on the ground, "we can get to work." He stands and addresses Shane. "I'll need an official legal document naming you as the acting CEO."

"It was in your inbox, and Emily's, an hour ago," Shane says. "And I need a heads-up when it goes out, since my phone is going to start ringing."

Senior looks at me, his eyes bloodshot, his complexion ruddy. "Send it." He glances at Shane. "You have your heads-up."

Shane inclines his head and starts to turn, but his father isn't ready for him to escape. "No one rules this company but a Brandon. Do you understand me?"

"One hundred percent," Shane confirms.

"You do whatever you have to do to keep it that way," Senior orders.

"I need every piece of controlling ammunition on anyone you consider an enemy," Shane responds.

Senior gives a sharp nod. "You'll get it."

"Before you leave," Shane presses.

"Yes," Senior agrees. "Before I leave." He turns and walks into his office and calls out, "I need that magical tea, Ms. Stevens."

And that's when the breeze under my dress makes my eyes go wide. Oh God. I look at Shane and mouth, *Panties. Do you have them?*

He gives a silent laugh and shakes his head, pointing to the office, while I let out a silent scream of, *No!!!!!*

"Afraid so," he says, smiling as he closes the small space between us. "You want to—"

"No," I say, "and stop smiling. This is not funny."

"It's a little funny."

"You go to your office. You have gotten me in enough trouble."

He lets out a low, deep, sexy chuckle, kisses my forehead, and takes off walking, and I swear, he owns every inch of this building just by being here. He darn sure just proved he owns me, but now his father will too. I press my hands to my desk. At least Shane was smiling, but I really have not had enough sleep for the roller coaster ride that this day has been and it's—I look at the clock—only eight fifteen. I straighten and hurry to the break room, warm up the tea, and then return to my workspace, pausing at the door of Senior's office. Maybe the panties are under his desk and he will never notice. Maybe . . .

He starts hacking and it's bad. Deep, vicious coughing, and I forget my panties. I rush into the office and find him leaning over his trashcan. I shut the door to offer him privacy, and then I'm across the room in an instant. Kneeling in front of him, I find myself staring in horror at the bloodstained tissues in his hand. It's so much blood. So very much blood, and I can't do anything but wait for the attack to end. Finally, he seems to wheeze and then pull in air. "Tea," he murmurs, and I hand it to him.

He quickly drinks. "It's hot. It's good." He tilts it back and takes a long swallow before scowling at me. "Why are you on your knees?"

"I—"

"Up. We have work to do." He turns forward.

I stand and move to the front of his desk and blanch at the sight of my panties hanging from a pencil in the pencil holder.

"It appears I have new décor," he says dryly, a rasp to his voice I think might be from the coughing attack. Or cancer. Or really, they are one in the same.

I snatch them up, and thank God I have a pocket in my dress, where I shove them. "Sorry. That was because . . . I was . . ." I purse my lips. "I should stop talking now and say nothing more."

"Nothing," he repeats flatly. "Frankly, Ms. Stevens, I hardly think your panties on my desk is nothing. Do you love him?"

The question takes me by surprise, but I do not miss a beat. "Yes. I do. I love him very much."

"My wife used to have that look on her face when she spoke of me."

I sit down in the chair. "She still does."

"She's fucking my best friend, Mike Rogers."

"I know."

"Of course you know. My son has a big mouth."

"No. I saw them."

"You saw them?"

"Yes," I say. "I saw them."

"Where? When?"

"Does it matter?"

"No," he bites out. "No, it does not. She's lying down for him. That's what matters."

My lips purse. "You do remember you're with someone else too, right?"

"He was my *best* friend."

The word "friend" is not one I expect from him, but he is

vehement on this point, proving there is more to him than meets the eye.

"And my wife is most likely helping him take over my company, so don't go throwing your moral high code on me. And don't fucking do it to my son or you'll get him killed. Go get that document to the stockholders and start with that bastard Mike. Call him and make sure he gets it."

"I will," I say, standing, and then walk toward the door.

"And, Ms. Stevens," he says as I reach for the knob, "too many people are getting fucked in this office. Don't let it happen again."

Despite being aware of the fact that he's lashing out, demoralizing me out of his own hurt and anger, I feel the blow of his words like a punch. I exit the office and shut the door, leaning against it, but it's not my panties on my mind. It's something else he said. *Don't go throwing your moral high code on me. And don't fucking do it to my son or you'll get him killed.*

That's what Shane thinks too. That's why he didn't come home last night, and I just don't know what to do with that information or what I feel right now.

CHAPTER ELEVEN

SHANE

I head through the lobby, the scent of Emily's perfume on my skin, which is exactly what I wanted. Now every decision I make today will be made with that scent reminding me of her. Reminding me that one wrong move and I could lose her, be it by way of my enemies or my own choices. But at least if it's from my own choices, she leaves me alive. As I reach the end of the hallway leading to my office and Derek's, I glance to his closed door, his secretary giving me a snide glower. I wink at her, enjoying the confused look on her face and wondering how she'd feel knowing my brother probably fucks her after he's been inside Teresa. And the minute Teresa finds out, Derek is dead. I wonder who's fucking who in that meeting with Mike and Derek, and I'm betting on Mike. That's not a good thing. This company is Brandon to the core, and it will stay that way.

Cutting left, I head toward my office, finding Jessica's desk empty but my door open. I pass her workspace and enter mine right as she is about to exit. I stop and do a double take at her hair. "Who are you and what have you done with my secretary?"

"What were you thinking, Shane?! In your father's office."

"There's the Jessica I know. There's a designer purse with an unlimited price tag on it if you stop talking about this and keep my coffee cup filled today." I walk around her and head to my desk, stepping behind it as she faces me. "And get ready. The entire board is going to call me today."

"I don't need to be bribed to do my job, Shane."

"Consider it a reward for doing it well."

"Oh God. How bad is this day going to be?"

"Bad. The board, remember?"

"Why exactly are they calling?"

"My father's been accepted into a cancer trial. He's leaving for Germany."

"How effective is the trial?"

"He's terminal. This is his last chance. That's the stat that matters."

"I'll read into that the way you'd assume I will. And why are the board members calling you, so I can be prepared? Are we giving them dates he'll be gone, or—"

"I'll be acting as CEO until he's at full capacity again."

She gapes at me and closes the space between herself and my desk. "And if he doesn't return to full capacity?"

"I'll have six months until a vote will be required to keep me in the role."

"And your father picked you over Derek?"

"I picked me over Derek. I wrote the amendment that made this mandatory."

"Of course you did. How's Derek taking it?"

"He's at breakfast with Mike Rogers and most likely plotting my undoing."

"That will be interesting to see. Are you sure you don't want whiskey instead of coffee? I do."

"Coffee. Lots of it. I didn't sleep last night."

"I won't ask—now. Later I will." She turns and starts walking.

"Jessica," I call out.

She rotates. "Yes."

"I like the hair."

She doesn't beam or glow. She just says, "Me too," and turns again, disappearing into the hallway.

I haven't even had time to sit down when Seth appears, and since he now has on a blue suit, tie and jacket in place, I assume he too managed to shower. He's followed by a tall, muscular man in a simple white T-shirt, tat sleeves lining his arms, who I assume to be Cody.

"I hope like hell you don't bring bad news about Ted," I say as Seth shuts the door and walks toward me.

"No news on our end," Seth says while the two of them cross to the front of my desk.

"Cody Rodriguez," the newcomer says, extending his hand.

"Shane Brandon," I say, sliding my palm to his and giving it a firm grip. "I understand you met Emily this morning."

"Indeed," he confirms, his hands settling on his hips. "I met her, and I have to say, she knows how to make a lasting impression."

I arch a brow and claim my seat, motioning for them to sit, which they do. "How so?" I ask, assessing Cody, who at this point reads as strong and confident to me.

"I took a call from one of Nick's men at the wrong time," Seth interjects.

"In other words," Cody says, "he didn't warn her I was about to introduce myself. So here I am. Mexican, in a hoodie, and approaching her in a hallway by a bathroom the night after Martina showed up at your apartment."

"She thought you were with him," I assume.

"One would assume that was her assessment," Cody confirms. "Bottom line, I spooked her and she was pissed. And she didn't mind letting me know."

"Or me," Seth inserts dryly.

"She's tough," Cody says, "but more so, she was alert and aware of her surroundings. That's good, but it's not enough. I'm going to tell you what I told her. I know the cartels and how they operate. I know how to protect her, but I need to be given the freedom to do so."

"I'm listening," I say. "What do you need me to do?"

"For starters," Seth interjects again, "you and Emily need to decide if he's going to openly watch over her or operate in the shadows."

"Which is the safest answer?" I ask.

"Openly shadowing her is going to make Emily and everyone around her nervous," Cody says, "which can become complicated and stir up questions you might not want to answer from your staff and board of directors. But hiding in the shadows slightly decreases my response time if she gets into trouble. I'll feel better about that if she carries a gun and knows how to use it. Does she and can she?"

"If she doesn't, we can remedy that," I say, eyeing Seth, who answers without me asking.

"I'll get her an appropriate firearm this afternoon."

"A Taser as well," Cody adds, "and Mace."

Unease slides down my spine. "You think the visit from Ramon is more than Martina trying to get in my head?"

"When you visited Teresa," Cody says, "you decided to play Russian roulette with a Mexican who doesn't mind pulling the trigger and really wants the bullet to end up in your head."

"I might not know cartels, Cody," I say, "but I read people really damn well. He needed to know he couldn't cow me. He needed to question what I really might do."

"And what are you willing to do?" Seth asks.

I cut him a look, not sure either of us is ready to hear me answer that out loud just yet. And I don't need to right now anyway. "It doesn't matter what I'm willing to do," I say. "It matters what he thinks I'll do. I evened the playing field again."

"And you got Ramon's attention in the process," Cody says. "A man who has a known interest in Teresa and a hell of a lot of anger that, because he can't have her, he takes out on everyone around him and her."

"Martina wants this partnership with me," I say. "Any wrong move by Ramon will destroy that and put Ramon in Martina's hot seat."

"That sounds logical to you and me," Cody says. "But my studies show him to be a wild card who's gone rogue more than once."

"Then I need you both to find a way to get him out of the picture," I say.

"Out of the picture?" Seth asks. "What does that mean?"

"I don't care if you send him back to Mexico in a wooden box. Get him out of the picture before it's my family who ends up dead." My office phone buzzes and I grimace, punching the button long enough to say, "Take a message from whoever it is," before releasing it.

"Even Mike Rogers?" she asks

I grimace. "No. Not Mike Rogers. Put him through." The line buzzes again and I pick it up, speaking before Mike has the chance. "If it isn't the ghost of the man called Mike Rogers himself," I say. "What did I do to finally merit communication?"

"From what I hear, you took over a company I'm vested in."

"You heard wrong then," I say. "My father is still very much in control as the document sent out this morning states. I'm simply on standby to fill in should he need a little recuperation time."

"You really think he's going to live?"

"Are you really hoping he's going to die?"

"Friends don't wish friends dead, but stockholders need straight answers."

Rarely do I have to bite back my choice words, but I do now. "What do you want, Mike?"

"Let's meet."

A chance to look into this man's eyes has appeal. "When?"

"Tonight at six for drinks."

Not about to do this on his terms and with sleep deprivation weighing on me, I counter. "Seven in the morning," I say, testing his loyalty to my father by adding, "the coffee shop here and my father can sit in."

"Caribou on Sixteenth Street and just you."

"My father can reassure you his health is on the mend."

"I want to talk about what happens if it's not, and that's not a conversation that feels appropriate with him present and on his way to treatment."

"All right then," I say, unsurprised the bastard doesn't want to face my father. "Us alone." I disconnect the line and look between

Seth and Cody. "He met with Derek this morning and Derek is aligned with Martina. I need to know if Mike is as well."

"We've found nothing that tells us he is," Seth says. "And meetings with Derek do not compute to alignment but rather Derek's attempt to earn his vote."

"A vote that isn't happening for at least six months," I say, "if it happens at all. No. There's more to this."

"If I might interject," Cody says, drawing our attention. "I know the cartels. I know Martina, but he doesn't know me."

"And the takeaway?"

"Adrian Martina is one of the shrewdest, most dangerous men I've ever studied. If he wants your company, and he does, he would not ignore a key stockholder such as Mike. But that said, he's calculating. He might not have made contact, but he damn sure has a plan to control Mike and use him if necessary. And let's just face it. Drugs and basketball equal a variety of scandals he could create for Mike."

All things I've already considered. "He claims he wants to go legitimate."

"And yet, Ted is missing," Cody says.

"Point made," I say, his assessment confirming mine. "Emily's smart with good common sense. We need her to be part of deciding how we address her protection." I look at Cody. "Follow your existing protocols for now. I'll talk to her tonight and arrange a sit-down."

"I'm in the hotel room around the clock when she's home," Cody says. "Just say the word and I'll be there."

I look at Seth and he reads my mind before I speak. "Mike. I know."

We all stand, but when Seth is about to leave, Cody isn't moving, his gaze locked on me. "In the old-school Mexican culture, brothers are possessive of their sisters," he says. "Teresa can protect Derek to some degree, but the minute Adrian feels he's locked you down, your brother becomes disposable. If Derek makes one wrong move with Teresa, Ramon will kill him."

The impact of his assessment hits me with the force of a hundred accurate blows. He's right, as Adrian already believes Derek used Teresa to get to him. "Since you're sharing your opinions," I say, "what will motivate Adrian to get out of our operation?"

"I might have more to offer once I get my feet wet, but for now . . . cartels know three things: money, trouble, and blood, but they always follow the money."

"We need to be the trouble and the blood," Seth says, eyeing a text message and then glancing at Cody. "Shane and I need to speak alone."

"Understood," Cody says, giving me a mock salute and heading for the door as Seth's phone now begins to ring.

"Nick," Seth tells me, taking the call while Cody exits and shuts the door.

I turn and face the window, hands sliding under my jacket to my hips, Cody's words in my mind: *The minute Adrian feels he's locked you down, your brother becomes disposable. . . . Ramon will kill him.* Even if I were to pull Derek to our side, which is unlikely, that relationship with Teresa is a thorn-covered rose.

Seth steps to my side. "Still no Ted. Still no leads. I don't think I have to tell you where my head is going on this."

He thinks Ted is dead. So do I. "No," I say. "You do not."

We stand there for several beats, heaviness in the air, and then I turn to him. "What's on your mind?"

He faces me. "Send him back to Mexico in a wooden box,"

he says, repeating my words. "You understand that might be what this comes down to, right?"

"I understand completely," I say, expecting regret or guilt that doesn't come. These people will kill everyone who has ever spoken to me, and they won't blink.

" 'See something, say something' is what Cody told Emily. All I want to hear from you is 'see something, do something,' and I'll protect you from the details."

"I don't want to be protected. See something, we'll do something."

He studies me for several beats, his stare probing, assessing, looking for a sign that this is my hesitation or weakness, but it is not. It's my full willingness to do what I have to do. He sees it too. It's in the shift of his eyes and the slow nod of his head before he walks toward the door. I face the window again, inhaling on the promise that I have never been more of a Brandon than I am in this moment.

EMILY

For two hours, I dodge and weave through one call after another as Brandon Senior shouts orders at me, but one good piece of news manages to find its way into the fold. The analyst Shane had me contact sometime back about our options for an acquisition in the fashion industry followed up with me. We now have a recommendation to bid on a company we can get at a steal of a price.

I'm about to sneak to Shane's office and talk to him about it when my intercom buzzes. "My office, Ms. Stevens."

I stand to do as ordered when Maggie appears in a wave of sweet-smelling perfume, stretching her normally all-black wardrobe by wearing a pale pink pantsuit, her eyes bloodshot and her skin washed out. She stops at my desk and punches the intercom. "Emily is taking a thirty-minute break from her desk." She eyes me. "Go."

"Are you okay?"

"No," she shocks me by saying. "I'm not okay. Please go."

I nod and step around my desk, hurrying through the lobby and down the hall. And while I do not think good things are going on in Brandon Senior's office right now, Maggie is here. They are together, and that is step one toward making peace. Or war. God. I hope it's peace they find, I think, reaching the end of the hallway leading to the alcove that houses Derek's and Shane's offices. I start to turn left toward Shane's, but Derek's secretary passes me and I stop dead when I realize his door is open. Maggie might be making peace at this very moment. Maybe I can at least open a door to some myself.

Steeling myself for probable failure and certain confrontation, I step forward and, decision made, charge in Derek's direction. Never pausing, I enter his office, shut the door, and turn to face him. He glances up from his desk, a look of surprise on his face before he tosses his pencil onto the desk and leans back. "Did you finally figure out I'm the right brother?"

"Shane's not your enemy."

"Says the woman banging him."

"Why do you have to be so crude?" I ask.

"My father taught me that skill with admirable insistence. I never put skills to waste."

"Shane's not your enemy," I repeat. "He had an amazing career in New York. He's only here, doing all he's doing, to save the company you seem to love."

"Take off the rose-colored glasses, Emily. Shane is not as admirable as you seem to think."

"Shane is not trying to take over the company, Derek. You're his brother—"

"Why are you here?"

"Wake up before it's too late. Martina will destroy you all, and he's not even the only person with his eyes on a takeover."

"What does that mean? Who else has eyes on the company?"

"Not just the company," I say, thinking of the combination of heartache in Maggie and anger in Brandon Senior that I've seen today. "Your family is falling apart now, but they could all be dead later."

"What are you talking about?"

"Martina's right-hand man followed me today, Derek, and of course that was a threat. I'm a target. I could end up dead. And you know what? You might not care, but just so you know, I don't want you to die, but you might. We all might before this is over." I turn to leave, but before I can even open the door, he's behind me, his hand on the wooden surface above me.

"No one is going to die," he says. "Who else has eyes on my company?"

"You mean Martina's company? Talk to Shane. Before it's too late." I tug on the door, and to my surprise, he allows me to leave, which I do. And at the exact moment I exit into the hallway, Shane steps out of his office, his eyes meeting mine, concern and a hundred questions in his gray eyes. I take a step toward him, and him me, but Derek overtakes me, outpacing me and charging toward Shane. And just that easily, I've forced a conversation between the brothers, but this one, I fear, will not end in peace.

CHAPTER TWELVE

SHANE

Only moments after Seth warns me that my mother is in the office, Derek stalks toward me, leaving Emily behind, his steps determined, his energy confrontational. His dark gray suit is less than pressed and perfect, when it's never so much as ill adjusted. He's rattled, on edge, ready for a fight with me, the wrong person. Martina and Mike are the enemies, but I am not sure he will understand this until it's too late, and I won't ever let that day come. I stand my ground, expecting some sort of snide remark about Emily perhaps before he moves on and lets me get back to trying to save us all. But that's not what I get. He stops in front of me, his eyes level with mine. "Let's talk."

A novel idea that, coming from him, and about as surprising as that demand being issued after Emily's been in his office, leaving me ever so curious as to what my woman said to my brother. Whatever the case, she got me his ear, and I'm going to use it any way I can. I give him a nod and move back into my office, standing my ground midway, expecting that confrontation to happen now.

Again, I'm surprised. Instead, my brother walks to the window and, giving me his back, stands there, looking out at the city the way I often do. I'm struck by the likeness in us, which I'd once claimed and wish I could deny now, and I wonder how many times we've stood at the windows of our offices, in the opposite direction. Opposite in all that we do, or so I'd thought days ago. Now I'm not so sure anymore, and I wonder how he went from being my big brother and idol to being an enemy. I step to the window myself, leaving several shoulder lengths separating us, the many spoken and unspoken words of the past few turbulent years thickening the air between us.

"Emily says you never wanted the company," he says finally, still looking at the skyline, though I doubt he's really seeing it any more than I am.

"She's correct."

"Then why come here and try to unravel everything I've worked for?" he asks, still not looking at me.

"I have some news for you, Derek. 'Everything,' as you put it, was unraveled before I got here or I wouldn't be here."

He glances over at me. "And yet this company, and the people working for it, managed to function for thirty years without you. Pops," he adds, "did okay by it, and so did I."

"Pops," I say, giving a humorless laugh at the childhood name we'd used for our father. "He hasn't been that person in decades."

"He was always the person he is now. We just didn't see it."

"But he isn't and wasn't the person who made these missteps."

Derek laughs this time, the sound bitter, choked, and in unison, as we often were in the past, we face each other. "Pops didn't make the missteps?" he asks incredulously. "Pops is king. He calls the shots. Who do you think is behind every move I've made since I stepped foot in this building? And I do mean every move."

"So he sent you to the FDA? I'm not buying it."

"Not directly," Derek says. "He never does things directly, but he makes it clear what he wants done and how."

"Your hunger for power makes you take things out of context."

"He said that I needed to convince the right people to approve that drug in whatever way necessary. Does that sound like I took his directive out of context?"

"And getting involved with a drug cartel?" I say, far from convinced. "Am I supposed to believe he told you to do that too?"

"He flung a picture of Teresa on my desk, along with her biography, and then told me he thought she needed a good fuck."

"Bullshit, Derek."

"You think I could even make this shit up? Really? Because I guess my imagination has run wild while good ol' *Pops* suddenly became a Boy Scout?"

I step to him and he to me. "If this is true—"

"It's true."

"Why the fuck would you do it then?"

"Which 'it' are we talking about?"

"All of it. Any of it."

His lips thin. "There are reasons."

"What damn reasons?" I demand tightly. "Make me understand."

"He has ways to destroy me."

"You're his son," I say. "Your scandal becomes his reputation, so I'm not buying that."

"He has ways around his own demise, I promise you. Why do you think the board, Mike Rogers included, stays so damn loyal to him? He has a file on everyone. He'll have a file on you too soon."

"His threats do not justify your bad deeds."

"Says the almighty Shane Brandon."

"That's not how it is."

"Isn't it? Well, talk to me a year from now when you aren't that person anymore. He'll change you if he lives long enough."

"That's a cop-out."

"Ask Mike Rogers about cop-outs. He's as captive as I am, which is exactly why I have his vote."

"Well, you must be proud to have the vote of the man fucking your mother. I guess nothing matters to you anymore."

He blanches. "What the hell are you talking about? Mom wouldn't do that."

"That's what I said too," I say, relieved that he's genuinely shocked rather than approving. "But it's true." I walk to my desk and pull open a drawer. "Seth provided proof." I remove a folder, flipping it open and tossing it onto my desk, a picture of my mother and Mike kissing on top. But Derek still stands two feet away, frozen, as if he dreads the truth I've just offered him. And I wonder if he too has her on a pedestal.

Finally though he caves to what I recognize as a need for answers, and crosses to my desk and looks at the photo, his jaw and pretty much every muscle in his body tensing. Abruptly his gaze cuts to mine. "When was this taken?"

"Recently."

"Fuck," he murmurs, his hand sliding over his chin. "Does Father know?"

"He knows and not because I told him. He told me."

"His comments at dinner," he says. "The wills. The Brandon family staying in control. He thinks Mike is plotting a takeover."

"And Mom is in Mike's bed. That equates to conspiring as far as Father's concerned."

His gaze sharpens on me. "And you? Do you think the two of them are conspiring?"

"You tell me," I say, folding my arms in front of me. "You're the one buddying up with Mike."

"For his vote, and my own control, not his, but for him to do this, he'd need to be certain that you or I didn't inherit the ammunition Father has on him."

"Mom's resourceful," I say, remembering my request for that information she has yet to deliver to me. "If it really exists—"

"It does."

"Then she might have it."

"I met with Mike this morning," he surprises me by admitting. "I don't believe he has it."

"Why did you meet with him?"

"To tell him you're the acting CEO and a fucking bastard," he says. "Why do you think?"

Translation: to plot how to unseat me. I move on, staying focused on gaining every drop of information this chat might deliver for my arsenal. "Does Mike know about Martina or the FDA?"

"Contrary to what you think, I don't hand anyone ammunition to use against me. I learned that lesson from our father. Anything Mike knows, Mom told him; I sure as hell haven't shared any of the details with her, and I know for a fact Father never tells her anything."

"But again, she's smart. She's capable of finding things out."

"This is Mom you're talking about," he argues. "Even if he cut her out of his will, she'd inherit a small fortune, and I can't believe she'd betray us, her sons."

"Unless Father's moved the money around so that it seems like there is nothing."

"He could have. It'd be lower than I give him credit for, but he could have. But if he did, we assume she's doing what?"

"Trying to be on the winning team that isn't us," I say. "And if that's true—"

"Mike's aggressively planning a hostile takeover and she thinks it will work," he supplies, his lips thinning.

"That's where my head is at," I confirm.

"And Pops? What does he think? Where's his head?"

"Mike's sleeping with Mom. Where do you think his head is?"

"He wants to ruin him."

"Or at least control him," I say.

"Control him how?"

"He's working on a plan," I say, offering no further detail.

"I'll make this easy on everyone," he says. "I have one. Use Martina against him."

I press my hands on the desk, leaning toward him. "Are you crazy? We don't know what Martina will do to him, and Mom could end up collateral damage in the process."

"Jesus, Shane. I'm not telling you to have Martina kill Mike. I'm telling you to make it clear to Mike that inheriting this company means inheriting Martina and his drug cartel family."

Relieved that he has not stooped to ordering hits on people, I absorb his meaning with a mixed reaction, hitching my hip on the edge of my desk. "You just said you didn't tell him about Martina or the FDA for a reason. You didn't want him to have ammunition on you."

"Which is why we need to turn the tables. Get ammunition on him that ensures if he tries to take us down, he goes down too. We need to connect him to Martina. Make it look like he's the instigator of the cartel relationship. Like he forced us into it. Then he's a captive. We control him."

His use of the word "we" is coming a little too easily after years of shunning me. I narrow my eyes at him. "Was this your plan? Get him on your side, set him up, and then use him to force me out?" I don't wait for a reply I don't think I can stomach. "Because if it was, you failed. It's not Martina's plan. Martina's plan is nothing shy of owning us all."

"How would you know anything about Martina's plan?"

"Adrian Martina came to see me last night. Made it to my door without authorization."

"How did he even get to your floor when I can't?"

"We'd have to ask the member of my security team who went missing last night, if he ever returns. And for the sake of his wife and young children, I hope the hell he does."

His eyes harden. "What did he want?"

"It was all about power. He wanted to send a message. He has it. We do not. Is that really how you want Brandon Enterprises to end up? Under his control?"

His expression tightens and he stares at me for several beats, his face unreadable before he walks back to the window. I join him, stepping to his side, both of us folding our arms in front of us at the same moment. The same, but different. Together, but apart. "Emily said Ramon followed her today."

"He did," I say. "And he made sure I knew. Just like Adrian made a point of telling me you're using Teresa to get to him."

We face each other, hands going under our jackets to our hips. Again the same, but different. "And you said?"

"I told him you fell for a girl and saw an opportunity. You are aware that Ramon is in love with Teresa, I assume."

"Believe me, I'm crystal clear on that point."

"Adrian only needs one of us, Derek. You're fucking Teresa. He's going to pick me."

Before I can blink, his hands are on my lapels and he's shoved me against the window. "Is that a threat?"

I shove him backward with enough force that he stumbles, and I get the hell off the glass. "It was a plea that we stand together. Clear the company of outsiders. Then if you want to fight with me, we'll fight it out—brother to brother—on our terms, one-on-one, the way it should be. Truce, brother. Choose family."

"Is that what you were doing when you drafted that document that just made you acting CEO? Choosing family?"

The fire alarm goes off, blasting through the overhead speakers. "Martina," I say, already walking. "I went to see Teresa today. He's making me pay. I need to get to Emily."

He grabs me again before I can make it to the door. "Why the hell did you go see Teresa?"

"Mom is in the building too," I tell him. "Martina is coming for our family and anyone we care about. We need to get everyone out."

"Damn it," he growls. "You did this. If anyone gets hurt, it's on you." He releases me, but the safety of everyone in this building is far more important to me right now than the reality check he deserves. Exiting the office, I find Jessica missing and I keep moving, leaving Derek to deal with his secretary, and when I reach the lobby as Seth does, both of us notice that the receptionist is still at her desk. "Get up and get outside," Seth orders.

She gives him a deer-in-headlights look. "Isn't it just a drill?"

I'm already past her desk and headed toward my father's office, where I hope like hell I find him and Emily.

"Jesus, woman," I hear Derek mutter behind me, clearly talking to our receptionist. "A fire alarm does not mean stay at your desk."

"Translation," Seth says, "get up and get out."

I round the corner and bring Emily's empty desk into view. "Damn it."

Derek appears by my side. "I'll get Mom and Dad." He charges toward the door and opens it. "Holy hell," I hear him curse as I walk to the hallway, followed by a barked, "put some clothes on."

I'd laugh if I weren't so fucking worried about Emily and Jessica, pushing onward to the lobby again, cutting left to the break room and then the copy room. There's no sign of Emily or Jessica. Moving toward the exterior lobby and elevators, I dig my phone from my pocket and punch in Emily's number, only to have it go straight to voice mail. My gaze catches on the ladies' room, and I push the door open and enter. "Emily! Jessica!"

Nothing.

"Damn it."

Urgency builds inside me, a tight ball that settles in my gut, and I rotate, exiting the bathroom. At the same moment, I find Emily and Jessica exiting the stairwell just as several staff members enter behind them. "What the hell are you doing coming up, not going down?" I demand, closing the small space between me and them, my focus on Emily. My hands come down on her arms and the relief I feel, the way just touching her and knowing she's okay, allows me to breathe again, speaks of how on edge Martina has me.

"Is this the kind of trouble I fear it is?" Emily asks softly, angling her body away from Jessica. "The kind that visited last night?"

"What does that mean?" Jessica asks. "The kind that visited last night?"

"It means," I say, glancing at her, "I'm going to have you escorted downstairs and out of the building."

"We can go down on our own, Shane," Jessica insists. "Go get your parents."

Emily's hands settle on my forearms. "Shane," she says, urgency in her voice as she presses for an answer to her question.

"I don't know," I say, and being as honest as I can be, I add, "but we're going to assume that it is until it isn't."

Seth exits the offices to join us. "Your father says he can't walk right now, and your mother refuses to leave him," he announces. "Derek's staying with them."

"They're all leaving," I assure him, the elevator dinging as Cody steps off.

Holding the door, he announces, "There is no fire. There's something else behind the evacuation, and I can't get an answer on what yet."

"Then do we still need to evacuate?" Jessica asks, stepping forward.

"Yes," I say in unison with Cody and Seth.

"The absence of a fire isn't the absence of danger," Cody states, his attention on my assistant. "In fact, the unknown is full of limitless possibilities."

"Just another day with the Brandon family," Jessica states dryly, her hands on her hips, eyes locked on Cody. "Obviously since you're hanging out with Seth, you're competent, but you started and then this happened. How do we know you aren't involved in all of this?"

"Because I said he's not," Seth says flatly. "And he's in charge right now. You and Emily need to go with him and get out of the building."

Jessica laughs. "Delicate delivery has never been your specialty. God, how I love you." She eyes Cody. "I'm ready. I don't take orders well, but if you say please, I'll call you Master."

"If you say please, I'll *let* you call me Master," he replies. "Now get in the damn car."

Jessica laughs. "Oh, I like him too. It's not love yet, but it feels good." She heads toward him.

I shake my head and focus on Emily. "You too, sweetheart. Go with Cody. But don't call him Master. That's me. And right now I have to get my parents to listen to reason and actually evacuate, even if I have to carry my damn father down. I'll catch up with you."

"I'm good at getting your father to do things," she argues. "Let me help. Then we can all leave safely."

"I'm not risking your safety over my father's stubbornness," I say, despite the fact that she's right. She has a strange ability that no one else does to soften that man.

"I'm not risking *your* safety over your father's stubbornness." She grabs the lapels of my jacket. "Let's do this together." She softens her voice. "All of this."

She's not talking about now. She's talking about last night. This morning. All of this.

"Sweetheart," I say, reaching for her hands. "I hear you. I do. I know what you want, but right now, I need you to go with Cody and do what he says. Please."

She wants to argue. I see it in her face, but all she says is, "This is killing me." Her grip on my jacket loosens.

And damn, I love how eager she is to help but how smartly she makes the decision. I cup her face and kiss her. "Do not leave Cody's side." I release her and eye Jessica. "That goes for you too."

"No worries there," Jessica assures, me, linking her arm with Emily's. "We'll see you outside, Boss," she says, setting them into motion, and Cody wastes no time herding them to the elevator car and sealing them inside.

Once I know they're on their way to safety, Seth and I step together. "It's a bomb threat," Seth says. "I didn't want Cody to create panic by telling them. I have men on every floor clearing them. Cody and two of his men are taking Emily and Jessica to the coffee shop a block down to get them out of the line of fire. Nick is waiting in the lobby to take you all there as well."

"How worried are we about this?" I ask.

"My gut says I should go to your father's office and pull a gun on your parents to get us all the hell out of here."

"Then let's go get them." We rotate and step forward, when Derek and my parents appear behind the glass in the lobby, walking in our direction.

"The gods of bitches and bastards answered my prayers," Seth murmurs.

"Hey now," I say. "This is my family."

He laughs. "Exactly," he says at the same moment my mother exits the lobby.

"Finally we're here," she announces, hugging herself, her dark hair a wavy wild mess. Her pale skin, which is as perfect as I once believed her to be, is now smeared with mascara, telling me she's been crying. My mother doesn't cry.

My father follows her, joining us, and immediately launches

into a hacking fit, a napkin to his mouth, his head down, the lion, the king, weak, defeated. Hating that we see him this way, and the truth is, I do too. I really fucking do. Derek does too. I see it in his eyes as he exits, then looks at me, his expression stormy and some mix of frustration and torment, which I think he's earned. The man just saw our parents fucking, followed by what preceded that discovery.

Seth crosses to the elevator panel and punches the call button, seeming more than a little eager to end this little hallway clash of the Titans, or rather, the Brandons. "Let's get everyone to a secure location."

My mother's brow furrows. "Isn't it unsafe to take the elevator in a fire?"

"There is no fire," Seth explains. "We're cleared to use the elevators, but we've been asked to move quickly. Once we're on the ground level, we'll be keeping you under lock and key until we know exactly what we're dealing with."

My mother lifts a frustrated hand. "I don't even want to try to read between the lines. I won't like what I find out." She grabs my father's arm, and he seems to recover, eyeing me and Derek.

"I'll expect an explanation," he says. "A good one." He turns and heads to the elevator, strong enough now that he has my mother in tow.

"A good one," Derek says dryly, stepping to my side, his voice low, biting. "The irony of that statement stretched continents. I'll be taking the next elevator down." Seth motions us forward, and Derek lifts a hand. "Shane and I need to finish a talk we were having."

Seth gives me an arched brow that I answer with a confirmation nod, hoping like hell Derek has some confession that will help me end this nightmare. Seth inclines his chin, his eyes reading his understanding. "I'll be waiting on the ground level," he says, disappearing into the car and allowing the doors to shut.

Derek puffs out a breath and rubs his hand on the back of his neck, punching the call button for another car. "How insane is it that I can't stand the idea of being around Mom right now? And yes. I know I'm a grown adult, but that doesn't seem to matter right now either."

"Been there, still doing that," I admit, "even after Emily logically reminded me that Mom's not only human, but that good ol' Pops has worn her down with a pocketful of women over the years."

Derek shoves his jacket back, hands settling on his hips. "I just saw our mother naked in our father's office, on top of him, after finding out she most likely was naked with another man last night. I'm a couple of bottles of Father's best Scotch, which I plan to swipe, away from logic working right now."

Small talk, no matter how reality based, doesn't suit us, and the minute the elevator dings, we face each other, that unfinished business between us demanding a conclusion I welcome. "Leave Teresa out of this," Derek warns. "Involving her will only lead to more trouble."

"This from the man who fucked her to get to her brother?" I demand, instinct driving me to push him, wanting to take him over the edge and hoping like hell I can be the hand that pulls him back to the top.

"I did fuck her," he says. "And I am fucking her and I will keep fucking her. Which is exactly why I know that any path that involves her leads to no place good for you."

"Is that a threat?"

"It's a dangerous territory, brother. One you don't want to face with Adrian Martina."

"You want reality? I'll give you reality. He wants to take what is ours. He'll kill you and he'll kill Emily and who knows who else. I won't let him take our company. I won't let him take the people I love, and he needs to know I will cut where it hurts. And if that means I involve Teresa, I will involve Teresa."

His eyes flash with challenge. "Now which one of us is in dangerous territory?"

"You paved this path I'm forced to travel to keep us all alive."

"Leave," he urges. "Go back to New York and then it's on me."

"You aren't the first to make that recommendation," I say, leaving out Emily's name. "But this is Adrian Martina we're talking about. Do you really think he'll let us walk away alive?"

"You mean you don't want to walk away from your newly inked CEO position."

"The one I may never assume? Martina wants me involved, and if I walk away, he'll kill you to get me back." I fix him with a hard look. "Our division is our weakness. I'm choosing family. When are you going to do the same?"

"Like you did when you left your legal career?"

"Yes," I say. "Like I did when I left my legal career."

"Like you did when you tricked me into signing a document that named you as CEO in the event Father was incapacitated?"

I feel those words like the whip they are intended to be, but with no regret. "I'd explain my reasons for that decision, but you won't hear me, and this isn't the time or place for us to fight personal wars. They have to wait or there will be nothing left to claim in victory. We have two mutual enemies. Adrian Martina and Mike Rogers."

He stares at me, his gray eyes cutting, sharp, before he walks to the panel and punches the button again. The elevator opens and we both walk inside, turning to face forward, side by side, every word we say now recorded, but as I watch him punch the button for the lobby level, that bandage still on his hand, I issue one final warning. "A blade in your hand now. A blade in your heart, or back, later."

He doesn't look at me. He doesn't reply. He simply steps into the spot next to me, both of us instinctively curling our fingers into our palms. Alike and so fucking different. The doors slide shut and we don't speak, a band of tension wrapping around us, tightening with each floor that passes, until we are at the lobby level. The elevator dings, the doors starting to open when Derek says, "I find myself wondering who is more likely to shove that blade into my heart. You or them?"

I don't have the chance to ask who "them" is. He steps out of the elevator, and the sound of shouts fills the air. Derek looks over his shoulder at me and I'm by his side in an instant, both of us jogging toward the noise and rounding the corner to the main lobby, where we both stop dead in our tracks. People pour in through the doors, running toward us and away from the thick smoke quickly overtaking the front of the building. My gaze scans and catches on a security guard and several men I recognize from our security team near the entrance, and they actually seem to be urging people in our direction.

"Out the back door!" a police officer shouts over a megaphone. "Proceed out the back door!"

"Whatever this is," I say to Derek, "it's on us, and we have to make it right." I don't wait for his reply. I start walking toward the problem, not away, trying to ensure everyone who could be affected is being supported and is safe.

Derek is instantly beside me, keeping pace, and for a moment, I contemplate that he might be part of this, whatever it is, and that is why he's staying with me. Maybe that's why he kept me upstairs, and I foolishly played into his hand. I do not like this idea, but I focus on getting to the front of the building, my strides longer now, quicker. Derek's stride matches mine as well, his energy too, my worries of moments before fading with them. He senses what I do. He fears what I fear. And we don't know what that is. The crowd is now behind us, and the smoke calls to me, *to us*, neither of us slowing, until we are standing just outside the wall of glass that encases the front of the building. I watch then as the smoke begins to dissipate, and in its depths sits an ominous-looking six-by-six wooden crate.

"Any idea what the hell that is?" I ask.

"What the hell is right," Derek says as the crate begins to rock back and forth.

CHAPTER THIRTEEN

SHANE

The crate continues to rock back and forth, and in all of thirty seconds there are a half dozen uniformed officers pointing guns at it but staying the hell away from it. My immediate thought is every possibility that box holds: a bomb, a person, an attack of some sort. My next is of Emily and my parents, and I reach for my phone, punching in Emily's auto-dial.

"Shane," she says, answering on the first ring, the sound of her voice delivering instant relief. "Where are you?"

"Derek and I are together at the front of the building," I say, the sound of my father's deep, gravelly coughs in the background telling me she's still with my parents. "Where are you?"

"We got caught in the smoke, and it's not treating your father well. Cody and two of his men are escorting us to our apartment so he can safely rest."

"Good," I approve, damn happy Cody was smart enough to get the hell away from here. "Text me when you get there." Derek points to the crate, and I watch as it splinters down the front. "I need to go, sweetheart."

"Wait, Shane."

"Stay with Cody," I say, ending the call as another splinter bulges the wood of the crate. Another blink and it bursts open, a naked man falling out of the wooden encasement and onto his side, his hands and feet bound. "Holy mother of Jesus," Derek murmurs.

Holy mother of Jesus is right, I think as cameras begin to flash, news crews pushing toward the scene while officials push them back, forming a perimeter. The naked man curls forward, hiding his face and as much of his body as he can from the many prying eyes I suspect he didn't know were waiting on him. Nick suddenly appears in my line of sight, an officer with him, the two of them approaching the circle of armed men around the crate and the naked man.

"I assume we've just found your missing security person?" Derek asks, and while I can feel his eyes on me, mine are on the man, anger burning in my belly at his demoralizing circumstances. Because of me. Because of Derek. Because of my fucking father. But Ted's alive. The way I told Adrian I expected to have him returned, but he's also paying for me forcing Adrian's hand.

"Shane—" Derek presses.

"Yes," I say, watching Nick rush through the line of officers to kneel next to the humiliated man. "That's him." Seconds tick by, and Nick motions to the officers, pulling out a knife to cut Ted's hands free, while EMS workers hurry forward and a blanket is pulled over Ted, but he doesn't move, which seems to indicate he's injured.

"He's telling you to heel," he says. "Or he'll make you pay the price."

All he did was piss me off, I think, *and when I'm pissed, I win and I win big.* "I'm not going to heel," I reply, glancing over at him. "And the brother I used to know wouldn't either."

"Who said I was going to heel?"

"Haven't you already?"

His expression tightens. "No. I have not and I never will."

The glass door just to the left of me opens and Seth appears, his gaze sliding between myself and Derek. "I need to get you out of sight before the police and the press corner one or both of you," he says, clearly in the role of head of security for the company. Before he's even finished the statement, Derek and I are walking with him, our strides long and quick.

"How's Ted?" I ask.

"Missing a finger, from what Nick just told me," he replies, cutting me a look, this news delivered with barely contained anger when Seth is never barely contained about anything.

"Damn it," I curse softly, my own anger momentarily blotted out with guilt and a sense of responsibility. This one is on me. I hired this man. I engaged with Martina and this was the outcome, a decision I'll analyze later, in private. "His finger was cut off and he still forced himself out of that box," I say, anger returning, along with a personal, silent promise to deliver the man the justice he deserves.

We round the corner to the elevator banks. "He's an ex-SEAL," Seth says, stopping at the garage-level car and hitting the call button. "He's trained to push through the pain. The only positive, if there is one, outside of him being alive, is that he seems unaware of being publicly exposed." He changes the subject.

"I need to wrap up a few things here, but Cody will be waiting on you in the garage of your apartment where your family's now located." He hands me a set of keys. "White Ford F-150 parked next to the Bentley."

"I'm gathering the plan, then," Derek says, breaking his short silence, "is to get us all in one obvious location and hope that seems too stupid for anyone to consider. Well, except for the fact that Adrian owns the staff there, and if he wants the press or the police to find us, they will."

The elevator opens and Seth holds the door with his foot and hand. "What do you know of the staff there?"

"Enough to know that unless you fired them all, you still have a problem." Derek walks into the elevator and faces forward. "But on the bright side: we'll all be together to get our stories straight before we get questioned, and daring to brainstorm right underneath Adrian's nose feels like a mighty nice 'fuck you' to him."

Seth's gaze shifts to me. "He could own everyone in every place you favor," he says. "What matters is how prepared we are. And we are."

Considering recent events, if this were anyone but Seth, I'd question him, but if he says we're prepared, I accept that answer, given the urgency of the situation. I give him a nod and step into the car next to Derek, while Seth steps between the doors and looks at him. "You know way more about Adrian Martina than you should."

"I'd have agreed with that statement two days ago," Derek surprises me by saying. "But right now, you need to know everything about him you can. For instance, Adrian revels in breaking those who think they can't be broken."

I digest this with discomfort, and not just for Ted, but in how easily that description could be used to describe me in pursuit of winning a courtroom brawl.

"And," Derek adds, "I guarantee you that Ted shoved his way out of that crate because he was led to believe staying in it had consequences."

Seth stares at Derek, his eyes hard, then harder, before he looks at me. "Cody will be waiting." He lets the door shut and leaves Derek and me alone once again. Side by side, and in an elevator. Enemies. Brothers. Allies if we are going to survive the mess our family has found, even if we must be uncomfortable allies. The ride is a short one floor, and we exit to the garage, where I unclick the locks of the truck, momentarily remembering the good times on our ranch my parents still own.

"You ever get to the ranch?" I ask.

"I can't stomach the memories," he says, and I get it. I do. It's the same reason I haven't been, despite loving the property and the experience.

"A time when they convinced us we were a happy little family."

He glances over at me. "You mean we weren't?"

It's a sarcastic, rhetorical question, and I give a humorless laugh. "Of course we were," I say, walking toward the driver's side of the truck while he does the same on the passenger's side. In unison, we climb inside and shut the doors, and for the first time since my return home, that mountain between us feels more like a hill. "Makes you wonder what was real, doesn't it?" I say, still talking about our family. But the idea behind the statement has me repeating, "You know more about Adrian Martina than you should," before a realization hits me. "But it's not him you know. It's Teresa."

"You already know this. What's your point? She was my gateway drug into Adrian's operation."

"That you got addicted to," I surmise.

He cuts his gaze from mine, looking forward, and does so a little too quickly for my comfort. "I told you," he says. "Leave her out of this."

"But you can't, can you? Because she *is* your drug, like Emily is mine."

He doesn't react or look at me, his gaze focused on the front window, where there is nothing but a wall to inspect. "Yes," he surprises me by conceding, his eyes meeting mine. "Yes, she is."

"Derek—"

"She isn't like them."

"She actively, willingly lives and works close to her brother," I say. "She's one of them."

"She's trapped."

"You're trapped. We're trapped. She is not. If she wanted to leave, they worship her. She could leave."

His cell phone starts to ring, and he removes it from his pocket and then glances at me. "Surprise, surprise," he says dryly. "It's Mike, no doubt wanting to know why our building is on the news. Aside from the fact that he's a pain in our fucking asses we don't need right now. Do we have a story we want to tell him?"

"We have no idea what Pops might have already told him," I say. "He could be cornering you into a conflicting story."

He hits decline. "That's the excuse I needed to ignore that call, but he won't be ignored for long. He'll call back."

My phone starts to ring, and I fish it from my pocket and glance at Mike's number on the screen. "No," I agree, showing the caller ID to Derek. "He won't." I end the call, return my phone to my pocket, and start the engine. "It's time to deal with our enemies, once and for all."

"Our enemies?" he queries.

"They are *our* enemies, Derek, Mike included."

"And what does that make our mother?" Derek asks.

"Indeed," I say, my agreement bitter on my tongue. "That's a question we have to ask."

"One with an answer we might not like."

He's right, and somehow, as I pull us out of the garage, I have this sense that not only are Derek and I alike but different, but circumstances now force us to be united despite our divisions. I'd call that progress if those circumstances weren't quite possibly life-and-death.

EMILY

The Escalade we ride in to the Four Seasons is large enough to allow myself, Jessica, Shane's parents, and two of Cody's men to ride with us. I don't ask questions about the smoke or the building evacuation with Jessica and Maggie present, nor do I say much about Shane's call, for fear I'll create questions none of us want them asking. For Maggie's part, she simply doesn't ask questions, which I can only assume comes from her role as the grandame of the Brandon family. And while I do not believe Jessica knows about the Martina family, she understands the secrets and lies that are the Brandons, and chooses to keep her lips as sealed as mine.

After a short few-block drive, the Escalade turns into the parking garage of the Four Seasons, at which time I have one thought. We might be out of the smoke, and Brandon Senior might be able to breathe again, but I can't. And that won't change until I'm back with Shane, touching him, kissing him, confirming that he's alive and well. I'm just not sure how we all stay that way with a man like Adrian Martina in our lives. Once we've parked, Cody and his men escort us to the elevators, though only Cody joins us in the actual car. The ride begins, and the silence is deafening until Brandon Senior begins to cough, a reminder to me that he's dying. It's also a sharp-edged knife in the heart of this family, a blade Derek handed to Adrian Martina to dig a little deeper.

We exit to the hallway, and Jessica tugs my arm, pulling me to the back of the group. "What's going on?"

"I really don't know," I say, and even if I did, I would not involve her in this.

"You asked Shane if this was related to last night."

"Shane's taking over as acting CEO," I say, grasping for a reasonable answer, and wishing like hell this woman didn't see and hear too much, too often. "Not everyone is happy about that."

"Derek?" she queries, but doesn't give me time to reply. "Of course," she says. "He wants the company to look in chaos under Shane's control."

"I thought so, but the smoke changed my opinion," I say, concerned now that I have eased her fears a little too much, when I want her to remain cautious. "It seems extreme," I add. "Maybe this isn't related to the family at all. Maybe it's terrorism or some other situation."

"Right," she says again. "It could be, but the timing does seem rather curious."

We reach the door to the apartment and head inside, where Cody locks up and sets the rules: "Don't leave. Don't answer the door. If you need something, I'll be on the balcony, making a few phone calls. Questions?"

Jessica shoves a lock of her now long blond hair behind her ear and folds her arms in front of her, concern furrowing her brow, her saucy attitude nowhere to be found. "Because the press is dangerous?"

"You're damn straight they're dangerous," Brandon Senior barks, his voice raspy, almost unrecognizable.

Cody's eyes meet Jessica's. "I'll be on the balcony," he says, and not for the first time, there is a fizzle of connection between them that has me wondering if that was an invitation.

Whatever the case, he steps down the hallway, and Brandon Senior motions toward the apartment. "I need an office to work in."

"I thought you'd want to lie down," I offer.

"He does," Maggie insists.

"I need to work," he counters.

"You won't be alive for the chemo if you kill yourself," she argues.

It's a good argument, but his phone rings, disrupting her efforts, and the minute he takes it out, looks at the screen, and says, "Mike," before declining the call, I know she's lost her influence tonight.

Clearly oblivious to this fact, Maggie looks displeased and questions him, "Why didn't you take that? Surely Mike wants to know what's going on."

This earns her Brandon Senior's scowl, which she doesn't see because he's focused on me. "For the last time," he tells me, "I need an office and a computer."

"Of course," I say, and, concerned about Shane's private documents being put on display, I motion toward the kitchen, rather than the office. "Let's set up in the dining room so you have plenty of room to work." I start walking, and I don't miss the way he offers Maggie his back, dismissing her, shutting her out, a bit like Shane did to me last night. It's a thought that guts me, stirring fears that Shane mimicked Brandon Senior's behavior without even knowing it. Worse, that Shane and I could become his parents.

"If you have to work," Maggie says, "I'll make some coffee or tea. Emily, do you have tea?"

"If Cody's okay with room service, they can make a green tea with honey," I suggest, following Brandon Senior into the dining room, where he claims the head of the table and now gives me a scowl. "I need a computer, Ms. Stevens. Are those letters out to the stockholders?"

"Hours ago," I assure him. "Should I call them and explain our silence this afternoon?"

"The less you say, the less that can be held against you or me," he says. "Until we know what that silence originated from, no." His phone rings again and he ignores it. "Get me that computer."

I nod and rotate back into the kitchen to find Jessica standing by the stove, while Maggie is at the bar, on the room phone. "What can I do?" Jessica asks.

"Go away," Brandon Senior calls out. "That's what you can do. My business can be your business when it's Shane's, because I'm dead. And I'm not dying."

"Soap operas and wine it is for me," Jessica bites out, and then looks at me. "You should join me."

"My business is her business," Brandon Senior calls out. "But my wife can join you."

The clear inference that his business is not his wife's has Jessica and me looking at Maggie, who laces her fingers together and looks toward the dining room, her usual fierce energy momentarily laced with defeat. A moment later, her jaw sets, her chest rising with a heavy breath, and I can almost feel her resolve form. "You mean your wife can join *you*," she says, marching forward.

Jessica and I share a look of discomfort, both of us moving into the living area. "I had no idea he treated her like the rest of us," she whispers. "If she's not immune, I wonder if his little girl-friend is?" She doesn't give me a chance to reply, motioning to the open patio door. "I'm going to go see if I can find out any-thing we don't already know about what happened back there." She lowers her voice. "I'll find you if I make progress."

I nod and take a step, intending to head to the office, when a thought hits me, and I follow Jessica to the patio, where I poke my head out of the doorway just as she reaches the balcony. Cody spots me instantly, pushing off the railing. "Is everything okay?"

"I just wanted you to know we ordered tea from room service."

"That's no problem," he says. "I have men watching the floor. I'll let them know." He reaches for his phone but hesitates, nar-rowing his gaze on me. "What's wrong?"

"Can you confirm Shane and Derek are safe?"

"The last time I communicated with Seth, which wasn't long ago, they were with him."

That's not a yes or a no, but it's better than nothing. Decid-ing I'll text Shane, I slip back into the living room, but I find my-self lingering just beyond the patio, observing as Cody and Jessica face the railing, my mind on that first night with Shane. Me lying against that glass. Me giving him my trust when I didn't know him and had every reason to distrust everyone around me. I still trust him and I know he trusts me. We aren't his parents. We won't become his parents.

Shaking off the thought, I hurry to the office and grab a spare MacBook, then make my way back to the dining room, sur-prised to find Brandon Senior alone, and on the phone, rather than with his wife. He glances up, motions for me to set the com-puter down. I do so and he immediately points at the door, dis-missing me. Unfazed by his typical behavior, I do as he says, but

I am bothered by Maggie's absence. Seeking her out, I head downstairs, find the bathroom door closed, and Lord help me, I don't know why, but before I can stop myself, I'm walking in that direction, stopping at the door, where I dare to listen. There is silence. Movement. Then words.

"No," she whispers. "You should have warned me about today. I don't think I can go through with this."

Feeling as if I've just been punched, I lower my head to my chest. Was Mike behind the evacuation and the smoke, not Martina? Or—oh God—is Martina working with Mike? The doorbell rings and I jolt, my heart in my throat as I race for the hallway. "Who is it?" I call out.

"Room service."

"You're clear to open the door," I hear, turning to find Cody standing behind me, but his eyes narrow at me again, awareness in their depths. "Is something wrong?"

"No," I say quickly, wanting to talk to Shane about this before anyone else. "I just—I'm nervous right now."

"With good reason," he says. "I'll get the tea."

"It's okay." I rotate and open the door, accepting the tea and willing my heart to slow, and I almost succeed. But then I shut the door and turn to find Maggie standing in the hallway.

"I'll take the tea to him," she says, but it's interesting to me that, as I hand it to her, she doesn't make eye contact.

She steps away from me and walks into the kitchen, and I find Cody lingering in the hallway, studying me. "What's bothering you?"

"Nothing," I say. "I need the ladies' room." I hurry forward, but when I try to pass, he catches my arm.

"I'm on your side," he promises softly.

It's an odd thing to say, but somehow the right thing as well.

And I want to believe him. I do believe him. He works for Shane.
And apparently, it's only Shane's blood that betrays him. "Thank
you," I say. "I just need to go upstairs and clear my head."

"Understood. And just so you know, I'm setting every
houseguest you have right now up in a room here in the hotel tonight. We want to them to stay, just to be sure the press is well
fed before we send them home."

"The press," I say. "Right. Of course."

He lingers a moment more and then turns away. I stand
there, waiting for him to leave, and then I dart forward, but instead of going upstairs, I cross the living area and enter the office, shutting the door behind me. I need the resources to do some
research on Mike Rogers. But for a moment I lean against the
door, trying to think of why Mike would have set this up today.
To make the company look lost and in need of his guidance? The
smoke, I think. Brandon Senior. To hurt Brandon Senior? To kill
him? It's a crazy idea. I mean, what would that solve? Shane would
still have control of the company. Another thought hits me hard.
What if the goal was to create some kind a situation where Maggie could contest Brandon Senior's will? Oh God. Did Maggie and
Mike plan to kill her husband? Is Derek in on it? And why, monster that he is, do I think he's not capable of such a thing?

All these questions lead me to the one I dread the most: How
am I going to even begin to tell Shane my suspicions about his
mother?

CHAPTER FOURTEEN

EMILY

I am not sure how long I lean against the office door, but my mind replays my encounters with Maggie, trying to give her an excuse for what I overhead. *You should have warned me about today.* Those words are fairly damning. *I don't think I can go through with this.* Those even more so. Without any question, she's up to some kind of trouble. But what? I pray her obvious hesitation to carry out her planned actions is about the love I still see in her eyes for Brandon Senior and that it will prevail. I want to believe this. I do, but it's hard to trust anyone except Shane right now. And Jessica. I trust Jessica.

Pushing off the door, I walk to Shane's desk and sit down, keying the computer to life. I then type in in Mike Rogers's name, wondering how this man is ever present in our lives yet never present at all. First things first though, I remove my phone from my purse, set it on the desk, and then slip my purse over my head. Opening a drawer, I intend to set my purse inside, but instead find myself staring down at a stack of eight-by-ten photos. I pick them up, staring at an image of Shane shaking hands with who I think is the mayor of New York. I thumb through another shot, and find him with one of the old-school New York Yankees, which I know because my father was an incessantly talkative baseball fan. There are more shots, at least five, all with prominent people. All of which most people would frame and put on the wall, but not Shane. They're his memories, not his bragging rights, which speak to me about his capacity to self-motivate his actions. It's a comforting realization. He'll remain true to himself. He won't become someone he isn't, when it seems, perhaps, that's what happened to Derek, who, by Shane's account, is far from the man of his past.

I flip through to the next photo, and a stack of smaller shots tumble from my hands and scatter onto the ground. I bend down to pick them up, finding there are about a dozen images now under the desk. Kicking off my high heels, I settle on my knees and begin picking them up, quite aware of my missing panties in this position but quickly distracted as the photos prove to be of Shane's college graduation, all of which include him and his family. One particular image, of Shane, Derek, and his father sitting at a table, holding whiskey glasses up for a toast, draws me in. They're laughing and smiling, even Brandon Senior, and you'd think that is what I'd linger on, but instead I'm struck by the absence of Maggie. Most likely it's a meaningless observation, as logically she's holding the camera, but somehow her anywhere but with her family feels quite profound right now. I shut the drawer and lean against it, dragging the skirt of my black dress over my knees, and staring at that same photo, feeling an inescapable sense of it trying to talk to me, but I just can't hear what it's saying.

The sound of the door opening freezes me in place. Brandon Senior's coughing follows, and my instincts have me recoiling under the desk, acting before I can even think. Seeking a shelter where I do not have to be subjected to Brandon Senior barking a list of commands at me, when all I want to do right now is talk to Shane, I sink back against the interior wall in the cubbyhole meant only for my legs, inside the darkness.

"What the hell happened back there at the building?" I hear him demand, assuming he's on the phone.

The door shuts with a thud. "Martina happened," Shane says, his voice delivering both relief and regret. I'm under the desk. I'm eavesdropping when that was not my intent. I want to get up. I *should* get up. I scoot forward, and Brandon Senior says, "In case you forgot, son, I'm headed to Germany, with a lot to do in advance. Save me the effort of leading questions and summarize."

"Gladly," Shane states. "Martina and his group of legit investors want to insert their illegal drug into a drug study and get it approved by the FDA. They don't, however, want to stop pushing it illegally through our operation, unless we corrupt a competitor and help them do so, in which case we're tied to it anyway. I drew a line in the sand. Without question, today's events amount to his answer."

Brandon Senior laughs. "A bomb threat and smoke are his answer. Sounds like Adrian is still playing frat-boy games. I don't see the problem here. Get rid of him."

"Says the man who wasn't around when the smoke cleared," Shane bites out, his voice tight, his anger palpable even to me. "Adrian left us a gift in that smoke. A crate holding my missing security person, who was naked, beaten, and missing a finger. A man with a family and kids."

I cover my mouth, forcing myself not to gasp, my lashes lowering with the effort. I can't even process what I've just heard, but Brandon Senior seems to have no trouble. "Now that we know the real story, what are we going to tell the press, our staff and stockholders, and your mother?"

I blink. That's all? I'm angry with Martina. I'm scared over what he might do next. I'm guilty for being the person Ted was guarding. And all Brandon Senior does is brush past it?

"That's all?" Shane demands, clearly agreeing with me. "A man with a wife and kids who was protecting us lost his finger and damn near his life, and you have nothing more to say?"

"Let me make myself perfectly clear to you, son," Brandon Senior states. "I'm not dying. I'm retaining control of this company, and overreactive, emotional responses are not productive and, in fact, most often, are destructive. Now, what is our cover story?"

"Today's events were unrelated to us" is the reply, and this time it's Derek's voice. "They appear to be directed at Ted, personally, as a potential act of revenge for a military operation he participated in some years ago."

Ted becomes the fall guy, I think. I don't know him, but I do know that he was on my security detail and now his life is forever changed. "Weigh in here, Shane," Brandon Senior presses, surprising me by caring about anyone's opinion but his own.

"It's an acceptable solution," Shane replies, "on the condition we write Ted a ridiculously large check."

"How ridiculously large?" Brandon Senior queries.

"As large as I see fit," Shane replies.

Senior's disapproval crackles in the air, but he concedes. "Do it," he says, and then changes the topic. "And get rid of Martina while I'm gone."

Footsteps following, and then the door opens. The instant it closes, Derek reacts. "I'm really fucking tired of being the ball boy picking up his fucking foul balls."

"Then don't be the ball boy," Shane says. "Especially when he throws the ball in puddles of shit the size of a lake."

"We can't just get Adrian out," Derek says. "You get that, right?"

"Do you want him out?"

"My answer to that question is irrelevant. This isn't a sandbox. We don't just throw sand in his eyes and he's gone. Because he'll come back with a baseball bat and start swinging."

"Do you *want* him out, Derek?" Shane presses, but a knock sounds on the door before Derek replies.

A moment later, Cody says, "I need to talk to you, Shane."

"Come in," Shane welcomes.

"Alone," Cody counters. "I need to see you alone."

"Derek stays," Shane states, rejecting his request. "What's happening?"

The door shuts, and Cody speaks again. "I didn't make the decision to bypass the coffee shop to come here for your father today. Ramon followed us when we left the building."

My heart starts to race and I sit up straighter, my hand on the wood above my head, bracing myself for whatever comes next.

"That said," Cody continues, "I do not think Adrian is a man of excess, and further action against you at this point would not fit his profile. But I wasn't taking a chance."

"He won't hurt Emily," Derek interjects. "There is a code in the cartel. The women—mother, sister, wife, girlfriend—are off-limits, at least until revenge is on the table."

"Agreed," Cody says, "*if* we're talking about Adrian. Ramon's another story. He's a wild card, known to have gone rogue on occasion, and not to Adrian's liking."

"And Adrian tolerates this why?" Shane asks.

"Ramon's really damn good at covering up Adrian's secrets," Cody explains. "He's his shield."

"Then we need to remove his shield," Shane states, his voice hardening. "If I wanted to get rid of Ramon, how would I go about that?"

I stiffen, my fingers curling in my palms, not quite sure what he's asking. Or maybe I am. Is he—could he—be suggesting . . .

"Definitely get rid of him," Cody urges, as if he's heard my thoughts.

"Any way that makes him disappear from my life and Emily's," Shane says, no hesitation in his response.

Oh God, I think, my hand going to my neck. He really is talking about killing Ramon.

"Give us a moment to talk, Cody," Derek orders.

"Stay, Cody," Shane counter-orders. "If I want to get rid of him, how do I do it?"

"Before I give you my answer," Cody says, "I want to preface it by saying that I just finished three years undercover inside a competing cartel. These people are not human. They're brutal. Ramon is one of the worst of them. Adrian's hands remain clean because Ramon allows him to keep them that way. Ramon has murdered and raped countless people. Why am I telling you this? Because if I could wipe the earth of that scum, I would."

"But you won't do it," Shane supplies for him.

"It's not a matter of won't. It's a matter of staying alive. All of us. You're on Adrian's radar. You're his challenger. If anything happens to Ramon, he'll look to you."

"He's right," Derek confirms. "Ramon's untouchable right now."

"Put him in jail," Shane counters. "Find one of those rapes and murders and make sure the charges stick."

"Same story," Cody replies. "Adrian looks to you."

"He's not untouchable," Shane says, his tone low but lethal, even vehement. "I don't accept that answer. Talk to Nick. Go see Ted. Get motivated."

Cody is silent for several beats, in which his resistance is palpable, but he finally concedes. "I'll have a discussion with Nick." Footsteps follow and the door opens and closes before Shane sideswipes me by attacking Derek. "What the hell were you thinking going into business with a drug cartel, Derek?"

"What was I thinking? I was thinking that our father ordered me to do it, and you were trying to take my place in the company I've lived for all my life. Did I think it would turn out like this? No. Am I on board to shut him down and get him out? Yes. But as you sit on that high horse, ride it on over to a mirror, baby brother. How quickly the golden boy decided to murder someone."

"You saw Ted's condition," Shane reminds him." You know what Ramon is capable of doing."

"And he has his eyes on Emily."

"He has his eyes on Teresa too. You say you care about her. He should be a problem for you as well."

I blink in surprise and confusion. Derek cares about Teresa? I had no idea he could care about anyone, but if he has mustered emotions for this woman, I have a feeling this complicates, rather than helps, our situation.

"How then," Shane continues, "can you care for Teresa and want Ramon free to hurt her?"

"Teresa's Adrian's sister," Derek replies. "He won't touch her."

"But he will hurt you. Ramon will put you in a crate the first chance he gets, and it will be personal. He didn't know Ted. Ted's condition will be mild compared to what he does to you."

"I'm not saying he doesn't need to die," Derek concedes. "But I'm not ready to say that yet, and you, my brother, got to that point in two seconds flat, the way Adrian would have. We are not the same, Shane. You and Adrian are. Why do you think he gravitates to you? You're cold. You're calculated. And you want power."

"I want our family name protected. I want it to mean something."

"Your name. Adrian's name. You both want to win, and you need to remember that staying alive is winning. And once the bodies start piling up, they just keep piling up."

"Ramon's the only person we're talking about here. Unless there's more you know about?"

"I'm done with this conversation. I'm going to go instruct Jessica to leak our newly created 'Ted story' to the whole damn planet in an effort to get the press of our backs. And if we can't get the hell out of this hotel, I'm going to expedite getting us all private rooms so we don't kill each other."

I hear him moving to the door. It opens, but Derek isn't quite done yet. "He killed his brother, you know," he says.

"Who?" Shane asks.

"Adrian."

"His father killed his brother."

"Adrian set his brother up. Made it look like his brother betrayed his father, when it was Adrian who did it."

There is silence then, followed by more silence, before the door shuts. Then there is no movement, no sound, and I think Shane has left with Derek, while Derek's words and accusations have not: Shane is like Adrian. And Adrian is a brutal monster. Derek believes it too. He's built Shane up to be the enemy when he is not. Yes, Shane wants to kill Ramon. I believe that 100 percent. I try to get my head around that. It's wrong. I get that too. It's murder, as Derek pointed out, but I simply can't condemn Shane for trying to protect us all, and for something he hasn't even done yet.

Suddenly a pair of familiar legs appears in front of me. Shane's legs. I swallow hard and scoot forward to be offered his hand. And when I press my palm to his, heat that has nothing to do with sex—okay, maybe a little to do with sex, but more so our connection—slides up my arm and across my chest. He pulls me to my feet, and I lean against the desk while he presses his hands on the wood on either side of me. "How long did you know I was there?"

"The entire time."

"How did you know I was there?"

"I could smell you, feel you."

I'm stunned. Confused. Pleased. Trapped by my own bad actions. "I'm sorry. Your father came in hacking when I was already bending down to get something, and I just . . . I couldn't deal with him again right at that moment. Only it wasn't just him looking for me, and I couldn't figure out how or when to make my presence known."

"Do you know one of the things I love about you?"

"What?"

"That even when it's painful, like now, even when things don't go as planned, you tell me the truth."

"You know about my family. You know honesty is important to me."

"And you know my family. You know me, Emily."

"I *do* know you."

"Then I think you know this as well. I *am* a Brandon. At my core, I know Derek is right. I am cold. I am calculating. I do want to win. And I will not let Martina win."

"I see all those things."

"The things that torment me relate to my family, and to you. I will not lose them. I will not lose you. I will, however, kill Ramon, and when it's done, I will wake up relieved, not tormented."

My hand settles on his chest, his heart thundering under my palm, telling me that beneath his calm, unaffected demeanor, he is, in fact, affected. And what he feels worries me more than what he says. "I'm afraid of this changing you."

"This is me, Emily. I'm not changing. I'm just being me in these circumstances. That's what I'm telling you."

"People change, Shane. Life changes them."

His fingers slide under my hair and wrap around my neck, dragging my mouth to his. "We won't change." His mouth brushes mine, tongue doing a sultry, slow lick before he vehemently murmurs, "I love you too damn much to lose you."

I want to respond, to tell him he won't, and that I love him too, but he doesn't give me a chance. He kisses me again, this time with a deep stroke of his tongue, followed by another, and I feel it everywhere, all over, inside and out. And he's different now, the torment of last night gone, as if he's stopped fighting who, and what, he believes himself to be. I don't know if that is good or bad. Good, I think, because he's clear-minded. Because he's being honest with himself and me.

I lean into him and he into me, and it's as if a charge ignites between us. Suddenly, our kiss is deeper, our hands are all over each other, and there is nothing but this need to feel each other. This hunger between us, this burn. There is no alarm. There is no smoke. No problems. There is just our need for more of each other, and I barely even know how my dress is up to my waist and how I'm sitting on the desk, my legs wide, as they were on his father's desk earlier. How his fingers find my naked sex and his pants get unzipped. There is just the moment he's inside me, driving deep. The moment when we are holding on to each other, him inside me, our lips lingering a breath from each other. The moment when that turns into another hot kiss and then him lifting me off the desk, one of his hands cupping my naked backside, my fingers gripping his jacket. And finally the eternity that is too short when I tumble into absolute bliss and he shakes and makes these sexy, intense sounds and follows.

He holds me, seeming as resistant to letting go of us right now as I am, but he caves and sets me down on the desk, his hands going to my face. "I can't seem to get our clothes off and make love to you."

"That wasn't what we needed. Not right now."

"I do," he says. "I very much need to make love to you properly. To tell you I love you at the right time and in the right way."

"Anytime you tell me you love me is the right time and in the right way."

There's a knock on the door. "Shane, can we talk?"

It's Seth, and Shane kisses my forehead, thankfully handing me a tissue he gets from I don't know where. He pulls out of me then, and I feel the absence, beyond our bodies, but there's no time to process why. He rights his pants, helps me right my dress, and sets me on the floor before crossing to the door. I slip on my shoes and round the desk to meet him and Seth in the center of the office.

"I closed the office for the afternoon," Seth states. "Nick and I handled the police. They believe this is related to a case Ted worked for Nick."

"And Ted was okay with that?" Shane asks. "Is he even able to communicate?"

"He's improving and agreeable," Seth says. "The man's a warrior. We're keeping the press away from him and planning to get him on a plane to a vacation destination with his family when he's able."

"What about the press?" I ask. "Do I need to do anything on that front?"

Seth gives a nod. "Derek and Jessica are actually working together. I'm not sure how or why that's happening, but they leaked the story to the press, and the stockholders want you or your father, and your father says you need to get your ass on the phone and handle it."

"Derek has decided that if we don't save the company, we have nothing to fight for," Shane says. "But his relationship with Teresa is a potential problem. She's in love with him, and he at least has some feelings for her."

"He's also sleeping with his secretary," I remind them. "The feelings he has can't be that profound."

"I'd point out that he's my father's son," Shane says, "but that's true of me as well." He looks at Seth. "What else do I need to know?"

"It's what I need to know," he counters. "Any word from Adrian?"

"Not a word," Shane says, "And I won't be giving him the reaction he's seeking, which is me begging him for mercy. He can come to me. He can ask for mercy."

Cody steps into the room, his expression puzzled, voice low. "Your mother saw images of Ted on TV and started shaking. She insisted on going downstairs for coffee and to get some air. I had one of our men take her."

I'm reminded of the call I overhead. "This," I say, "would be a good time for me to talk to Shane alone."

Shane glances over at me. "You know something about my mother?"

"Yes."

"Just say it, sweetheart," he urges. "I'm not a delicate flower."

Only the truth is that his mother's shortfalls bother him deeply. Still, time is of the essence, and I push forward. "I overheard her on a phone call. She asked why she wasn't warned about today and then said she didn't think she could go through with 'this,' whatever that means."

Shane presses fingers to his temples, while Seth folds his arms in front of him and Cody shows no reaction at all. "The many possibilities this represents are innumerable," Seth states. "We need to know what Derek knows and then confront her."

"I'll talk to both of them," Shane says.

"Let me talk to her," I suggest. "If she's trapped and needs an escape, it won't come in the form of her angry, scorned son. It's at least an option."

"All right," Shane says. "I'll talk to Derek first."

Seth shakes his head. "I'd recommend you talk to Derek while she heads down to talk to your mother. If there's something else planned, and her comment about not being able to go through with this indicates there is, we need to know what it is and by who."

Shane looks at me. "He's right. I'll text you when I get answers from Derek."

I nod and walk to the desk for my purse, slipping it back over my head and across my chest. "I'm ready."

Seth reaches into his pocket and produces a can of pepper spray. "Just in case, I want you to have this. Cody can show you how to use it on the way down."

"I was a single girl before coming here," I say, accepting it and slipping it into my purse. "I know how to use it and do the most damage."

"Do you know how to use a gun?" he asks.

"Yes," I say, offering nothing more, aware that this isn't the time or place to discuss why I was armed back in Texas long before my family was corrupted by a hacker operation. Instead I say, "I won't be the girl who went down without one hell of a fight."

CHAPTER FIFTEEN

EMILY

Cody and I step into the elevator, and we both know enough not to have any conversation of merit with cameras rolling. We face forward, both folding our arms in front of our chests, and he clears his throat, but before the doors shut, Jessica appears and holds the door. "As I thought," she says, handing me a tissue. "You need this."

My brow furrows, but I accept the tissue. "I'm not going to cry, if that is what you think."

"Unless you're making a fashion statement," she says, "and Lord knows with my hair extensions, I get it, your lipstick is on your cheek, not your lips."

I whirl around to look in the mirror, laughing as I confirm that, indeed, I have pink all over the place. "At least it's me, not Shane," I say, cleaning myself up.

"He was a mess too when he told me where you were headed," she says, "which is what alerted me to your potential problem as well. I didn't think you'd want to talk to his mother in your current state. Aside from the fact that she's scornful of any hair any of us has out of place, it would have pretty much announced you'd been making out with her son."

"That would have been bad," I agree, facing forward. "Thank you."

"Friends don't let friends look like they put their makeup on drunk."

"It wasn't *that* bad," I object.

"It was bad, honey," she says, turning her attention to Cody. "Why didn't you tell her? You're supposed to be protecting her, not letting Shane's mother attack her for having her tongue down her son's throat."

I shake my head. "Good grief, Jessica."

"I was going to tell her," he replies.

Jessica scowls. "No, you were not."

The elevator starts dinging over and over, the door jerking against Jessica's grip. "That means let it go," Cody informs her. "We need to get downstairs. You'll have plenty of time to reprimand me later."

"I don't reprimand," she states, clearly missing the invitation I'm certain was in his words. "I simply point out logical conclusions and actions," she adds, glancing at me. "I was sitting with Shane's mother when the Ted story came on the news. She started to tremble, like he was her son or something. Like it was personal. Something wasn't right about it."

I nod my understanding and she glances at Cody, the two of them exchanging a look I tune out, my mind processing the observations shared with me. Jessica's astute and observant. If she thinks Maggie's personally involved, and I'm of the opinion that she is, I'm not going to like the details, which is all the more reason why I have to get Maggie to talk to me.

"I would have told you about the lipstick," Cody assures me as the doors shut and the car starts moving. "I'm here to protect you, and I will. I have your back. That's what I'm telling you."

I glance over at him. "I appreciate that. It's Shane's back I'm worried about."

"We all have his back and we're one hell of a team, you included."

"Jessica—"

"Is bossy, arrogant, and beautiful," he says. "She's also loyal, but that doesn't change the reality here. She's going to have to learn that we Mexican men like to be in charge."

I'm not sure if he's talking about his job, or something more personal, but whatever the case, the elevator dings and I laugh. "Good luck with that one."

He winks at me and holds the door, and really, truly, he's incredibly charming and good-looking. The kind of man I'd wish for Jessica. Except for one thing, I think, stepping into the corridor, with him by my side. At any moment, he could end up like Ted. But then again, at any moment, I fear Shane could as well. I could too. We all could. And this idea seals my pledge to get the answers I need from Maggie. "She sitting in the bar area," Cody tells me as we turn left into the main lobby and start walking in that direction, our steps determined, no words spoken.

We turn left again, our path now framed by couches and tables, as well as a bar to our left, but Maggie is nowhere to be found. Cody's cell phone buzzes and he glances at the screen then at me. "She moved to the back corner of the restaurant, which is all but empty, since it's midafternoon."

Midafternoon, I think, as we walk toward the archway leading to the restaurant, wondering how I've lost my concept of time today. "Table for two?" the cute, blond twentysomething hostess asks.

"One," Cody informs her, glancing at me. "There's no exit inside the restaurant and my presence might intimidate her. I'll wait here by the door."

Giving a quick, agreeable incline of my chin, I instruct the hostess that I'm meeting Maggie, and she allows me to find her on my own. Moving through rows of empty tables, I cut left and seek her out, finally locating her hidden in a corner, behind a large pillar. I approach the table, expecting to find her on the phone. What I find instead is her sitting there, elbow on the table, fingers curled under her chin. She's also holding a tissue and seemingly oblivious to my approach.

I sit down in the brown leather chair across from her, and she jolts, balling her fist at her chest, mascara smudging the ivory skin just beneath her blue eyes. "You scared me," she declares, and I don't miss the absence of coffee on the table, instead noting the presence of whiskey.

"I was worried about you," I say. "I heard you were rattled by what happened to Ted."

"Aren't you?" She downs the amber liquid in her glass and motions to the waitress. "I mean, this is one of Shane's security people. It hits home."

"It wasn't related to us," I say, watching her closely, looking for a blink, a reaction, but the waitress appears and gives Maggie a reason to focus elsewhere.

"Another, please," she tells the woman, holding up her glass and then looking at me. "Do you want a drink?"

"No, thank you," I say. "I still have press and stockholders to manage."

"Right," she says, waving off the waitress. That tremble to

her hand mentioned to me by Cody and Jessica is easily seen now as she adds, "Of course you do."

I narrow my eyes at her and then lean forward, softening my voice. "I know we are just getting to know each other, and I don't want to be presumptive, but you are not yourself. I know you as the queen of the family, always in radiant control. Is this about Brandon Senior's cancer?"

"You mean the cancer that might or might not kill him in the next two months? No. Why would it be about that?" Her tone is sharp, snappy. Sarcastic. "You know, of course, that my husband keeps his mistress here in this very hotel." The waitress sets her drink down and then Maggie lifts it. "And yet he wants me to go to Germany with him."

"Don't you want to go with him?"

She downs her drink and stares at the empty glass. "I do," she admits, her tone stark now. "I just want him to want me there."

"He wants you there. He loves you."

Her gaze cuts sharply to me. "I wonder if you'll feel loved when Shane finds a woman on the side."

"Nastiness is unbecoming," I say, calling her on her words and shaking off their bite. "Ted's situation has obviously triggered some sort of emotions in you." I home in on what I believe to be her guilty conscience. "Are you worried about your own sons being next?"

She pales two shades and sets her glass down. "A mother always worries for her sons." She stands. "You'll excuse me, I'm sure. I need to go to the ladies' room."

I've hit the nerve I intended, and now I just need to decide how to use it, but first things first: I open my purse to remove my phone and make sure that Cody warns me if she tries to escape.

Better yet, I think, zipping my purse back up, I'll make sure. I stand and start walking, making fast tracks for the exit, where Cody greets me. "Is she in the bathroom?" I ask, eying the alcove beside the bar where I know it to be.

"She is," he confirms, "and she was crying."

I give a quick nod and cut left, walking under the archway and into the ladies' room, where I find Maggie sitting on a vanity seat immediately to my right. "Oh good gracious," she exclaims, swiping a tissue over her tear-streaked cheeks. "Can I not get a moment or two alone?"

I walk to her, standing above her. "What did you do?"

She blinks, and unshed tears pool in her eyes. "What?"

"What did you do, Maggie?" I demand, pressing her. Forcing her to face whatever she's done. "Tell me now before it's too late. Tell me so we can fix it."

"We *can't* fix it," she declares. "Ted's finger is already gone." She bursts into tears.

Knots form in my gut, and I kneel in front of her, my hands going to her knees. "He's alive, but he wouldn't have been if Shane didn't lay down the law with Martina. Why are you involved with Martina?"

"I can't tell you. Shane and Derek will hate me."

"You have to tell me, Maggie."

"No. No, I won't." The words are strong, but she follows them with a sob.

I dig my fingers into her knees. "Pull yourself together," I command, "and tell me now. You're strong. You can do this."

"I'm stupid. And I was lonely. I'd been alone so long and Mike and I just happened. But I don't love him; I love my husband. I want him to live and I want him—"

"What does this have to do with Martina? And don't tell me

you don't know who that is, because he's the one who ordered Ted's torture."

"Martina found out about the affair. A man who works for him came to me. Ramon. He was scary. Very nasty and perverted. I thought for sure he'd rape me."

"He might. He'll come back. That's why you have to tell me everything."

"There's not a lot to tell. He threatened to tell my husband about Mike if I didn't help Martina get to your apartment. He said he just wanted to talk to Shane. Just talk. I swear I knew nothing about Ted being kidnapped and hurt. I mean, I met Ted. I distracted him to allow Martina to get by him. I didn't think there was more to it than that. I just . . . I was desperate. I didn't want my husband to live or die from cancer, knowing his wife and his best friend were together."

"And you and Mike decided the two of you would take over the company?"

"What? No. No, I would never do that. The company is my husband's and mine, not Mike's."

"What about the hostile takeover?" I ask.

"What hostile takeover? By Mike? Are you talking about Mike?" She doesn't give me time to respond, her torment becoming anger. "That bastard. I'll kill him. I will kill him." She hops to her feet, and I follow, my hands going to her arms.

"No," I say. "You can't do anything of the sort. We need to get help. Sit, please."

"No, I—"

"Sit down, Maggie," I order harshly.

She sinks back onto the chair. "They're all going to hate me and I was just confused. I love my family."

I believe her. But I don't respect her. This isn't about money and power for her, at least not in the way I feared. I reach for my purse and unzip it, removing my phone. She grabs my hand where I hold it. "What are you doing?"

"Adrian Martina is a dangerous man. Ramon a brutal monster. He will rape you. And they will use you to hurt your family. We need help."

"Seth," she says. "Let's talk to Seth."

"Maggie," I say. "We *need* to tell Shane. He's the one Martina is targeting."

"He will *never* forgive me," she says, shoving her dark hair behind her ear, her hand and her voice trembling now. "Go to Derek."

"Shane will forgive you over time," I say. "I'll help him. And I'll help you. But he has to be told what's going on. I'll talk to him first. Okay?"

"I don't want my husband knowing about this. He can't know, at least not until we know he's going to make it through this treatment."

"I'll talk to Shane, but I think that makes sense. Can I call him?"

"Yes."

I dial Shane and he answers immediately. "What's happening, sweetheart?"

"Can you please meet me in the bar?"

"Now?"

"Most definitely now."

He's silent for several beats. "I'll be right there."

I end the call and refocus on Maggie. "Stay here or go back to your table. I'll talk to him at the bar and we'll go from there."

"Yes." She grabs my hand. "Thank you."

There is this desperate fragility about her right now, nothing like the woman I've known her to be, or that her sons have known her to be. And I am reminded of my own mother, who became someone I didn't recognize. I lost the woman who'd been my rock long before she was gone. It hurt. It made me resentful. And these are things Shane and Derek will feel at the worst possible time. I stand up and walk to the door.

SHANE

I walk through the lobby of the hotel I now call home because of Emily, because of my family, dread in my gut over my mother's certain betrayal. Seth is by my side, a rock ready to smash my enemies, trust between us that I share with only one other person: Emily. We round the corner to the bar, and I spot Cody and Emily sitting in a corner on an L-shaped couch, but it's her and her alone who I see. Her who creates that punch in my chest I always feel when I see her. Not so long ago, I believed it to be a deep, clawing, physical need that she stirred in me. Now I know that need is a result of a bond, one part physical and one part something far deeper. A deep connection that I feel with her that I have never felt with anyone before in my life. I want a calmer day when I can make love to her and when I can propose. When I can make her my wife, and know what that means isn't this life I'm offering her now. Rather one where my enemies are gone and hers are forgotten.

Pulling away from Seth, I approach the couch, while Cody stands, gives me a nod, and leaves Emily and me alone. I claim the cushion catty-corner to her. "Hey," she says softly, scooting to the edge of her seat, holding her dress primly at her thighs when, not so long ago, I had her alone, dress to her waist. The way I wish I had her now.

"Stop looking like you want to crawl into a hole," I tell her, my hand settling on her knee. "I already assumed my mother betrayed us before you came down here. I mentally prepared myself."

"It wasn't really a betrayal," she says, her hand covering mine. "More a series of misplaced decisions. Though I think right now, in the heat of everything happening, you'll see it as a betrayal."

"Tell me," I urge.

She inhales and lets it out. "She was an absolute mess when I got down here. I pushed her and she retreated to the bathroom, where I found her in a complete meltdown."

"As in my mother was crying?"

She gives a grim nod and whispers, "Yes."

"Are you sure we're talking about the same person?"

"No. Yes. I mean, this is how it was with my mother too, Shane. It's hard to see our parents change and become weak. But I know you want me to get on with this and tell you what she did or didn't do. So. Here goes. First, she says she doesn't love Mike. She said she was lonely and it just happened. She also says she doesn't have a clue about a takeover, and got irate and ready to attack Mike when I said he was up to no good."

"And you believe her?"

"Yes. I do believe her. I also believe she loves your father and regrets her affair with Mike, which is what left her vulnerable to Martina's threat to expose her affair."

A muscle in my jaw begins to spasm. "What did she agree to do?"

"Helped him get to our door last night. Nothing more. She had no idea Ted was going to be hurt, and the idea that she allowed that to happen shook her badly, Shane. Ramon is the one who threatened her. He visited her. She thought he might rape her."

Anger, red-hot and fierce, pours through me, and I lace my fingers together, containing it, ruling it the way I plan to rule Ramon and Adrian. Seconds tick by, and I remove my phone from my pocket and dial Derek. "Come down to the bar," I say when he answers. "It's important." I end the call and lift a finger, silently calling Seth and Cody to our sides. They join us, Cody beside Emily and Seth beside me. I look at Emily. "Tell them what you told me."

She gives a tiny nod and quickly, succinctly relays the information before I look at Seth and ask, "How, if we were watching her, did they get to her?"

"She and Mike met at a hotel last night," he says. "Obviously Ramon had a plan to sneak her out and get her here. And I do not like Ramon's involvement. I recommend we put your parents on a plane to Germany tomorrow morning. Get your mother out of here."

"Agreed," I say, glancing at Emily and Cody. "Where is my mother now?"

"The bathroom," Emily says. "She's been in there a long time now too."

I look at Emily. "Derek needs to understand what Martina is doing to our family. Tell him." She nods, and I stand up, suddenly angry all over again at my mother's actions. Emily grabs my hand and stands.

"I know you're angry with her. I am too, but remember. She's human. And if there is one thing I learned from losing my father, guilt can be a brutal pill to swallow." She releases my hands and I turn away, rejecting her words, that anger I'm feeling already rooted in a hot spot that refuses to cool.

Crossing the bar, I reach the bathroom door, and without even a blink, enter the women's bathroom as I did once before to find Emily. My mother is sitting on a chair to my right, and the instant she sees me, she pops to her feet and bursts into tears. "I'm sorry. I'm sorry. I just . . . I just . . . I don't what to say, Shane."

Her torment and pain rip through me, clawing away at my anger and leaving something far starker that I cannot name. But it drives me forward, and toward her, and she flings herself into my arms. I close my arms around her, holding her as she sobs. My mother, the queen herself, is sobbing. I hold her like this, and time stands still, but my emotions do not. I know Emily says she's human, but I don't know this woman I'm holding who can be this weak. But I do know she's a creation of the Brandon family name.

The bathroom door opens, and my mother doesn't seem to notice, keeping her face plastered against my shoulder. Or maybe she's afraid of what she must now face: my brother. Derek walks in, stepping to us, his expression as stark as those emotions I cannot name. We stare at each other across her head, brothers again, for a reason neither of us wants to exist: this is an attack on our family. And while I've thought it and said it many times before, this is a war we are fighting, and it has never been so real.

I release my mother, and she turns to Derek, the two of them staring at each other, no words, no tears. It's their way of coping, and I step to the door to allow them their private reconciliation. Exiting the bathroom, I find Emily standing there. I wrap her in my arms, and those stark emotions I'm battling are suddenly bearable. I cup her face and stare down at her. "When this is over, I'm going to properly propose, and you're going to say yes. Because I'm going to make sure you love me so much, you can't say no."

"I already do, Shane."

I press my forehead to hers, my lashes lowering, savoring her words, her smell, her body next to mine, until the bathroom door opens behind me. Emily reacts immediately, pulling us closer and kissing me. "I'll be nearby." She backs up and disappears as Derek steps to my side.

"Mom's freshening up."

"Mom," I say. "Like Pops. We never call them those names anymore."

"Maybe it's time we do," he says as Seth steps in front of us. "And maybe," Derek adds, "it's time Ramon dies."

Seth doesn't react. He never does. He's stone-cold. The bathroom door opens again, and my mother, Mom, steps to Derek's side, lacing her arm with his. "I'm ready to go back upstairs."

"I need a word with Shane," Seth says.

"We'll go on up," Derek says, looking at me, hatred in his eyes, but it's no longer for me. He starts walking, leaving Seth and me alone.

"You spoke to Cody instead of me about Ramon," Seth says, "because you knew he wouldn't do it. And you know, even if you don't like to admit it, that part of the reason I'm so close to you is that you understand me and what I've done in my life. You know what I'm capable of doing. And you knew if you came to me about Ramon, I would find a way to end him without recourse. You want him dead. You come to me when you're really ready." He turns and starts walking.

My lips quirk, that stark feeling completely gone. "Seth." He stops walking and turns to face me. "I'm ready."

CHAPTER SIXTEEN

EMILY

From a nearby table in the bar, I watch Shane in the moments after his mother departs with Derek, as he and Seth have an exchange, standing there in the archway by the bathrooms, his blue suit hugging every athletic line of his tall, powerful body. On the surface he is simply a gorgeous man who owns the room, and every situation he so chooses to own. But it's the man beneath that presence who calls to me, who knows me as I know him, in ways that simply can't be defined. And now, with Seth departing, Shane's gaze lifts, seeking me out, and it's an amazing thing, the way his eyes warm when they fall on me. The way he makes me feel like I'm the light in the emotional storm he's just traveled through with his mother. Like he has been the light in the storm of my past that delivered me to Denver, and to him.

I stand up and close the distance between us, and he watches my every step, and I his, the room fading away to just us, if only for these few precious moments. And when the space dividing us is erased, his arm automatically slides around my shoulders, our path leading us toward the main hotel, our steps automatically falling into sync. "How bad was it with your mother?"

"Was that my mother?"

"Shane," I say softly. "Just remember—"

"She's human," he supplies. "I know. And that's all the more reason to get her and my father to Germany sooner rather than later. We're working on getting them on a plane by morning."

I sense the relief in him with this plan. His mother will be out of the sights of Ramon and Mike. And it is, indeed, a good plan, but I am instantly aware of the good-bye to his father that he will soon share, and it could come sooner than he expected. I don't say this to him though. Not now. And I really don't have a chance to have that conversation with him anyway. We round the corner to the main hotel area and start walking toward the elevator. "Will they stay the night here?"

"That remains the plan," he says.

"And Jessica?"

"We'll use the press situation to keep her here for the night," he says, "and then reassess her situation once I talk to Adrian."

"And you're making him come to you."

"That's right."

"And he's making you go to him," I say.

"He's an impatient man who hates to be ignored," he says. "He'll come to me, but not before he tries to force me to be reactive first." He turns us to the elevator banks, where Cody catches up with us.

"An update," Cody says, punching the call button, his dark eyes instantly engaging, his dark hair curling at the longish ends. His attention is on Shane as he adds, "One of my men is escorting Derek, who's setting your mother up in a private suite for your parents to share. Derek seemed to think she needed to pull herself together before she's with your father again."

"I forget how smart my brother is sometimes," Shane approves, the elevator doors opening, the three of us stepping inside, where we are silenced by the risk of recording devices represent. And while this is something I've been aware of before now, the idea that Ramon might be watching just plain gives me chills. It also creates a new concern for me regarding Jessica's safety that I wait to express until we've exited the elevator, just outside the car, where I pause to ensure I have both men's attention.

"Won't Jessica being here tonight actually bring attention to her and make her a target?" I ask. "I mean, Derek's secretary isn't here. With Jessica here when she's not, it makes Jessica look important, which isn't the way you want Martina or Ramon to see her. And Jessica doesn't know about Martina at this point, but she's smart. If you keep her around here long enough, she'll figure it out."

"Seth actually brought up those very concerns a few minutes ago," Cody says. "He wants to get her home tonight and have her place monitored, but not until late. We want every second we have to see how things develop." He glances at Shane. "Unless you have a problem with this strategy."

"Not at all," Shane says, urging me forward, down the hallway toward our apartment, and while I am actually impressed with how forward-thinking Seth is, that "how things develop" comment is bothering me. It speaks of dangerous unknowns, and without question, if we don't find leverage to get Adrian Martina to walk away, someone else will get hurt. But as we reach our door, I decide voicing the obvious does nothing. Shane and everyone on his team—even Derek, of all people—are clearly working their backsides off to get us out of this.

Whatever the case, Shane opens the door, and it's time to put this aside and show Jessica a happy face. Only Jessica isn't the one who wants my attention. I step inside the apartment, and almost instantly Brandon Senior shouts, "Ms. Stevens, I need you in here!"

Cody locks up behind us, then heads into the apartment, while I sigh and take a step toward the kitchen, my path to Brandon Senior where he still sits in the dining room. Shane catches my hand, snagging my fingers and walking me back to him. "Ms. Stevens," he says softly. "I need you upstairs."

My eyes go wide. "No. Your father and Jessica are here."

His eyes alight with mischief. "That didn't stop us earlier." He kisses me. "I'll behave, but just know this. Every time I want to throttle someone this afternoon, I'll distract myself by thinking of you with no panties on." He cups my backside through my dress, his cheek sliding to mine, lips near my ear. "I really love your ass." He nips my lobe, and I yelp as his father calls out again, "Ms. Stevens!"

"Jesus," Shane growls, easing back to look at me. "I don't know how you put up with that. I'm going in the office to call Ted's wife, and then I'll come rescue you from the hell that is my father."

"You're calling Ted's wife?"

"And Ted too if he's up to talking, though I'd doubt it. But I do think he needs to hear our appreciation, and they both need to know we're going to take care of them."

"My heart just melted," I confess. "I think I just fell more in love with you."

His sexy, full lips quirk. "Remember that the next time I piss you off the way I did this morning." He kisses my hand and walks away, cool and confident, seemingly unaffected by all that has slammed into him these past few days. But there is something beneath his surface, a darkness—anger, even. I wonder what will happen when it surfaces.

And who will get hurt.

The next few hours see afternoon become evening, for most of which Shane and Derek are behind closed doors in the dining room with their father, though each of them come and go randomly for meetings I don't question. For the most part, Jessica and I remain curled on the floor in the office, in front of the couch, our shoes off, coffee on fast pour. Turns out that together we are a dynamic team, efficiently handling all leftover business matters for the Brandon men and clearing their slates and ours. It's not long after that, nosy bee that she is, Jessica discovers my file on the fashion brand I've proposed for Bandon Enterprises, and her excitement that follows is nothing short of addictive. We start making plans and drafting ideas, and without knowing she's doing it, she's helped me keep my mind off Adrian Martina.

"I think you should have a Jessica line," she says. "And, of course, I'll approve the designs. They have to live up to my very high standards."

"Of course." I laugh. "And they are high."

She strokes her new long blond hair. "We have hair extensions. And so many shoes. Like, two floors of shoes."

"We aren't a department store." I laugh again. "A brand name."

"We could do both."

From there, we talk for hours, and in that time, I learn little things here and there about Jessica. Turns out that underneath her shell of confidence and perfection is pain. She's adopted, but her parents are no longer alive, and little hints tell me they weren't such nice people anyway. And while I knew she was burned in a relationship before, I discover he was older than her, worked with her in some way, and that she is affected by that past in some deep, damaging way. I've known for quite some time that Shane helped her after that relationship, but I don't ask details, and I won't. When she's ready, it's her right to tell me, not him. But for me, certain things are clear. He's like a brother to her, and we are her family. Incredibly, the Brandon family, in all its destructive glory, has managed to heal us both through Shane. He saved her, like he did me.

The seven o'clock hour arrives, a long day closing up, and the Brandon clan, along with several of Nick's men, head to the family house to pack for an early morning flight to Germany. It's also time for Jessica to depart, and it's at the door, after Cody has explained her security escort as a way to avoid the press, that I find myself giving her a big hug and silently vowing that we won't allow her to be hurt.

Suddenly, the energy in the apartment is at a low, with my only guest, Cody, hanging out on the couch, watching television. I retreat to the office and, feeling a growing need to get us out of pharmaceuticals and drugs, I leave a voice mail for the analyst I've been working with on fashion acquisitions, hoping to hear from him soon. With that done, I dive into my research on Mike, which leads to one of my list-making frenzies that are all about control, of which I have none right now. I write down the names of Mike's close friends, with Brandon Senior at the top of the list. Then names of known rivals, followed by principals in companies he's invested in.

While working, my eyes keep catching on my wrist, where

I used to wear the bracelet that was once my mother's. That I can no longer wear without fear of exposing a link to a past I can never claim. This leads me to thoughts of Maggie and her transition to this unrecognizable person, the comparison to my mother refusing to be ignored. As does my brother, who decides to pop into my head, as does his involvement with hackers as nasty as Martina. For all I know, he has found his own crate, with no way out. Inevitably, those things lead me to another place: my father. Or maybe it's more watching Brandon Senior interact here today, the way he barks orders, familiar now, when my own father would have been kind and respectful.

At least until he was selfish and brutal by killing himself.

Irritated at the direction of my thoughts, and recognizing that today has been full of old triggers I normally control better, I'm ready for a break. After careful consideration, I decide my lists are all public record and therefore safe to e-mail. I punch in Shane's address and shoot them off to him in the hopes they help in some way. Task complete, and trying to shake off the uneasy feeling clawing at me, I stand up and stretch. Still uneasy, I exit the office to find Cody in the kitchen, his back to me as he makes coffee, which allows me a quick escape upstairs. Once there, I shut the door and walk into our room, where I find two cases sitting on the bed. Gun cases. A familiar—but long ago extinguished—fire in my chest starts burning, and with it, my hesitation to walk to those guns.

No. No. No. I have been past this for a long time. This doesn't make sense. I cross the small space between me and the bed and reach for the smaller of the two cases. Inside is a shiny new Luger, a compact weapon with a limited recoil, which makes it a top choice for women. I pick it up to sample the weight, and that burn in me intensifies, and images long put to rest begin to flicker in

my mind. My father. Blood. Heartache. That burn again that I
know as heartache, which takes me back to blood and vivid images long suppressed. I all but drop the gun on the bed, which
isn't a smart thing to do, but my hands go to my hips—not it. It
sucks this is happening. It sucks big-time, but I remind myself
that I know how to manage this.

I reach for the gun to put it away, but I think better, leaving
it on the bed, and turn to walk into the bathroom. The room is
never fully dark, natural moonlight entering from two overhead
panels, so I don't turn on the light. I just strip off my clothes, turn
on the shower, and step inside. Once I'm there, I angle the show-
erhead toward the corner and sit down, pulling my knees to my
chest. The water is hot and it pours over me, and I try to think of
it, just it. It works for a few minutes, but then I'm seeing blood.
Dripping. Running. Pooling. So much blood.

"Emily? Sweetheart?"

I blink and Shane is standing in the shower door, his jacket
and tie gone. "Shane. I didn't hear you come in."

"Why is the gun lying on the bed?"

"I should have put it away. I'm sorry."

"What's wrong?"

"Nothing. I just needed to escape from everything for a
while."

He begins to strip, and in a matter of moments, he's a gorgeous naked distraction, and that burn in my chest eases. He steps
into the shower and, to my surprise, sits down next to me, then
pulls me between his legs, facing him. My knees go back to my
chest, and his hands settle on top of them. "Talk to me," he orders.

"You talk to me. Have you talked to Adrian?"

"No. But I will tomorrow."

"What about Ted? I never got to find out what happened on the call."

"His wife cried. It gutted me. I made financial promises Seth is going to solidify for them tomorrow." He pauses. "Emily. Sweetheart. You're avoiding what brought you to this shower. If this is getting to you—"

"No. Or yes. Of course it's getting to all of us. It's not that."

"The gun is for your protection. I know it's hard to think—"

"I've carried for years, Shane. I couldn't take my weapon on the plane when I left Texas, so I ended up without it. Guns used to be a problem for me though. I took lessons and bought one to overcome that."

He strokes my cheek. "Why was it a problem?"

I inhale, and that burn is back. "It just . . . was. And I saw someone, a therapist, and he said to use the water to mentally erase my bad thoughts." I shove away from Shane and sit under the direct spray, my legs still at my chest, eyes closed, my face to the water. "And so that was what I was doing."

"What bad thoughts?"

"He said to imagine it washing away the blood."

The minute I say the word "blood," he drags me to him again, cupping my face over my knees. "What blood, Emily?"

"This is not the time for this."

"It can't be your stepfather. You haven't seen a therapist since then. What blood?"

"Shane—"

"Oh shit. Your father. Did you find your father?"

I swallow hard. "Yes. I found my father after he shot himself. I tried to save him and I was covered in it. You know. It. In his blood."

"Holy fuck. You were a teenager."

"Yes, which means I've had lots of time to deal with this. It's honestly not logical that I'm thinking about this now."

"Tell me what you were thinking about tonight."

"Your mother is so different from what mine was, and yet they are alike. Our brothers are . . ."

"A mess," he supplies.

"Yes, but we both still want to save them. And our fathers." My eyes burn. "Your father . . . I like that he's real. He's mean. He's underhanded. He's dying. But my father. He was kind and sweet. He was alive and had so much ahead of him, and he just quit." Realization hits me hard and fast. "I know why this is affecting me."

"Tell me," he urges.

"It's not about me. It's about you."

"Me?"

"Yes. All night, all day, I've known that I have to make you think about tomorrow morning. Really think about it, Shane, and I've dreaded that. I hate it now."

"You mean that I may never see my father again."

"Yes," I say, the word rasping from my throat.

"I know. I drew that meeting out with him today because of that. I knew I was doing it. Derek knew I was doing it. My father knew too. Pops knew."

"Pops?"

"The name we called him as kids." He laughs without humor. "And he was still a total dick today."

I give a sad smile. "He is what he is."

"I guess we can never say he wasn't true to himself. Come." He stands up and takes me with him. "The water is getting cold and we're both in need of rest."

He leads me out of the shower and wraps me in a towel, tenderness in his eyes, in his touch, that has nothing to do with sex. It's about intimacy. It's about the emotional whirlwind we share compliments of our families, and each other. Returning the favor he's given me, I grab a towel and knot it at his hips, which earns me one of his sexy smiles. His fingers snag mine and he leads me to the bedroom, and bed, where he's thankfully already moved the guns out of sight. "Where's Cody?" I ask as he pulls the blankets back. "It's strange to have someone else here."

"He's in his suite," he says. "We're alone." We climb into the bed, underneath the soft sheets, facing each other, our legs tangled, and he is hard now, thick, his shaft nestled inside the V of my body, and that burn in my chest has become the burn in my belly. But he is in no rush, the way he was in the office today. He touches my arm, caresses it, the gentleness in him sending a shivering of sensation and random, expanding emotions through me. He kisses me, a soft brush of our mouths. He caresses my nipple. Then he touches my arm again. Tender. Sexy. I never knew a touch on the arm could be so powerful. *My hand* rests on the hard wall of his chest, over his heart, the feel of it thrumming just plain everything to me right now. *His hand* curves my hip, palm on my naked backside, and he slides his shaft against me, oh so slowly and sensually. My eyes won't stay open and my teeth find my bottom lip. And when he presses inside me, stretching me, filling me, there is nothing but sensations and the sounds of our breathing, which is heavy and in unison. He pushes into me slowly, deeply, until I have all of him, and then he just holds me, his hand sliding over my hair and dragging my face to his.

"Have I told you I love you?" he asks.

"Three times," I say. "And I love you too, so that's three for me too. I think. Or two."

His lips curve. "We're counting?"

"Yes."

"Then let's keep counting," he says. "So we never forget to say it. I love you."

"Four," I whisper. "I love you too."

He pulls his shaft back and drives into me. I gasp. "That's one," he says.

"One what?"

"One gasp. One thrust. I hope you aren't tired after all, because I really need to spend this night inside you. *Making love to you*, Emily."

Emily. I am Emily now, not Reagan, and with him, making love to him, is exactly how I want to spend this night. Letting him know that on the eve of a good-bye, he is not alone.

SHANE

Long after Emily has fallen asleep, I lie in bed, holding her, and I've decided I was right. As long as I have her with me, I won't lose the part of me that isn't my father or my brother. Though I believe I've been walking that line these past few days without knowing I was walking it. Thinking like them, not me. But now I'm back, thinking like the calculating, smart attorney who, I am proud to say, was one of the best in the nation. I see things differently than they do. I see potential solutions I did not see yesterday, plans forming in my mind, trying to take root.

Kissing Emily's head, I slip out of the bed and walk to the closet, pulling on pajama bottoms, then head back to the bedroom to slip my phone into my pocket. I start for the door. "Where are

you going?" Emily asks, and I rotate to find her sitting up, clutch-
ing the blanket to her chest. "Is something wrong?"

"Nothing at all," I say, moving to sit next to her. "You've inspired me. My mind is working overtime. I have some ideas on
how we end this hell we're in without anyone dying. I just need
to work through the plan, which means a lot of pacing and planning. Lie down and rest."

"I inspired you?"

"Yes." I caress her cheek. "You did. I'll explain how later.
Rest. I'll be back to bed soon." I stand and head toward the door.

"Shane."

I turn to find her still sitting up. "Yes, sweetheart?"

"Do you want me to pace with you?"

"Many times, but not now. This process of mine is a lonely
but effective one."

"Okay, then just one thought to mull over as you pace. There
was a mass grave of fifty people found in Mexico, all beheaded.
Ramon is thought to be behind it. While you're figuring out this
plan of yours, if you decide someone has to die, I'd choose him.
Before he chooses someone else."

"I'll keep that in mind," I say, heading down the stairs, aware
of how out of character it was for her to speak the dirtiness of
those words, and how certain I am they would haunt her should
she learn of his death. But she's right. Ramon still has to die, but
this has to be my secret with Seth. My cross to bear.

DEREK

I lie in the bed with Teresa next to me, curled to my side, staring
at the ceiling. Ted's naked, bloody body haunts me. I've tried to
get it out of my mind, but guilt grinds through me, proving to be

a vicious monster. It wants to finish the job of destroying me. The one I started myself by allowing our involvement with Martina. Ironically, had we not though, Teresa would not be next to me now. And I love this woman. I've tried to deny it. I tried to fuck her out of my system, and when that didn't work, I went to other women, reminding myself of the pleasure of variety. She knew too. I made sure Teresa knew I'd been with other women, drenching myself in their perfume, thinking she'd leave me, or maybe it was just that window of time, when I had a death wish no one knows about, even her.

But she just kept hanging on to me, and now I don't seem to be able to let go of her. Which means I can't let go of me. And it sucks because love sucks. I mean, look how well that's worked for my parents. It hasn't worked. Neither has me trying to get their departure to Germany out of my mind tonight. My father's a bona fide bastard, but tomorrow might be the last time I see him. Then there is my mother. Her many betrayals are too raw for me to claim any objectivity, but the idea of her being alone with my father, the man she's loved all her life, when he dies, is a brutal thought. But so is leaving with them, and allowing my father to survive his cancer, and lose his company.

My cell phone vibrates on the nightstand, and I grab it, noting Shane's number. "What's wrong?" I answer softly, standing and walking into the bathroom to keep from waking Teresa.

"You're with Teresa."

And he's officially in high-and-mighty mode. "What the hell do you want, Shane?"

"What if I said I have a plan to get us out of this and you get to keep seeing her?"

I go still. "I'm listening."

"Not on the phone. After the airport in the morning." He ends the call.

I walk back into the bedroom to find Teresa awake, the light now on, her pale pink gown covering her knees that she's pulled to her chest. "I have millions of dollars in a trust."

"What?"

"Enough that we can run away and be together."

I'm stunned by her words, but more so by how much this woman loves me despite all I have let myself become, and all I have done to her. I sit down next to her, drawing her hand in mine. "No," I say. "We aren't running. And we aren't using your money. I have money. I'll take care of you. That's what I'm supposed to do for my woman. It's the one thing my father did teach me right. The one thing he did right by my mother."

"You're a target because of me. Adrian and Ramon hate you just for being with me. We have to get out of sight and out of mind."

"Shane and I have a plan. Everything is going to be okay, and we're okay."

"Shane? You hate Shane."

She's right. I hate Shane. I hate how he always wins. I hate how he's always the one who Pops references with pride. I hate how he gets anything he wants. "We want the same things."

"Which is what?"

I lower her to the bed with me so that we face each other. "To win."

"And how do you define winning?"

"We don't die."

"That's why we leave, Derek. That's how we win. Please. Let's run away together."

"No running. No dying."

"Derek—"

I kiss her, silencing her fears, before they become mine.

No one dies, including my bastard father and golden-boy brother. And most definitely not this woman, who's the reason I've decided life is good, and maybe I should be too. For her.

CHAPTER SEVENTEEN

SHANE

Morning comes, and with the promise of it being a big day, I opt to wear my gray power suit I bought to celebrate my first win in the courtroom, pairing it with a gray silk tie and gray shirt. I head downstairs and find Emily standing at the island in the kitchen. Her cell phone is at her ear, a smile on her lips that she's glossed the same pale pink as her fitted skirt and matching silk blouse. Her long dark hair, which I happen to know smells like a bouquet of flowers, softly tumbles around her shoulders. And when she looks up at me, her eyes lighting up with the contact, in that moment, I think she looks like an angel who doesn't know she's trapped in hell.

"I'll see you at the office, Jessica," she says, ending the call and then smiling at me. "She found out about my fashion brand proposal and now she's pitching a 'Jessica' fashion line, Shane. She sat up drawing sketches last night."

"Let me guess," I say, stopping at the counter opposite her. "There're *really* expensive purses involved."

Emily gives me one of her sweet, musical laughs. "Well, yes. There are. But there's a lot of money in purses." She turns somber. "I know I've said this, like, ten times since we woke up this morning, but I really want to go to the airport with you."

"Someone needs to be at the office, making it look normal," I say. "And that's you and Jessica."

"I can make it look normal an hour later, after I go with you to the airport."

"I'm okay," I say. "I promise you."

"You think you're okay," she insists. "It won't hit you until he's on the plane."

"It won't hit me until I'm home tonight," I assure her. "I have a way of compartmentalizing, especially when I'm focused on a goal, like I am today."

"Getting us out of this."

"Yes. Getting us out of this." My cell phone vibrates with a text, and I fish it out of my pocket, glancing at the message from Seth, then back at Emily. "Apparently my parents are on the road with Seth. My mother forgot something at the house. And Derek's in the garage, waiting on me." I walk around the counter and pull Emily close, taking a moment to nuzzle her hair and inhale those flowers. "Damn, you smell good." I stroke her cheek. "I may not be into the office until later, but call me or text me if you need anything."

"Be careful."

"I told you, sweetheart. No one dies. My plan is a good plan."

"And that plan is what?"

"A work in progress. I'll tell you all about it tonight." I kiss her forehead and turn for the door, pulling it open to hear, "Shane!"

"Yes?"

"I love you. That's number five."

"I love you too, and, sweetheart? No one dies." I leave her with that promise, and certainty, and exit into the hallway. And I don't doubt those words until Derek and I settle into my Bentley and reality comes at me fast and hard.

"You said no one dies," Derek says, his voice low, tight. "You forgot that cancer is less forgiving than Adrian Martina."

"You forget what a stubborn ass our father is," I say, starting the engine. "He won't die until he's ready to die. And that man isn't ready." I reach behind me and produce a gun case. "Because you aren't ready to die either."

He removes a gun from the case and tests the weight. "Beats the hell out of our hunting rifles." He glances over at me. "What if I want to shoot you?" He points the gun at me.

Adrenaline courses through me, and my agitation is instant. I grab it, shoving it to my forehead. "Do it."

"I could, you know. I've thought about it at times. And yet you handed me a gun."

"Pull the trigger if you're going to pull the trigger, Derek," I order. "Man up. Be who you are."

"Who am I, Shane? Who the hell am I to you?"

"The only person you are right now is the person holding a gun on me."

He puffs out several breaths and releases the trigger, and we both pull back. "Who I am is the one who trusts no one." He indicates the gun. "I would never have given this to you. You trust too easily. If you do that with Adrian's people, you'll get us both killed."

My lips thin and I face forward. "The gun at my ankle is loaded," I say. "Yours isn't for a reason."

He gives a bitter laugh. "You were testing me."

"Yes."

"And did I pass?" he queries.

"I won't be buying you bullets anytime soon."

I put the car in drive.

The short ride to my parents' place is silent, our confrontation over the gun heavy between us, and the irony of us both testing each other is hard to miss. It's a bit of cold comfort to know Derek didn't pull the trigger. I wanted to know how much I dared to trust him, and the answer is, as I suspected, not much. He's insecure, and acts rashly, with poor judgment. And our father knows that, regularly using it to manipulate Derek into doing his bad deeds. But Derek still does them.

Thankfully, we arrive at the house just as Seth is pulling out of the driveway again, allowing us to follow them without going inside and risking a houseful of Brandon personalities, leading to conflict. Still Derek and I don't speak, and as the minutes pass, so does the bite of our gun incident. The mood shifts, still jagged-edged, still dark, but it's not about us, the brothers, anymore. It's about conversations we don't want to have about how final this good-bye might become. For forty minutes this doesn't change, until finally, we pull onto the tarmac of the private airstrip, a few feet from where Seth has just pulled in.

"Here we go," I say, popping open my door at the same time Derek pops open his.

We both exit the car and I pocket my keys, no hesitation in either of us as we walk toward the black sedan Seth has exited along with our parents. My mother is dressed in a black pantsuit, a Chanel jacket to her knees, her hair perfect, her normal air of confidence back in place as she frets over the bags that Seth is retrieving. "Don't forget the small one in the corner," she says, pointing to the back of the trunk. "That's my jewelry."

My father, in dress pants and a pullover collared shirt, scowls at her. "I don't know why you needed jewels for my cancer treatment."

"Because it's going to go well and we're going to celebrate."

"I've got the bag," Derek says, snatching it up as another sedan parks in the drive. Two men step out of the back of the vehicle before the driver pulls away.

"Nick's men," Seth says, setting down the bags in his hands. "I need to introduce them to the pilot."

"I'll get the bags on the plane," Derek offers, and it's then that I notice he's wearing a black suit and a black tie, looking way too much like he's attending a funeral.

He loads up and takes off walking, while my mother comes to me. "We'll be back in two weeks, but if you can fly up and see us—"

"You know I can't right now."

"Well. I guess it's okay. He has an eighty percent survival rate. I think that might be better than we all have on the Denver highways every day."

The reminder that that 80 percent is really 20 percent delivers an unwelcome punch to the stomach, as does my mother hugging me and squeezing me a little too hard and long, a hint of the fragility she showed yesterday still in her energy.

"Bags loaded," Derek announces, to then find himself in a similar embrace to the one I've just encountered, his eyes meeting mine, his expression as stark as the emotions I felt yesterday but refuse to allow myself today.

Which is easier said than done as my father orders my

mother to the plane and steps in front of Derek and me. "I need the documentation you have on the stockholders you promised us," I say to him.

"I have no such information."

"You said—"

"What I say is that I expect normalcy to be restored when I return. Is that understood?"

"No," I say. "Because your definition of normal, Pops, is what got us into this."

"Just make sure your definition is more profitable than mine." He turns and starts walking, and all of a sudden, I need to stop him.

"Pops!" I call out at the same moment Derek does the same, alike again. We're both tormented. We're both fighting a million conflicting feelings.

He halts, shoulders squaring, but he doesn't turn. "Don't fuck up my company while I'm gone." He starts walking again, and as he climbs the steps, entering the plane, my fingers curl into my palms by my sides. Seth steps off the plane, giving me a two-finger wave, and then heads to his car, his business elsewhere, taking care of Ted and his family as I promised his wife yesterday, and ensuring Emily and the office staff stay safe today.

Refocused on the plane, Derek and I watch the staircase being removed, the steel door shutting. And when the engine roars and the wheels start to move, there is a finality in the air that I do not want to read into. "I don't want to watch it take off," Derek says, as if he senses it as well.

"Agreed," I say, and in unison, we turn to the car, halting with the discovery of a sleek black Jaguar a short distance across the tarmac, with Adrian Martina leaning on the hood, his arms folded, his legs stretched out and crossed.

"Unless he's here to kill me," Derek says, "I think this calling card is for you."

"Agreed again," I say, fishing the keys from my pocket and handing them to him, but he closes his hand over mine.

"I didn't pull the trigger," he says. "But if that man ever holds a gun to your head, he will." He releases my hand, and I don't analyze how I feel about that warning. I am in my zone. I'm focused on my enemy, and that enemy right now is Adrian Martina.

I turn and start walking, my steps even, pace unrushed, calculated like my plans, to eradicate him from my company and our lives, until finally I'm standing in front of him. He doesn't stand but continues to lean on the expensive car, his tan suit probably double the cost of mine, his dark hair slicked back as if he's freshly showered.

"Two in-person visits in a week," I say. "I'm starting to feel important to you, Adrian."

"You're pissed about Ted."

"Pissed? I don't get pissed, Adrian."

"He's alive."

"And humiliated, beaten, and without a finger."

"Someone close to me got carried away. He's been reprimanded."

"I'm quite clear on the way you use Ramon to do your dirty work and claim naiveté we both know you didn't possess the day you were born."

"He's been reprimanded," he repeats.

"You crossed the line, and not just with Ted. Ramon threatened to rape my mother. *My mother.* And you think this convinces me you want to do legitimate business with me?"

"I know nothing of this situation with your mother."

"And that is the answer that's supposed to convince me to

forget this? *My mother,* Adrian. Let me be clear. I know your reach. I know the reasons people fear you. But I do not. An eye for an eye. You hurt one of mine—"

"And you visited my sister."

"Ramon visited Emily. We aren't even, and no one does successful business together when they are not even."

"What do you want?"

"Ramon gone."

"Done."

I arch a brow. "That easily?"

"I didn't sanction his actions. They do not please me. Nor does my desire to go legitimate please him. Now, can I trust that you'll get my drug into that study?"

"When you get the drugs out of my facility."

"You know my terms." He pushes off the car. "The drugs stay until we have another distribution outlet. Otherwise my father will pay us a visit, and if you think yours is a bastard, mine's the devil himself." He walks to the driver's side of the vehicle. "I'll get rid of Ramon. Then I expect to move forward with the drug study."

He climbs into the car and I watch him drive away, my lips curving at the sides. He played right into my hands. I've bought time and protection for our women. I've removed Ramon from our direct circle, allowing Seth to work his magic, with no path back to him or us.

I walk to the Bentley, the car my father gave me, that until this moment I've hated. It was bribery to get me to look the other way and forgive his many sins. Now it's a reminder to me of everything the Brandon family was and will not be again. I'm here. I'm staying. And Adrian Martina is not. I slide into the driver's seat, next to a brother I thought would never be shotgun to me, or me him, again.

"Well?" Derek asks.

"Ramon is gone. He's sending him away."

"If he agreed to that, it won't be for long. He'll be back."

I start the engine, deciding that the sins of our father became the sins of my brother, regardless of Derek's own role in his demise. My sins don't need to become his too. I'll keep Ramon's fate to myself. "A little time to play a good game of poker is exactly what we need, which I'll explain on the way to our next stop."

"Which is where?"

"Mike Rogers's office."

Derek and I park in the lot in front of the all-glass mega sports complex where Mike's pro-ball team operates. "So let me get this straight," Derek says. "Your plan is an almost plan that's stewing in your mind."

"That's how I operate," I say. "I have something brilliant that sits just out of reach but leads me through a discovery process. It's close. It's really close."

"And this discovery process tells you that we need to suck up to Mike. To the man who fucked our mother and is trying to fuck us."

"That's right." I open the door of the Bentley and get out, typing a quick text to Emily: *Parents in the air. Went as expected. Working on that plan. Let me know all is well there.*

"What are you hoping to gain by doing this?" Derek presses, meeting me at the hood of the car.

"He's been working to divide us," I say, falling into step with him and heading toward the door. "We're uniting and removing that option. That means he'll make a move that shows his hand."

My phone beeps with Emily's reply: *So calm here, I feel like I'm at the wrong place.*

Satisfied she's safe and all is well, I slide my phone back into my pocket. "It seems to me like his efforts to divide us keep him distracted and buy us time. I wrote our bylaws and they're damn good. No move he can make will be fast or easy. I'm working toward an endgame."

"That's still floating around in your mind and I'm supposed to blindly follow."

"I'm a better bet than Pops. I promise you, brother."

We enter the lobby, where the basketball team's logo is etched in every other tile beneath our feet, and on the front of the oval reception desk. We approach, announcing our presence. "If you could let Mike Rogers know we're here and it's urgent."

"Of course," the twentysomething woman says, dialing his number.

In all of thirty seconds, she's on her feet, rounding the desk. "This way," she says, indicating a hallway to our right that we quickly enter before stopping at door number one. "Mr. Rogers will be with you shortly," the woman says, opening the door and granting us access to a tiny room with a schoolroom-style round table and wooden chairs that I suspect are used for application processing.

Derek takes a seat at the table while I lean against the wall and check my watch, setting the timer. "We wait fifteen minutes to look respectably agitated and we leave."

"You don't think he's going to see us?"

"At this point. I know he's not."

"Then why put us in this room?"

"The shithole of a room is the telltale sign that he's not going to see us." I glance at my watch again. "Three minutes. Twelve more to go." And so we wait. No words. Just Derek tapping the table incessantly, another telltale sign, this one of his nerves over a meeting that isn't going to happen.

At exactly fifteen minutes, I lift my arm to indicate my watch, and Derek stands. "Now what?"

I push off the wall and reach into my jacket, removing two envelopes marked URGENT. "We leave him one of the two messages I've found always get me the attention I want. I'll let you pick." We step into the hallway. "Letter A says simply: IRS. Letter B says simply: Bankruptcy."

Derek laughs. "Priceless. I choose Bankruptcy. Just thinking about how he'll shit his pants pretty much makes my day."

"Bankruptcy it is," I say, sticking the IRS note back into my pocket and walking to reception.

"Please give this to Mr. Rogers, and I'd appreciate it if you read him the note inside immediately. It's a time-sensitive legal matter."

"Of course," she promises, and Derek and I head for the door, exiting the building.

"How long do you think it will take for him to reply?"

"The average is the same fifteen minutes we waited," I say, clicking the locks to the Bentley, and I've just opened my door when I hear, "Shane!"

At the sound of Mike's voice, Derek and I share an amused look over the roof of the car. I check my watch. "One minute. A new record." And proof he was lingering nearby when we were sitting in that room. I motion to the front of the car, and Derek and I come together there, sending the "united we stand" message that we came here to deliver.

Mike stalks toward us, a team logo on his collared shirt, his arms as ripped as a linebacker's beneath the short sleeves. The scowl on his face is fitting for a football player who just got hit wrong and wants to hit back. He stops in front of us. "I knew there were problems you boys couldn't handle, and I knew your father wasn't on his game anymore. I'm going to petition to take over the company. Expect paperwork by Monday." He says nothing more, turning and stalking away, his reaction bigger and better than I could have imagined it to be.

"We aren't in bankruptcy," I say to his back. "Not even close. We just wanted to get your attention."

He rotates to face me, that scowl deepening, furrowing his forehead with heavy lines. "I'm still petitioning to take over the company." He turns, and this time I let him leave.

"What the hell?" Derek demands. "Shane. This is a major problem."

I motion to the car, where no one can observe our interactions, and the instant we're inside, Derek is showing that reactive side of himself again. "I told you, we need to let Adrian deal with him."

My lips curve and I look at Derek. "That plan of mine, that was out of reach, isn't out of reach anymore. You're right. We do need to let Adrian deal with him. And Monday, or whenever Mike attempts legal action, is when the party starts. We'll counteroffer his takeover by offering him the pharmaceutical company, for a healthy fee, of course, that allows us to transition our business. And he'll then inherit Adrian Martina."

"The pharmaceutical branch is our most profitable."

"Which is why he'll have to pay us to take it over and pay us well."

"That seems a little too easy and clean for what we're dealing with here."

"It won't be easy. Mike won't agree to what I'm proposing. He'll try to take everything and I'll have to force his hand."

"How?"

"Aside from photos of him sleeping with the CEO's wife, that I can spin in all kinds of ways to at least taint a judge's opinion of him, Adrian will be in my pocket."

"In your pocket? Doubtful. And you said you couldn't get out. He wants you involved."

"I'm going to be when I convince him Mike is the perfect little bitch he needs and hand him his new business partner. One he'll want to ensure signs that deal."

"Assuming this works, are you authorized to sign off on a deal like this in place of Pops?"

"Not unless Pops is incapacitated, and now that I let him get on the plane without coming up with this plan first, that becomes complicated. I need to get to the office, draft the paperwork, and put Seth on a plane to Germany to get his signatures."

"Too bad your idea wasn't a real idea until now."

I text Seth to meet me at the office and then slide my phone back into my pocket, revving the engine. "This is going to work. I promise you, brother. We're a few short weeks from the end."

I pull us out of the parking spot, eager to get to work and address the legality and strategy behind this plan. Even more eager to close the book on Martina and start a real life with Emily. In fact, by the time I pull us into the office parking garage only a few minutes away, I've decided it's time to look for a ring. But while I'm thinking of new beginnings for myself and Emily, Derek is brooding, and once I park in my reserved spot, he makes no attempt to exit the car. "Teresa says I'm a target for Adrian and Ramon because of her," he says. "Not because of our business dealings."

"She's the sister and daughter of a drug lord," I say. "We can remove you from her brother's business, but I'm not sure how dating her ends well. Pops should have never sent that directive and you should never have gone."

He looks at me. "She's not like her family. She's good in a way I don't deserve, and that's just it. Eventually she'll figure that out, and then Adrian or Ramon will decide that I should pay for hurting her. I'll be dead."

"No," I say, rejecting that idea. "There's a way to get you out of this."

"Really? I'm listening."

"Give me time. We'll figure it out."

"In other words, your claim that I could be with her was at my own risk."

"We're Brandons. She's a Martina. We can't change the blood running through our veins. I'll negotiate your safety in the deal."

"How?"

"I'll figure it out."

He reaches under the seat and lifts the gun. "And I'll buy those bullets."

CHAPTER EIGHTEEN

SHANE

The minute Derek and I walk into Brandon Enterprises, he cuts right toward his office, and I cut left toward Emily's, finding her desk empty and my father's door open, his office dark. It's then that I feel the punch of his absence, and when I turn around and Emily is standing in her private lobby area in front of me, I grab her, cup her head, and kiss her. It's not until I force my mouth from hers that I realize Jessica is standing next to her.

"I take it this is going to be a closed-office kind of day," she comments dryly. "Should I leave now?"

"It's actually going to be a busy work day," I say, releasing Emily. "I have some detailed contract work for us to attack with urgency."

"Oh, my favorite," she adds. "Are we talking one Snickers bar kind of detail or a box of chocolate survival kit?"

"Survival kit."

"Got it," she says. "Headed to my desk to break open the emergency drawer." She disappears down the hall, and Emily flattens her hand on my chest, her eyes meeting mine, under-standing in their depths. "I hate the empty office too. It bothers me every time I walk around the corner, but he'll be back and barking orders at me in no time."

She tries to sound convinced, but she fails, and deep in my gut, which never fails me, I'm not sure he'll ever come home. "Any problems this morning?" I ask as her intercom buzzes.

"It's been smooth sailing here," she says, moving behind her desk and punching the intercom button while I sit on the edge facing her.

"There's a delivery for Brandon Senior that ended up in the copy center," the receptionist says over the intercom. "Do you want me to get it on my break?"

"No," Emily says. "I'll grab some coffee in a few and get it." She releases the intercom button and refocuses on me. "How's that plan of yours going?"

I give her a quick summary of my morning. "Wow," she says when I'm done, sitting down in her chair. "So Ramon is gone?"

"Not yet," I say. "But soon. And Seth and Nick's team will make sure it really happens."

"But for how long?"

"I'll negotiate that when I negotiate the sale of the pharma-ceutical brand."

"Yes," she says. "About that." She tilts her head to study me. "Are you sure you want to do that? The pharmaceutical brand is your baby."

"That became our hell," I say. "I can't get this deal negoti-ated fast enough."

"How fast do you think?"

"Once I have proof Mike is coming after us, which he says will be by Monday. I plan to be prepared for sooner."

"This is good news then, right?"

"It's a reason for optimism," I say. "And we'll know quickly how this is going to roll out. We should have the details hashed out two weeks from now."

"Won't we lose a lot of income when we shed the pharmaceutical brand?" she asks, radiating toward the same concern Derek had expressed when I'd told him.

"We'll leave the deal with cash to transition the business."

Her eyes light up. "Is this a good time then to talk about the fashion brand again?" She slides a file across the desk. "This is the one I think we need to buy. But it's rather urgent we act now. The analyst just told me this morning that it's undervalued, but that could change if we give another buyer time to weigh in."

I pick up the file. "Does this include an official evaluation?"

"It does. And mine, which is a detailed plan for making it our own successful brand. It's all there."

"Then I'll take a look and we'll talk about it over dinner." I stand, and so does she. "How about room service? Just the two of us, and we'll put everything else on hold. And tomorrow we'll get up and run together."

"I'd like that very much."

I give her a quick kiss and head down the hallway to turn toward my office, finding Derek's secretary's desk empty. Turning left, I halt at the sight of him standing at Jessica's desk. "Did you just call me 'Jessica'?" Jessica asks him, her voice radiating exaggerated disbelief.

"That is your name, right?" Derek asks.

"But you never call me by my name."

He arches a brow. "And you call me by mine?"

"Of course I do," she says. "You just wouldn't like the name I've taken the liberty to choose for you."

"In other words, I should go back to calling you 'bitch.'"

She nods. "Yes, please. I'm much more comfortable with that from you. Now that we've solved that, what did you need?"

"A new secretary."

"I thought you liked yours? As in really like her."

Derek scowls. "Can you coordinate with HR or not?"

"She can," I say, closing the space between them and me.

Jessica looks at me and then at him. "I can. What happened to your old one?"

"Moved her to another department," he says, avoiding eye contact with me and walking to his office, where he shuts the door.

"Why are you frowning?" Jessica asks the moment we're officially alone.

Because despite my chat with Derek in the car, my brother just made a move to prove his loyalty to a drug cartel's princess, but I don't say that. "Send Seth to my office when he gets here," I say, walking in that direction.

"I hate when you ignore my questions," she calls after me.

"And I hate when you don't let me ignore them," I reply, stepping behind my desk and setting the file down, only to have the intercom buzz and Jessica announce, "Seth is here."

Seth appears in the doorway a moment later, shutting the door behind him. We exchange a look of understanding, both of us stepping to my window, staring out at the city, while I update him on my morning. "This is not a good time for me to leave the country," he says.

"I don't trust anyone else to go to my father and A, keep this confidential and B, actually convince him to sign the documents."

He glances at me, his expression tight. "There isn't anyone else," he concedes. "I don't trust Ramon to leave and stay gone.

I'll need to meet with Nick and ensure he has Ramon under his thumb while I'm away."

"Just make sure your people let me know when he does leave."

"Just assume he hasn't left even if he seems to have left," Seth says. "That's the safe bet here."

It's not the answer I want, but I give a nod, and he immediately moves back to the topic of Germany. "When will you have the contracts ready for me to take?"

"A few hours."

"Then I'll book the last flight out tonight to ensure they're ready." He heads to the door, and I'm already sitting at my desk, opening the file Emily gave me, my mind on the need to have my father sign off on a purchase if we make one. And after a quick scan of the numbers Emily has promised look good, I'm impressed enough to pick up the phone and call the analyst I have working with Emily.

"Make an offer," I order. "But keep this between us. I want it to be a surprise for Emily."

We talk through terms, and when I end the call, a smile curves my lips. Emily was forced to give up her legal career or risk being found by her brother's hacker thugs, but this fashion brand excites her. So I'm planning on offering her more than a ring when I propose. I'm going to give her a future that's her creation and pride and joy, not just mine.

EMILY

I text Cody my plan to go downstairs to the mail center, as well as to the coffee shop, giving him an FYI on my every move, even in the building, as he's instructed me to do. Once I've sent the

message, my phone in hand, I head to the elevator, stepping onto
the car, where I punch the button for the lobby level. The car
starts to move, and my phone buzzes with Cody's reply: *We've got
eyes on you.*

Stuffing my phone into my dress pocket, I crinkle my nose,
finding it a bit unnerving to know that if I make a funny face in
the mirror or fix my hose, someone has eyes on me. But it's short-
term, as little as two weeks, it seems, and I can handle that, and
do so with a smile. I mean, I'm in love with a brilliant, charming,
sexy, smart man who I can bare my soul to, be just plain naked
inside and out with, and feel safe with. How can I not smile?

The elevator dings with my arrival to the lobby, and I exit,
my steps light as I walk to the mail center and stop at the desk.
"You should have a delivery for Mr. Brandon of Brandon Enterprises," I say to the fortysomething female customer service rep.

"I do," the woman confirms, handing me an envelope
marked *David Brandon—Urgent.* Brow furrowing, I step away
from the desk and open it, finding a handwritten note:

Emily,

*This is Teresa. I'm Adrian Martina's sister, and I'm in
love with Derek. I need to talk to you. I'm in the coffee
shop. I know you have to call your people. And that's
fine. Just please don't let them make a big scene. I can't let
it be known I was here, and I mean you no harm at all,
but, of course, they will worry that I do.*

A friend,
Teresa

I inhale, remove my phone from my dress pocket, and dial Cody, filling him in on the situation when he answers and then reading him the note. "What do you think?" I ask.

"I think it's odd," he says, offering nothing more. "I'm in the building. Stay there, and I'll walk with you to the coffee shop."

"You think it's okay for me to talk to her?"

"If she's really alone, then I don't see why not. But I'm going to have our team check the security footage before we head that way. I'll see you in about one minute."

"Got it," I say. "I'll be here waiting." We end the call, and I pace the tiny mail center until Cody rounds the corner, dressed in jeans and a black T-shirt, no gun in sight, but I am comforted by the idea that somewhere on his person, there's one hidden.

"We're just waiting for a call from my team to clear us to go to the coffee shop," he says, taking the letter from me and reading it himself before handing it back to me. "This is interesting, for sure."

"You said it's odd."

"And interesting."

"I think it's about Derek," I say.

"Seems like a reasonable assumption." His phone buzzes with a text, and he pulls it from his front pocket and glances at it before looking at me. "We're good to go," he says, sticking his cell back into his pants pocket. "Nothing suspicious on the security feed, aside from a drug cartel princess being in the building. She's wearing a blue scarf over her head that looks suited for the blue dress she's wearing, which kept her from being flagged." He motions to the lobby. "Let's do this if we're going to do it."

Anxious to find out what Teresa has to say, worried for Derek, but also worried she might deliver news that jeopardizes Shane's plan to exit Brandon Pharmaceuticals, I start a brisk walk across the lobby to the coffee shop. "I'm staying with you," Cody announces as we arrive, both of us pausing in the entryway and scanning to find Teresa sitting at a back corner table, reading a book, unaware we've arrived and clearly prepared to wait all day if she has to.

"She won't talk with you at the table," I say. "You can't sit with us. You can see me from here."

"I'll sit at the table next to you," he stubbornly insists.

"Cody—"

"This isn't a negotiation."

I sigh. "Fine. But let me sit down with her first and tell her who you are."

He gives a short incline of his head and I step forward, weaving through displays and small tables, until I am sliding into the seat across from Teresa. She looks up and then jumps, her brown eyes going wide before recognition fills them and then relief. "You're here."

"Yes," I say, struck by the sweet quality she naturally radiates. "And so is my security person." As if on cue, Cody claims a chair at the next table, just out of hearing range.

Teresa glances at him and waves, which isn't at all what I expect. "He's smart to protect you," she says, looking at me. "My family isn't exactly angelic."

"I'm glad you understand."

"Completely. Thank you for talking with me."

"Of course," I say.

She laces her fingers together. "You know Derek and I are dating, I assume."

"I do," I say.

"I love him. Lord knows, he makes that hard at times, but I

do, which is why I need to know something from you. I hope you can help."

"I'm listening."

"He says Shane has a plan to get them out of business with my brother."

Warning bells go up, my fear that she's setting a trap for Shane with Adrian by going through me. "I have no idea what they are doing with your brother," I say, deciding to play dumb. "Shane is very protective of me, but I know he wouldn't be foolish enough to burn your brother."

"You're afraid I'm setting you up." She shakes her head. "I knew you'd think that, and really, I don't know what I thought you could say to make me feel better." Tears pool in her eyes, and she opens her book and slides an envelope toward me. "Can you give this to Derek?"

"What is it?"

"Good-bye."

"What? Why?"

"Because I can't change who I am, and even if Shane is brilliant enough to convince my brother to move on from Brandon Pharmaceuticals, I'm still a Martina. I'm still the woman in a family of old-fashioned Mexican men who just happen to take everything to the extreme. When they get mad, you die."

Emotions well in my chest, her love for Derek affecting me. "He needs someone to love him. You can't leave him."

"You will regret convincing me to stay later," she says. "I'm going to spare you that pain." She swipes her eyes. "I've been up all night thinking about this. I asked him to run away with me. I still want him to, but that is a mistake as well. My family would find us."

"Not if you created new identities. I can help you. I can—"

"No," she says. "I won't ask him to walk away from everything for me."

"I would for Shane."

She pats the letter. "Just give this to him, please. You read it, not your security people. I don't want anyone else to read my private thoughts. You're a woman in love. I'm sure you understand."

"I do," I say, tears streaming down my cheeks now.

She starts to get up, and I catch her arm. "If you ever need anything. Come to me."

"Thank you. I wish—I think perhaps we could have been friends."

"Me too." I release her arm, and she leaves.

I reach for the letter, my hand trembling as Cody claims the seat in front of me. "You're crying. What the hell happened?"

"She's leaving to save Derek from her brother." I open the letter. "She wrote him a letter and asked that I read it, and no one else."

He scrubs his jaw, his hand rasping over the one-day stubble there. "Fuck. Derek's erratic as it is. I'm worried as hell about how he's going to react."

"Me too. I need to read this."

He nods. And I pull out the rose-scented piece of paper.

My love:

I just need you to know how much you meant to me. You were my escape from the family who enslaves me to their brutality. And yet I became the one to enslave you. I became the danger lurking at every corner, the demon with a blade in her hand, waiting to destroy the man I love.

I am leaving. I am telling Adrian it's because he killed our brother.

I am never coming back.

You won't find me, so don't look.

But you will find the right woman and you will be a good man for her. I order it. Make that my impact on your life. Honor what we have by letting it make you a better man. Do not become a Martina. Make the Brandon name mean something more. Don't look for me. I know how to disappear.

And don't worry. Adrian won't blame you for my disappearance. I've left him a letter telling him how much I both love and hate him.

Forever yours,
Teresa

I'm all but bawling when I finish reading it, and Cody shoves napkins at me. "I'm not good with tears, woman. You're killing me here."

"Good thing I don't usually cry, I guess," I say, wiping my face. "The letter is pretty simple. She loves him. She's saving him. She's challenging him to be a better man. I need to see Shane."

"You need to fix your face. You have mascara dripping down your cheeks, and Jessica is not going to let that slide."

"I don't have my purse. I'll just have to wipe it off and go on upstairs." I swipe at my cheeks. "Better?"

"Not at all."

"Dang it." I stand up. "We'll stop by the bathroom."

A few minutes later, I've cleaned up my face the best I can and returned to the office, but Cody's right. Jessica will spot a makeup nightmare, and I don't want to risk questions I can't answer. I stop by my desk, using the makeup in my purse to repair the damage the tears created, and then head to Shane's office. Rounding the corner, I find Derek's office door open, and I swear, I can't help but dart in the other direction a little faster for fear he will exit and somehow know what is happening.

Luckily, Jessica is focused on her work, looking frazzled, and Shane's door is open, which allows me to breeze past her, enter his office, shut the door, and lean on it. Shane looks up from his desk, giving me a keen inspection. "What's wrong?"

"Teresa came to see me."

"As in Adrian's sister?"

"Yes." I cross to his desk, rounding it. He rotates his chair to face me, and I rest a hip on a bank of closed drawers. "She's leaving him to protect him. Leaving for good. She wanted me to tell her that you had some way to let them be together, but ultimately she'd already made the decision. She gave me a letter to give him."

"Holy fuck. He's not going to take this well. Where's the letter?"

"She made me promise not to let anyone else read it. Just me and Derek. It just says she loves him and she challenges him to be a better man. What do we do?"

He presses his fingers to his temples. "If I tell him now, I risk him going ballistic on Adrian and getting himself killed. If I don't tell him now, he'll go ballistic because she's missing."

The door bursts open and Derek charges into the room, slamming the door. "Why was Teresa just in the building talking to Emily and now she won't answer her phone? Yes. I have people working for me too. I know things."

My stomach knots and I look at Shane, not sure what to do.

His lashes lower and lift, and he stands. "That conversation we had about her saying she was going to get you killed?"

"What about it?"

"If you do anything rash, you'll end up dead and never see her again. You understand that."

"What the hell is going on?" Derek demands.

"She left. She said it's the only way to protect you."

"I don't believe you. She wouldn't leave her family. Not without me."

"She said they'd hunt you down if you went with her," I say. "I offered to create new identities for both of you, but she said that wasn't fair to you." I glance at Shane and remove the letter from my pocket. He nods, and I slide it onto the edge of the desk.

Derek stares at it, as if he's afraid to read it, but finally curses, dragging a hand through the long layers of his dark hair, and snatches it up. He opens it and reads it, crumpling it in his hand when he's done, his lashes lowering, his breath gushing out.

"Tell me you aren't going to go after Adrian," Shane says.

Derek opens his eyes. "She'd hate me if I killed her brother or her father, but the sooner you get him the hell away from our company, the better." He turns and walks to the door, opening it and disappearing into the hallway.

Shane wraps his arm around my waist and turns me to him, resting his head on my belly, his torment over his brother's pain palpable. My hand comes down on his hair, and I lean over and into him. And for long minutes, we just hold on to each other. We just hold on, a silent promise between us to never let go.

CHAPTER NINETEEN

SHANE

Emily and I try to convince Derek to join us for dinner, but he declines, leaving us both weighted down with worry for him, but I am comforted by the knowledge that Nick has a man watching over him. And knowing through that contact that Derek hits the gym and orders takeout before staying in for the night is enough to allow Emily and me the ability to enjoy our evening together. We order room service. We talk through her plans for the fashion and beauty line, which are both thoughtful and smart. We make love more than once, and I can't help but hold her just a little too tightly when we head to bed.

We wake early, with the knowledge that Seth has just landed in Germany, and head out for a chilly run. By the time we've done five miles, the day has turned warm, and we stop in a coffee shop we've come to enjoy, settling into a couple of leather chairs in a corner.

"He's still on your mind," Emily says, and sips her coffee.

"*He* could be a lot of people right about now. My father. Derek. Adrian. Mike. Ramon."

"All of them, I'm sure," she says. "But Derek is who I was talking about."

I think back to my many recent exchanges with Derek. "I gave him a gun yesterday and he pulled it on me."

Her eyes go wide. "What? Oh my God."

"I didn't load it and he put it down without firing. The point is, it showed me how erratic his behavior can be. I need him stable and strong to get through these negotiations."

"And you don't think he can be that person?"

"Do you?"

"He's changing. I can see that, but that's hard to do with a dying father and the love of your life leaving you. Maybe you should send him to Germany to be with your family. It gets him out of the picture for a while."

"I wish I could, but looking united in this Mike Rogers deal could be win or lose."

"Your father has cancer. It seems reasonable Derek would be with him, since you have to run the company."

"But when he's there, what happens when my father starts talking in his head again? What happens when he turns Derek against him or this deal?"

"But Seth is getting your father to sign off on your plans."

"That doesn't mean Derek couldn't go to Mike and work against me."

"Right," she says as we stand and head for the door, both of us falling into deep thought as we walk home, me about the execution of my plans, and, it appears, she's still focused on Derek. "Well," she says after five minutes of walking, as if we're still in the middle of our prior conversation, "we just need to keep Derek close to us. If he's close to us, we can control him. Nothing can go wrong."

It's not a perfect plan. It's not even close to a perfect plan. But for two weeks, we're going to make it work. Because one thing's for certain. She's right. Nothing can go wrong. Not if we're going to survive our brush with the Martina cartel. My cell phone rings, and I fish it from my pocket, finding Seth's number. "Seth," I tell Emily before answering the call.

"You're there?" I ask.

"I'm at the hospital and I won't be getting those contracts signed."

Irritated, I stop walking. "You have to convince him, Seth. I need—"

"He's not good, Shane."

I feel the words like a punch that flattens me, and I sit down on a bench. "What do you mean by 'not good'?"

"Apparently he wasn't doing well when he arrived," he says. "They fast-tracked his treatment, and he had a bad reaction. He's fully incapacitated at the moment."

I squeeze my eyes shut with the impact of those words. "And his prognosis?"

"Your mother's here. She's probably better to speak on this."

"Put her on."

Emily goes down on her knees in front of me. "How bad is it?"

"Really bad, I think," I say, a moment before my mother comes on the line.

"Shane."

"Mom."

"They said that sometimes this happens. It's not the end."

I let out a breath I didn't know I was holding. "That's good news."

"It's just news," she says. "But I'm giving Seth paperwork that proves he's incapacitated. Save the company for him, okay?"

Damn it, that was another punch to my chest. "I will. I am."

"Good. And that Mike Rogers bastard. I didn't find the dirt on him. It's all on you, son."

"I can handle Mike and Adrian Martina, Mom. I've got this. I promise you. I've got this."

"You always do, son. Here's Seth."

"Wait," I say.

"I'm here," my mother says.

"You can't tell Derek. Let me tell you when I know he can handle it."

"That's hard for me. He'll want to know."

"You have to leave this to me, for everyone's best interests."

"Okay, then. It really is *all* on you. Handing off to Seth." There are muffled voices, and then I hear Seth say, "Shane."

"I'm here."

"I have one piece of good news," he says. "Ramon got on a plane to Mexico this morning."

"That's definitely welcome news right now."

"I knew it would be. I'll be on a plane in a few hours and back to you by morning."

"Good," I say, then hesitate, because I know he'll tell me the truth, but I have to ask. "Seth, man. How bad is it?"

"I hacked his records while I was in the waiting area. I agree with your mother. This isn't the end. It's just not a good beginning to his treatment."

"Thanks. Safe travels." I end the call, shove my phone back

into my pocket, and stand, taking Emily with me. "I need to run again."

"Okay. Let's run."

"You aren't going to ask what happened?"

"You can tell me when you're ready."

I cup her face and kiss her. "You couldn't be more perfect for me than you are in this moment." I release her and we start running again, my mind and body both tormenting me. The idea that I am now CEO of our company, now able to manage whatever is needed with Mike and Adrian because my father is dying, stirs guilt in me that I know is misplaced. But it's still real. And I still have to cope with it to get by it. I have to cope with it because I have to keep my promise and save Brandon Enterprises.

Another five miles later and I've found my zone, that place where I am in control, where my emotions are nonexistent. We slow to a walk, and I bring Emily up to speed on my phone call with Seth and my mother, as well as my changing thoughts on Derek. "I can't keep this from him until we know more and trust my mother won't let it slip. I need to control how he hears the news."

"I agree," she says, and I'm already pulling my phone from my pocket again and dialing my brother, who answers on ring number one. "You do know I'll be at work in an hour, right?"

"Pops had a reaction to his medication. He's incapacitated."

"I want our company back," he says, sounding remarkably calm. "What does this mean?"

"I'm CEO and I can sign in his behalf, but I don't want to announce that until we have to."

"Why?" he asks.

"I want to hold our cards close to the vest and play them as Mike tries to play us."

"Understood. Just make sure you fuck Mike and fuck him well. You don't beat a man when he's down, and that's what he's trying to do to Pops."

"We won't let him," I say, ending the call, and a few minutes later, when I step into the shower with Emily, I don't need the water to wash away anything. I push her against the wall, tangle my fingers in her hair, and let her know exactly what to expect. "Hard and fast is what I can promise you right now. No making love about it."

"Bring it on," she replies, and I drive into her. Hard. Fast. Because that's what I promised, and I keep my promises.

Once Emily and I arrive at work, she joins me in my office, and we bring Jessica in as well, filling her in on our plan to dump Brandon Pharmaceuticals.

"I'm confused," she says, folding her arms in front of the blinding canary-yellow blouse she's wearing. "Why?"

"Liability," I say, claiming my seat and pulling out my calendar. "And that's all you need to know," I add. "But what I need to know is any critical problem happening in the company that I need to address." I look at Emily. "And a meeting no later than tomorrow afternoon with the banker my father met with about the sports complex. Can you work your magic and make that happen?"

"Consider it done," Emily says, hands settling on the waistline-fitted navy skirt she put on this morning for me to take off. Twice.

"Anything else?" Jessica asks.

"Let me know when Derek arrives," I say. "I need him to help run the company while I work to change how we do business."

"Will do, Boss," she says, hurrying toward the outer office, while Emily lingers.

"He might not show up," she says. "He's going to look for Teresa. I know he will."

"Let's hope not," I say. "Because the last thing I need right now is Adrian thinking Derek's behind her disappearance. You seem to work magic on the Brandon men. Can you try to reach him?"

"I will," she promises. "I'll let you know."

She disappears into the hallway, and I tap the calendar in front of me. It's Wednesday. Mike threw out Monday as a deadline. I know attorneys and strategy. I'm going to get a legal filing on Friday at closing, when his people think I can't do anything about it. I need to be ready to hit back over the weekend. I open my e-mail and find the information I was sent on Adrian's consortium, and dial the operations manager to set up a meeting. If I want Adrian to work for me, I'm going to have to do a little work for him.

Thursday morning arrives much the same as Wednesday, with only a few variations. Like yesterday, Emily and I go for a run, and we manage to talk to my mother on our walk back. And when she offers no good news about my father, my mood edges on the darker side. That leads to a good, hard shower fuck. Also like yesterday, when I pull the Bentley into the office garage, Derek's car is missing. "We're early," Emily says. "It's only seven. And you know from Nick that Derek spent the night at a strip club."

"Exactly why I'm irritated," I say, exiting the vehicle and rounding the hood to get Emily's door, before adding, "We're trying to save the company, and he's out partying with strippers."

"Teresa left him and he got bad news about your father," she reminds me, stepping out of the Bentley.

I shut the door and we start walking. "All the more reason to defeat Adrian and save the company."

"I know," she says, and we step onto the elevator, making the quick ride to the lobby level before stepping into another car leading to our floor.

Once we're inside and the doors are sealed, she steps in front of me, her tiny hands at my waist, under my jacket, and I am struck by how easily she touches me now. How much I want her to. How close I am to this woman. "He's not you, Shane. He's not all hard steel and unbreakable strength."

"That's how you see me?"

"Yes," she says, those beautiful eyes of hers filled with warmth and pride, her hand brushing my cheek. "Yes, I do."

"And you know what?" I say, snagging her hand and kissing it, fierceness in my answer. "When you say things like that to me, when you look at me like you are now, I want to live up to your expectations. I *really* want to live up to them."

"And you think Derek just talks," she supplies, reading my thoughts.

"Don't you?"

"I think he has good intentions."

"Intentions don't run this company or save it."

"He's hurt right now. He's damaged." She flattens her hand on my heart. "He's your brother."

"Who pulled a gun on me."

"Right. I did say damaged, remember?"

"I'm not trying to be coldhearted, sweetheart. But the clock

is ticking on our father's life and the survival of his company."
The elevator dings, the doors opening on our floor, and we step
into the corridor as I add, "And Lord help us all if Derek looks
for Teresa and somehow gains Adrian's attention again."

"He won't," she says, walking with me toward the lobby.
"He's not that foolish. That's my gut, and I think it's right."

I reach for the glass door and hold it open for her. "Because
you have a way with the Brandon men."

"I'm good with you," she says, pausing beside me. "You said
so this morning in the shower." She gives me a gorgeous, sexy
smile and darts away, and while my blood heats and my heart
warms for this woman, I find myself staring after her for another
reason. It's not just me she's good with. Emily handles the Brandon men like a lion tamer who knows her different beasts, and
by the time I'm at my desk, I dial hers. "You're the one who talked
to Derek and shook some sense into him the other day. He came
to me because of you."

"If you're about to ask me to call him, I've tried. Yesterday
and today, but I'll keep trying. And it's still early. We're the only
ones here. He could show up."

"Right," I say, releasing the intercom button and removing
my cell from my pocket to hit Nick's auto-dial. "If my brother isn't
here by noon, get someone to shake him out of bed. We have a
meeting with a group of investors at three."

"That could get brutal," he says.

"So will Adrian if I don't control him, and that means getting him here and keeping him busy."

"Got it. Will do."

He hangs up and I get to work. By noon, I've finished a meeting with the operations manager for Adrian's consortium. Impressed with their investors and the resources they represent,

I send the man away with the registration form for the drug study. He's barely had time to leave the building when my cell phone rings with an unknown number.

And I know exactly who it is. I answer the call and say, "Hello, Adrian."

"What's the timeline on the drug study?" he asks, unsurprised I know he's my caller.

"Paperwork takes time," I say. "But we've begun the process."

"Then we have an agreement? You will support our efforts to take our drug to the market?"

"We have a beginning," I reply. "We'll see where that leads."

"I do not approve of that response."

I laugh. "You're the one who wanted me, not Derek, as your lead contact."

"And do I have you as my lead contact now?"

"You'll keep calling me," I say. "Whether I want you to or not."

He laughs. "Indeed. Do you speak Spanish?"

"If I did, I wouldn't tell you."

"You do," he says. "You took two years in school."

"If you looking into my college record is supposed to rattle me, you failed. Now, I have work to do. I'm hanging up." And I do, immediately picking up the line to dial Jessica. "How do we look for this afternoon's meeting?"

"Emily just buzzed me, and every banker your father met with is confirmed for a meeting with you."

"And is Derek here?"

"No. No-show so far, and Seth is on the phone for you."

"Seth," I say. "Are you here?"

"I am, and I hear Derek punched one of Nick's men about fifteen minutes ago. Derek's on his way to you now."

"Jesus," I growl. "I do not have time for this. Any word on where Teresa might be located?"

"She's completely MIA. No travel, phone, or credit card pings. And if we can't find her, he can't."

I look up to see Derek standing in my doorway, his suit wrinkled, his tie missing. "I need to call you back, Seth." I end the call.

"I'm here," Derek says. "What now?"

"I have a group of investors showing up here soon. Go home and shower."

"I don't think I will."

"Derek," I bite out. "You told me to save the company."

"And you will." He presses his hand on his head and closes his eyes. "I just need a day. I need a fucking day, Shane." He looks at me and then shuts the door. "I need something."

"I'm listening."

"If your people can find Teresa, so can Ramon or Adrian. Make sure they can't."

"And if we find her? Do you want to know?"

"If you were me, what would you want to know?"

"Do you really want me to answer that?"

"Yes. I do."

"No. Because if I knew, I'd go after her, even though I'd know it wasn't right for her or me."

"And why is it wrong for her?"

"Right now, you're too close to her family. Later. Later, maybe it can be different."

"Fuck you, Shane."

"You asked."

"I know. And you're right. Again. You are always right. *Fuck you*." He looks at the ceiling, then at me, and then turns and leaves.

A moment later, Emily steps inside my office. "Shane, go after him," she pleads.

And it hits me as I look at her—beautiful, determined, headstrong—that she touches every part of my life. I have her for every little moment, like this one, no matter how good or bad. When I thought I'd lost her, I lost it. And now Derek has lost Teresa and he's losing his mind. The same but different, I think again. I stand up and cross the room, long strides carrying me past Emily and down the hallway, but by the time I reach the lobby, he's gone. I dial his number and it goes to voice mail.

Emily exits into the corridor and walks to me. "How do you save someone who keeps self-destructing?" I ask her.

"If I had that answer, I wouldn't be worried my brother was lying dead in a ditch somewhere."

"Your brother almost got you killed. My brother just might do the same for all of us if I don't get him under control."

CHAPTER TWENTY

EMILY

Friday morning arrives, and Shane and I fall into what is fast becoming our routine: a run, coffee, conversation, and yes, usually sex. But the part I really am coming to love is this one right now, where I stand in front of him, in the closet, and loop his tie for him, then flatten my hand over it and his heart.

"I love you in gray," I say, smoothing the silk over his always impressively hard chest. "It matches your eyes. Cool, calculating."

He laughs, this low, sexy, smooth sound that I feel in my belly, and oh, how I love that feeling and this man. "And I love you in nothing at all," he says, cupping my backside over my emerald-green sheath dress. "However, you, my woman, look good in green, blue, sweats, and with brown hair—though I am curious about your blond hair."

"I was thinking I could get a wig," I say. "Didn't we talk about that before? Then I could be the other woman here or there."

"Hmmm," he says. "I like that idea. I command you to make it happen."

I laugh. "Yes, Master." I shake my head. "That was a joke. You are not my master."

"I bet I could get you to call me Master."

"Me too," I say, "but I'd have to hurt you when it was over."

"That would earn you another spanking."

My teeth worry my bottom lip and my cheeks heat. "We were a little intense that night."

He sobers. "I liked it, sweetheart. I want to do it again. Can I?"

"Everything's okay when it's with you."

He reaches up and slides a strand of hair behind my ear. "I have a surprise for you."

"I like surprises. Tell me."

"Then it won't be a surprise."

"When will you tell me?"

"Maybe today." He kisses me. "Which is why we should get to the office."

I run my hand over his stubble and he scrubs his chin. "And," he says, "you're telling me that I forgot to shave."

"Indeed you did." I push to my toes, and this time I kiss him. "I'll go make us some coffee to go while you break out the razor." I turn away, and he smacks my backside. I yelp and look over my shoulder. "Watch that, you."

"Just making sure you remember what my hand feels like."

Grinning, I start walking, wondering how this man thinks I could ever forget his hands on my body. I snatch my purse off the bed and head down the stairs, setting it on the counter to make our coffee. I've just started one cup brewing when my phone rings. Unzipping my purse, I pull out my cell to see Derek's number. I hit answer. "Derek. Hey."

"Emily?" he says, his voice deep, gravelly.

"Yes."

"I meant to call my mother. Fuck."

"Were you checking on your father?"

"Yeah. You know anything?"

"Your mother calls every morning during our run. Nothing has changed. He's still—"

"Got it. Still not good."

"But he's not bad. He's just not good."

"Right. Not bad. Not good."

"And you?"

"Fine."

"Are you coming in today?"

He's silent a moment. Then two. "I hate him, you know."

"Your father's a hard man."

"Shane. I hate Shane."

"Oh," I say, fighting a defensive, protective response. "He doesn't hate you."

"You know why I hate him? Because he always gets everything he wants. He got you."

"But you didn't want me."

"But I wanted Teresa."

"I know. I do. And it hurts right now. It'll—"

"Get better? Would it get better for you if it were Shane?"

My throat thickens. "No. No, it would not. Derek—"

"You know what really sucks about Shane? I love him as much as I hate him. I mean, he's just so fucking good at everything. Does he have to be good at everything?"

"Let's have lunch. Can you do lunch?"

"I don't know."

It's not a no, and so I push for more. "Please."

"I'll think about it." The line goes dead.

I sigh and stick my phone back into my purse, looking up as Shane rounds the corner, looking tall, dark, and gorgeous in his gray suit. His face chiseled. His dark hair just long enough to be a bit wild when I run my fingers through it. And the light in those gray eyes right now, just plain mischievous. He stops in front of me, hands settling on my shoulders. "That surprise I mentioned. I wanted to wait to tell you, but I just got off the phone and I really want to tell you now."

"Okay. I'm going nuts here. Tell me."

"I made an offer on the fashion company you want."

"We did? We made an offer?"

"We did. Days ago."

"Days ago? When? How? What did they say?"

"It's yours, sweetheart. You are now CEO of a fashion line. I'm delaying the signing of the paperwork to ensure we get this Mike stuff behind us, but—"

I wrap my hand around his neck to bring his head down to mine and kiss him. "Thank you. I'm going to make this so good for the company. For you. For us. It's going to be huge. Amazing. I think I'm going to cry." I swipe at my eyes. "I mean. My law degree. My brother. And now I have you and this, and how did that happen?"

He turns me to the counter, and his big legs frame mine in that wonderful, brutishly sexy way they often do, and he says, "I got lucky when you drank out of the wrong coffee cup."

"I got lucky."

"*We* got lucky."

"Yes." I smile. "Can we do the Jessica line?"

"This is yours. You can do what you want. You can even give her a small slice of stock if you want."

"We can?"

"Of course."

"We should take her to dinner tonight and tell her."

He strokes hair from my eyes. "If I'm correct, Mike is going to strike today, and I'll have my hands full. But why don't you take her if I can't make it? We'll celebrate this weekend when I give you your second surprise."

"I can't handle another surprise."

He kisses my forehead. "You're going to have to. Now, forget the coffee. I need to get to work and be ready for Mike." He steps away from me and I grab my purse, following him to the door, Derek back on my mind.

"Derek called me," I say as Shane reaches for the door.

"And?" he asks, turning to face me, hope in his eyes that says he is a brother who hasn't given up on his brother, and I'm not going to let him.

"We might be having lunch soon. He's just hurt and healing. He'll be okay."

"Okay," he says. "Well. I guess that's better than not okay."

He opens the door and we step outside, his arm sliding around my shoulders, together, when Derek is just so very alone.

SHANE

I've barely sat down behind my desk when I hear Jessica call out. "Hey! What are you doing? Shane!" My intercom goes off. "Mike Rogers—"

"Is here," I supply as the brute of a man steps into my office in his typical uniform of jeans and a pullover sports shirt, and he's not alone. Beside him is a twentysomething man in an ill-fitting shirt and tie.

"Do it," Mike orders, waving the kid forward.

The man steps forward, sets a piece of paper on my desk, and says, "You've been served," before turning and leaving the office.

"I told you that was coming," Mike says. "I'm not letting the kids run the ship."

"And when my father returns?"

"He won't return."

"You're wrong, but it really doesn't matter." I open my desk and slide a file forward. "We no longer wish to do business with you. This is a proposal to split the company and have you, and whatever investors you've gathered to take us over, buy out Brandon Pharmaceuticals."

He laughs. "Why would I settle for less than all?"

"Because you fucked my mother."

The door shuts behind Mike and he rotates as we both take in the sight of Derek standing at the door in a perfectly pressed blue suit. He is the picture of professionalism. "And I'm not the attorney here, my brother is, but I don't think juries favor people who fuck their best friend and business partner's wife while he's fighting for his life. And since my brother is one of the best attorneys in the country, I'm certain he must know a law or two that breaks."

"I do know a law or two or ten," I say. "And I have to tell you, Mike, I love a good day in the courtroom." I tap the file in front of me. "I put some pictures in there for you. Examples of some of the evidence I'll present in discovery."

Mike steps forward and snaps up the file, flipping it open, his jaw clenching at the sight of the photos inside. His gaze jerks to mine. "You wouldn't show the court naked images of your mother."

"She fucked you," Derek says. "She's not our mother anymore."

"You have until Monday to withdraw your lawsuit or the deal is off the table," I say. "Because my time to reply to your legal action is valuable. Once I start working on it, it's game on, as you basketball lovers say."

Derek steps aside and opens the door. Mike stares at me, his eyes as cold as ice, but in their depths, there is just a hint of fear. He turns and starts walking. The minute he's out of the room, Derek shuts the door and walks to the window, leaning a fist on the glass. "I think that went well," he says.

I stand and hitch a hip onto my desk. "It did. Not well enough though. He'll need extra incentive, which I plan to give him."

He glances over at me. "Adrian?"

"Yes. And if I play the hand right, I get the drugs out of our operation and a promise for your safety as part of the deal."

"I don't know how you plan to do that, but knowing you, it'll work." He faces me, folding his arms in front of his chest. "You're just so fucking good at everything."

"That doesn't sound like a compliment."

"I'm good too. The problem is that I try to be your kind of good. I'm better when I'm my kind of good, and I haven't been that in a long time."

"What are you saying?"

"That I hate you and I love you. And I'm here to fight with you to save the company, but I can't work with you long-term. I want you to buy me out."

I push off the desk and narrow my eyes on him. "Emily said

you called her and you weren't in the best place. Now you're here. Dressed to work. On your game with Mike. Teresa called you. You're running away with her."

"No. Teresa didn't call me."

"I don't believe you."

"Teresa *didn't* call me."

"Something happened." I tilt my head and study him. "You know where she is."

"No," he says. "But as I was reading her letter again this morning, I had a realization. Teresa was brave enough to choose another path. You chose another path when you went to New York. This is all I've ever been, and yet it's never been all I could be. I need to let go of the company. The way she let go of her family and me."

"You know where she is," I repeat.

"It doesn't matter if I know where she is. I would never go to her again the way I am now. I need to be that better man she told me to be. And I can't be him when I'm trying to be Pops or you. There's no war between us anymore. The company's yours." He starts walking toward the door, and I turn to watch him leave, a knot forming in my chest.

"You can always change your mind," I call out.

"But I won't," he says, and then he's gone. I stand there, staring after him, trying to identify what it is I feel. And one word comes to my mind. Pride. I am proud of my brother, and I know he will be that better man. Now it's time for me to give him the gift of freedom by cleaning up our mess. I pull my phone from my pocket and dial Adrian Martina. "Shane Brandon," he answers. "What great news do you have for me?"

"I have a proposal to talk about."

"A proposal. I'm intrigued. Come to the restaurant."

"Starbucks on Sixteenth Street in fifteen minutes."

"You presume I have nothing better to do. That's obnoxiously demanding."

"And my proposal involves an obnoxious amount of money." I end the call.

I walk into the Starbucks with Seth by my side to find Adrian sitting at a table in a corner with another burly older man standing behind him. Seth and I walk toward them, and I sit across from Adrian while Seth remains standing, mimicking the other man.

"This is Pedro," Adrian says.

I don't look at Pedro. I don't care about Pedro. And Adrian already knows Seth. "I'll get to the point. Mike Rogers, the owner of the Denver Mavericks—"

"I know who he is. The stockholder who's fucking your mother."

"*Was* fucking my mother," I bite out. "He's trying to force a hostile takeover of Brandon Enterprises, which means I won't be in control of the pharmaceuticals brand."

"Except you're too damn good to let him win."

"But you want him to win," I say. "You want him to buy out the pharmaceuticals brand. And you want this because he's the kind of little bitch you can control."

"I've looked into him. He *is* a little bitch."

"I gave him a proposal, and he needs encouragement to take it—which I'm quite confident you can give him."

"I can," he says. "What about my drug study?"

"I'll submit the paperwork before the deal is signed, to ensure it happens." I slide a file toward him. "In case you need encouragement. The profit statements will get your attention."

"And what do you get out of this?"

"Money from the buyout and freedom from you."

"I do like that you're honest. It's not something I see a lot of." He flips open the documents and looks at the highlighted number. "You have my attention. I'll look it over, and if it's acceptable, I'll ensure he goes along with your proposal."

"I need you to pull the illegal drugs out of the operation until this is done."

"I told you—"

"Short-term loss for bigger long-term gains."

He studies me for a few long, intense beats. "If I decide to do this, then I'll pull them out."

"Let me give you some extra incentive." I shift the papers in the folder and set a new page on top.

He studies it for a moment and then looks at me. "This is a proposal to buy out the sports center where Mike's team plays."

"Yes. I have an investment team and half the funds. Your team would need to supply the other half. But it's legitimate. It's obnoxiously profitable, and you'd be primed to buy a team or just pick up a piece of Mike's."

"And what do you get from this? Are you a partner?"

I flip to another sheet of paper. "Broker fee and I'm out."

"Smart move, but I expect nothing less from you. You get money and freedom. And I'd own Mike every which way and back."

"That's right. And I'd venture to say you'd be richer than your father without having to hide your money. You'd change the legacy of the Martina name. And that's what you said you want to do."

"And how will you change the Brandon name?"

"Fashion. We're going into fashion."

"Fashion," he says. "Interesting. I'll call an emergency board meeting about the sports center. And since I know you'd never cheat me, consider Mike my new possession. I'll have the illicit operation removed from your facility by Monday morning. Anything else?"

"Yes. There is. My brother."

"What about Derek?"

"He lives. He keeps his fingers. He's untouchable."

"You're asking for my word?"

"Yes. I'm asking for your word."

"And you trust my word."

"I believe you are a killer. I believe you are vicious. But I believe you're a man of your word."

"That I am." He lifts the folder. "And you've paid for your brother's freedom. I'll be in touch. And so will Mike." He stands and leaves, and I shut my eyes, relief washing over me, daring to believe this might be over.

An hour later, I walk into the lobby of the office, a bag in my hand, then round the corner to Emily's desk and motion for her to join me in my father's office.

"What's going on?" she asks.

"I'll tell you in a minute." I buzz Derek's desk. "Derek, man. Come to Pops's office. It's important. And no, nothing is wrong with him."

Emily gives me a curious look. "You look happy."

"I am." I pull the whiskey from the bag and grab three glasses from the cabinet in the corner. "Which is why we're drinking obnoxiously expensive whiskey." I start filling the glasses, and Derek walks in.

"That's some damn good whiskey," he says, joining us at the desk. "There's either really bad news or really good news."

"Adrian guaranteed me your safety after agreeing to force Mike into making the deal. And he's going in on a deal to buy the sport center that we're brokering for a massive chunk of change. In other words, brother, if you do cash out, do it after this deal. You'll have the money to do whatever the hell you want."

Emily's gaze jerks to Derek. "You're leaving?"

"I know you'll miss my sweetness," he says dryly. "But you can call. I won't tell Shane. But yeah. I think it's time I try something new."

"We're going to get crazy rich with a new fashion line. You might want to stay."

He arches a brow. "Fashion? There's a way to tempt me to stay. Or not. But good luck."

I lift my glass. "To luck," I say. "And to new beginnings and happy endings."

We clink glasses, and Derek and Emily repeat, "To new beginnings and happy endings."

CHAPTER TWENTY-ONE

EMILY

Since Jessica has a Friday night date, we schedule dinner with her for Sunday night to talk about the fashion line, and with Friday night to ourselves, Shane and I end up eating downtown and walking the neighborhood. We wake Saturday to news that Brandon Senior is recovering from his allergic reaction and actually showing progress with his cancer treatment. Life simply feels good. But even good times require bumps, and come Sunday night, Shane is in a heavy exchange of phone calls with Adrian, working through numbers on the sports center, and he simply can't make dinner.

At almost seven o'clock, I've showered and dressed in black jeans a black silk top with boots to match, and per Shane's insistence, I'm carrying a purse large enough to hold my gun at my hip. Heading downstairs, I find him in the kitchen, and I swear, dressed in a snug white tee and sweats, keying away on his MacBook, he looks almost sexier than he does in a suit. "Hey," I say, joining him and leaning on the island beside him.

"Hey, sweetheart," he says, setting aside his computer and giving me a quick, sexy inspection before snagging my hips and walking me to him. "I like you in jeans."

"I like you at dinner with me," I say, my hands settling on his arms. "Any chance you finished that work and can go?"

"I wish I could, but anything to do with Adrian needs to get done and be over."

I sigh. "I know." The doorbell rings, and knowing who to expect, I grimace. "I like Cody, but do I really still need him now that you've made this agreement with Adrian?"

"Yes," he says firmly. "And you know why. Per Seth—"

"Ramon went off the grid in Mexico. Until he's located him again, and until we're well past this deal with Adrian, we need to be cautious."

"Exactly."

I cup his face and kiss him. "I love you. That's twenty times."

"I love you. Go make Jessica a happy stockholder. I'll be done when you get back, and I'll make up my missed dinner in any way you like."

"Any way?"

"Any way," he confirms, mischief in his eyes. "Preferably without clothes."

"That works for me," I say, backstepping and giving him a wave before I head for the door, but not before he gives me a smack on the backside that has me yelping and smiling.

I step into the hallway and greet Cody, my cell ringing as I do. Fishing it from my purse, I glance at the Caller ID. "Unknown caller," I say with a smirk. "Not answering that." I stick my phone back into my purse, but for some reason, a shiver slides down my spine.

It's not long after that we're at street level, the night cool and comfortable as we walk toward the restaurant, pedestrians mill-ing about here and there, a horse carriage as well. We're almost to our destination when my cell phone rings for a second time, and sure enough, it's an unknown number again. And sure enough, despite the warm evening, another shiver slides down my spine, almost like a warning. It's unsettling, as is the crazy sense of being followed I suddenly experience. Which is just odd since Cody is the one who is always following me and he's here now. It's a sensation that takes my mind back to Ramon. I turn to Cody. "When Seth says Ramon is off the grid, what does that mean?"

"He's intentionally disappeared," he says, "and going to Mexico to do that isn't uncommon. The problem is you don't al-ways know when they cross back to the States."

"So Ramon could be back here and we don't know it," I say.

"He most likely still in Mexico."

"Most likely," I say. "That isn't comforting, and no wonder I have the creeps tonight."

"Talking about Ramon will do that to a person. Stop talk-ing about him and thinking about him. I'm here. You're safe."

"I know," I say, but for some reason, despite trusting him, I don't really mean the words.

Moments later, we arrive at the restaurant, and the sparks between Jessica and Cody are so intense, I insist he join us for din-ner. And with them chatting up a storm, I'll save the good fash-ion news for dessert. We order our drinks, and while Jessica and I choose wine, Cody sticks with coffee. "On duty, ladies. I can't protect you if I'm falling all over the place." He lifts his coffee. "This is as strong as it gets for me."

And funny he says that because I take only two sips of my wine and I start feeling buzzed. No. It's more than that. I start feeling sick to my stomach. "I need to go to the ladies' room,"

I announce, pushing to my feet, my belly burning now. This is not good. It feels wrong. And I feel dizzy, my vision a bit foggy.

Somehow though, I make it to the bathroom, a one-stall room, and I don't even try to lock the door. I go down on my knees and start heaving. Something isn't right.

"Emily," Cody calls out. "Are you okay?"

"No. No something—" I throw up again.

He opens the door and I turn to face him, only to find him falling to his knees and then on top of me. "Cody," I whisper. "Cody."

His body is lifted off me and I am staring up at not one, but two men, their faces fading in and out. And then everything goes black.

I blink awake to a slightly spicy scent and the feel of carpet against my face, not to mention a throbbing headache. Sitting up, I try to clear my foggy vision and bring a man sitting directly across from me into focus. I blink again and then blanch. "Derek?"

"Emily," he says, and breaths out, his voice raspy. "You're okay. We're going to be okay."

"My arms hurt." I try to move them, and suddenly I realize my wrists are bound in front of me. And his are too. My heart starts to thunder in my chest. "What is this? What's happening?" I twist around to inspect my surroundings, finding us in an office with a big oak desk at my back. "Where are we?" I ask, turning back to Derek.

"Adrian's office inside his restaurant."

"Why? How? Oh God." A memory assails me. "Cody. They hurt him. Where is he?"

"I don't know. I was drugged just like you. I woke up here."

"Why would Adrian do this? Shane has such a good deal set up for him."

"I have literally no answers. I've seen no one since I woke up."

The door opens, and the rough-looking, muscular, hard-eyed man I know as Ramon walks in. "You're awake. Good. I've been looking forward to this."

"Why are you doing this?" I ask.

"Why? Because your fucking boyfriend ruined my empire. I told Adrian to put this brother in charge." He points at Derek. "I can control this brother. But no. He chose Shane and this ridiculous idea of going legitimate with my drug. Sub-Zero was *my* creation. Mine. Not his to sell in a pill bottle." He grinds his teeth and growls low before abruptly shouting, "Mine! It was mine." He kneels by Derek. "You will replace Shane again when he's dead. You will do as I say and I will pay you well."

"Adrian will kill you for this," Derek says.

"He has a Sunday fuck date. He doesn't come here on Sundays. He will never know what happened if you don't tell him, and you won't. Because you like power and money and I will give them to you."

"I'll tell Adrian," Derek promises, spitting in Ramon's face. "I will not work for you."

Ramon curses and stands up, kicking Derek in the face so hard, he tumbles over.

I cover my mouth, fighting a scream I somehow know will infuriate Ramon, and then suddenly Ramon is kneeling in front of me, cupping my face, his breath thick with onion. "Shane will watch you die before he dies. He will watch me fuck you many times. You are too delicious to not fuck." He licks my face, and my stomach rolls all over again, but somehow I remain calm. I don't cry or scream. I just try to think of how to free myself and Derek.

Ramon stands up and shouts, "Pedro!" A burly older man, his nose flat, his eyes hard, enters the room, and Ramon commands him, "Call Shane Brandon and get him here now."

SHANE

I have just finished crunching the numbers that I promised Adrian by morning when my phone rings where it sits on the island next to me. I frown when the caller ID says it's Adrian's restaurant, finding it odd that he would call from it, not his private line.

"Adrian," I say, answering.

"This is Pedro from the coffee shop meeting with Adrian."

Unease rolls through me. "Right, Pedro. What's up?"

"Adrian is managing a problem with an investor. He wants you to meet him here at the restaurant as soon as possible and explain the details to him in person."

"Which investor?"

"I don't know. He didn't say, and I don't deal in such things."

"All right then. I'll be there soon." I end the call and something just feels off to me. I dial Adrian, and like the three times before this tonight, I get his voice mail. That doesn't feel right either. I dial Seth and explain the situation.

"I don't like it," he says.

"I have to go to this meeting. I need to make sure this deal happens."

"I know," he says. "I'll meet you in the parking garage."

I hurry upstairs and change into jeans and a thin black

leather jacket that allow me to pack not one, but two guns. I'm in the garage in ten minutes, inside my Bentley, Seth riding shotgun. "What is your gut telling you about this?" I ask him, pulling us onto the highway.

"That this is trouble. A deal gone bad." He pulls his phone out. "I'm going to tell Cody to get Emily home safe."

"Yes. Do it. That's a good idea."

I turn left onto a new street, placing us only a few blocks from Martina's restaurant when Seth ends the call and announces. "Cody's not answering."

"Why the hell wouldn't he answer?" I demand, a bad feeling clawing at me, my hand on my phone. I punch in Emily's number and it goes to voice mail. "She's not answering either."

"It could be the building they're in," Seth says, dialing his phone again, "but I'm having Nick go check on them."

"Jessica was with her." I halt us at a light and dial her number.

"Shane," she says, panting, her breathing so raspy that my heart skips a beat. "Where's Emily?" she asks. "Cody and I are sick . . . oh . . . God . . . so severe . . . food poisoning. And we can't find her. Or I can't. Cody's on a stretcher."

"I'll send someone to the hospital to help you," I say, ending the call and glancing at Seth. "Emily's missing. Cody and Jessica were poisoned. Cody's condition doesn't sound good."

"Fuck," Seth says. "I'm calling for help."

He punches in a number and I dial Adrian. He doesn't answer. I curse and start to call him again when my phone rings with his number. "What the fuck are you doing to Emily?" I demand, answering the call. "I will kill you if you hurt her."

"What are you talking about?"

"You called me to the restaurant. She's gone. I'm not stupid."

"Shane," he says, "I did not call you to the restaurant. Fuck. Ramon is back in town. Not by my choice. I'll meet you there." He ends the call and I pound the steering wheel.

"Damn it, Seth. Ramon has her. Why the fuck is he still alive?"

"You know why. You know he couldn't die when he could be connected to us."

"Well, he's connected now. And he will end this night with a bullet in his head." I turn a corner and pull to the curb in front of Adrian's restaurant, barely killing the engine before I reach for my door.

Seth grabs my arm. "You need to wait on backup."

"Not a chance in hell." I exit the car and stalk toward the restaurant entrance, and Seth is by my side in an instant.

"You are never rash," he says. "Don't start now."

The restaurant door opens, and Pedro greets me, eyeing Seth. "Just you," Pedro says to me.

"To fuck with that," Seth says, to which Pedro replies by pulling a gun on him.

"To fuck with you," Pedro says, motioning me forward.

I don't hesitate. I hurry into the restaurant, and suddenly Emily is screaming. "No! No! Get back! No!"

And then another voice, a familiar male voice. "Stop it! Let her go!"

Derek.

My heart lurches at the sound of my brother's voice, and I start running toward his and Emily's voices, cutting around a bar to a hallway.

"No!" Emily screams. "No!"

I run toward the doorway I now know leads me to her and Derek, and when I enter the room, Emily is in the center of the office, fighting one of the four men in the room, who rips her shirt open. Two others are beating Derek to a pulp while Ramon stands in front of it all, smiling. I pull my gun. "Stop. Stop!"

Ramon gives a deep laugh. "We aren't going to stop," he says. "Not until she's fucked upside and down while you watch."

Suddenly, Adrian's voice bellows out in Spanish. Angry. Forceful. Everyone goes still. The men beating Derek release him, and Emily is flung to the ground, her eyes meeting mine, fear I never wanted her to feel burning in her eyes. Ramon looks at me. "She will die for your sins and then you will die."

Everything seems to go into slow motion then. He points the gun at Emily, and I know he is really going to shoot her. "No!" I shout, firing my weapon at him, but in that blink of time, Derek has thrown himself in between Emily and Ramon. Ramon falls to the ground, but so do Derek and Emily, Derek on top of her. I rush for them and go to my knees. And there is blood. So much blood. Derek. Emily. Derek. Emily. I don't know who is bleeding. I don't know who is alive. I grab Derek, and I move him but he is limp. I roll him over, and there is Emily. Her eyes shut. Blood all over her. I maneuver in between them, blood all over me now that I will never wash away, and I lift my face to the ceiling, a scream ripping from the very depths of my soul, pain I can barely endure gutting me. And when Adrian Martina steps in front of me, I look up at him and I make a promise. "I will live to hurt you. I will live to torture you. You will die a slow, painful death for this."

Dear Readers,

I know this is a rough cliffhanger, but in my defense, I've known this would be the ending to *Bad Deeds* from the beginning. I also thought I knew the outcome of this scene. But as I type the end tonight, I don't know anymore. So this is now a cliffhanger for me as well. I know only this. Life isn't all roses, but through my characters, I try to deliver one message: we can, we must, always survive.

Lisa

ABOUT THE AUTHOR

New York Times and *USA Today* bestselling author Lisa Renee Jones is the author of the highly acclaimed Inside Out series. Suzanne Todd (producer of *Alice in Wonderland*) says, on the Inside Out series: "Lisa has created a beautiful, complicated, and sensual world that is filled with intrigue and suspense. Sara's character is strong, flawed, complex, and sexy—a modern girl we all can identify with."

In addition to the success of Lisa's Inside Out series, she has published many successful titles. The Tall, Dark, and Deadly series and The Secret Life of Amy Bensen series both spent several months on the *New York Times* and *USA Today* bestseller lists. Lisa is presently working on the dark, edgy Dirty Money series for St. Martin's Press.

Prior to publishing books, Lisa owned a multistate staffing agency that was recognized many times by *Austin Business Journal* and also praised by *Dallas Woman* magazine. In 1998, Lisa's agency was listed as the #7 growing women-owned business in *Entrepreneur* magazine.

Lisa loves to hear from her readers. You can reach her at www.lisareneejones.com and she is active on Twitter and Facebook daily.

The **DIRTY MONEY** series is
"EDGY, BRILLIANT, AND ALL-CONSUMING!
A MUST-READ!"
—KATY EVANS, *NEW YORK TIMES* BESTSELLER

READ THE ENTIRE SERIES FROM
NEW YORK TIMES BESTSELLING AUTHOR
LISA RENEE JONES

DAMAGE CONTROL • *BAD DEEDS*

🦁 ST. MARTIN'S GRIFFIN